DOUBLE-WOLF

DOUBLE-WOLF

Brian Castro

ALLEN & UNWIN

First published in 1991
Second impression 1991
Allen & Unwin Pty Ltd
8 Napier Street, North Sydney, NSW 2059

National Library of Australia
Cataloguing-in-Publication entry:

Castro, Brian, 1950–
Double-wolf.

ISBN 0 04 442347 0.

I. Title.

A 823.3

Set in 10.5/12pt Palatino by Excel Imaging Pty Ltd, NSW
Printed by Australian Print Group, Maryborough

Creative writing program assisted by the Australia Council, the
Australian Government's arts funding and advisory body.

Jo

Acknowledgments

The quotation from the Wolf-Man on page 94 is from Lemaire, Anika *Jacques Lacan*, trans. D. Macey. London: Routledge & Kegan Paul, 1977, p. 241

The quotations from Karl Kraus on page 143 are from Kraus, Karl *Half-Truths and One-and-a-Half Truths*. London: Carcanet Press, 1986, pp. 33, 79.

'he seemed to me the sort of man to whom one should give orchids.'

Karin Obholzer
Gespräche mit dem Wolfsmann

'he used to threaten me with eating me up...'

Sigmund Freud
*From the History of an
Infantile Neurosis*

'Only for the egoist and the dogmatist (and maybe they're one and the same, although I'm thinking of two different friends of mine) is there one "history" only. The rest of us live with the suspicion that there are as many histories as there are people and maybe a few more...'

Robert Coover
*Whatever Happened to Gloomy Gus
of the Chicago Bears?*

KATOOMBA

Winter, 1978

(A misty rain is falling.

It smears the glass like somebody's spit. Somebody talking too loud, too fast.

It is cold, but not cold enough. Not yet. In the late afternoon when it is almost dark there will be rumours of snow. Perhaps one of the last snowfalls here for all time. The eucalypts brood in the chasms, as black as the shelf of rocks worn and wet on the other side. Far better than trying to outrun fires roaring up the gorges in those mad summers. Wet black rocks fired from the bowels of another millenia.

This used to be a coal siding. 'The Crushers' it was called then, subsiding escarpments and waterfalls crushing the breath out of you a thousand metres above sea level on an uplifted plateau outside of Sydney. Nowadays Katoomba is littered with hotels, hospitals, mental institutions.

The mist drifts into old boarding houses, finds the damp courses, settles into rotting floorboards, drips into the stew of vegetation underneath. It's so cold you can no longer smell anything. Your urine steams, traces a line of pain from kidneys to bladder, makes patterns of blood in the snow. But you'll have to wait until it snows for *that* morsel of creativity. If it happens then you'll have to go out in it . . . purge everything. The indistinction of the valleys, happily, guards against the possibility of romance and sentiment. You get tired of views.

There is a house here in Katoomba worth visiting. Nobody knows about it. Tourists visit it by chance, perhaps as an afterthought, nostalgically trying to recover the twenties or the thirties, searching for stories. They wouldn't believe what you tell them . . . that a wolf once escaped from somebody's private menagerie and roams these ridges and plateaux . . . or

1

that the imagination held in check might gnaw itself to death. True, in the valley below they keep wolves. It's illegal, not a Southern Hemisphere thing to do, un-neighbourly, what with sheep and deer farms nearby.

If you stand still now, among the low, smoky cottages you will hear somebody playing Satie's 'Monotones', pausing, plunging onto what sounds like wrong notes, wrong moods, like the houses about to tumble into chasms, weatherboard, low-roofed, pitched between escarpments and valleys, out of joint even in summer when the paper petals of Bougainvillea cling gaudily to their walls in a brief climax of colour.

Many years ago you stood not far from here and said: This is a place for neurotics. Katoomba is libidinal, pleasurable, exciting, depressing. They used to come up here for cures, the mentally ill, the pulmonary, the artistic. Entrepreneurs made it sound as though the place was spuming with spas instead of mudbaths. The sick unknowingly drank artesian water. They come up now to eat . . . displaced, cosmopolitan, wealthy, buying their illnesses. Sniff. They wear furs flavoured with mothballs. Leather still stinking of carcasses. Up the street, in the plush hotel known as the Alpine Lodge, you can hear a palm court orchestra playing 'The Dying Swan'. They are really straining. You stand here in one of the last decaying boarding houses, hungry, naked, with only a handful of memories. Ah! Here's a butt someone's dropped. You roll flaky, cheap cigar tobacco in cigarette paper. When you smoke it the ash is black. That guarantees poor quality.

'I'll tell you a dark story,' you say to those who are peering in at the door, at the sight of a whitebeard from whom they expected felicitations, prophecies, a Yuletide greeting at least . . . a popular thing up here . . . but what is popular is, well, a matter of bad taste and overstatement . . . 'I'll tell you the story of a life lived and not lived,' you say.

They move about. Maybe you're one of those buskers. Not even an instrument for accompaniment. A voice like a scratched recording of an ancient poet. They never permit an old man his long-windedness. That's because he knows that life is short. It can be summed up in a paragraph. They know that if they allow him to go on they will not stop him and there will be implacable malevolence . . . etc. Some are already dropping coins into the beanie you're about to put on. But while there is breath . . . they have to allow at least this cheap sentiment . . . breath smelling of garlic, rough port, stinking tobacco . . . there is a chance of some truth.

You begin to tell. The listeners shuffle and nod. 'It must have been a hell of a life,' they say, wanting to get on their way.

'His name was Sergei,' you sigh, and as you say his name betrayal enters backstage like an opportunist, and a dark rain begins to fall on Katoomba.

Falls upon your head.

Vienna

1972

Shreee. A north wind. From about three-thirty in the afternoon these places become tombs. Something about the sun. A solitary child, singing and skipping, marks time. A deserted car park. The wind, unwanted, springs up and stirs the trees. Leaves. All those deaths. The hour of our death. The English prayers of his Russian childhood repeated in the way history hums. If you walk up the path to the Steinhof you will hear the coughs from the pulmonary pavilion and the screams from the mental pavilion. Coughing and screaming. Sometimes screaming and coughing. From the other direction. If these sounds are any guide to the layout of the hospital, then it's pretty disorienting.

Behind is the crematorium. You'd think they'd have more taste. But there's no smoke. Modern technology. Business. The families get a discount because they don't need a hearse. Just a short walk along a ramp lined with flowers. 'We are gathered here today . . . ,' someone says to the flowers. Today. Tomorrow. As if time were that important. The lilies in the field don't know about time. They bloom; they die. The number of women named after flowers. Sergei knew a Lily once, or was it a Loulou? She went mad. Totalled. Used to pull books off his shelf and flip them with a finger. Said she read them that way. Flowers. Put petals in pages. They stank. Marriage, kids. Maybe that's the way to go. A woman said to him once: 'Now that I've had these children, my life is over.' A stone is rolled over the crypt. The kids don't give thanks. They double the emptiness. Then her body goes . . . goodbye sweet hysteria. Merciful menopause puts a stop to the travelling womb. Rock a bye baby. An empty cradle. It must have been like swinging on a giant pendulum. He had a menopausal governess called

4

Ovens. A British nanny. A tyrant. Years later there were ovens all over Europe. Women plagued him. First because he was rich, then because he became poor and famous. It was in his nature to be a pauper with style. He gave away his money and then regretted it. For him, fame and fortune have never gone together. Women burrowed in like ticks, sucked him dry, abandoned him. His wife was the only one he could trust. Even then . . .

Standing here like Rodin's statue of Balzac. A favourite author since his cure. He's robust now. Likes to watch old movies. Humphrey Bogart. He has on a long dark green Bavarian greatcoat which reaches to his ankles, fashionable again now, with a flap over the shoulders. His pockets are cut so he can reach the essentials. In his hand he holds a terracotta penis. A lucky charm.

Life sometimes is like one of those little priapic Greek statuettes . . . unbalanced . . . out of proportion. He's just attended a conference. He said to them: All writers are wankers. His advice to writers? Get a proper job. He wanted to discourage the herd. You can only speak the truth once. After that, all is paradox.

Later a middle-aged woman came up to him. 'Mr Wespe,' she exclaimed, 'I really didn't think that was *necessary*.' She took off her spectacles. 'What about your audience?' she scolded. 'You never think of them.'

'Let them eat words,' said Wespe.

He was tired of being a curiosity and was in a particularly bad mood, thinking of his Thérèse in the hospital mortuary, turning blue, her lungs still filled with gas.

In the Steinhof the clock says four. He does not go up yet. At this hour they patrol the corridors and watch the rooms carefully. Suicides are common, doing the rounds like a shadow in the afternoon. The tea trolley clanks like the coffin cart. The nurses turn frivolous. 'Permit me to be frivolous.' No. They don't talk that way anymore. This is the twentieth century. But they joke because it is the hour of death. They are coming off their shift, the fag end of the day, with death folded in their sleeves. Through their starched uniforms he can make out their underwear.

'Give me a shot, baby,' he says. A hypodermic you know where. It catapults out like a cuckoo. Numbing sleep. The somnolence of overheated pipes. Settle back. Soporifia. Damn. The warmth makes him erect, watchful. Not bad for a man of eighty-five.

'Gin or whisky?' they joke.

Blood. A wave of blood. The unconscious surfaces out of the black liquid. It is the hour of the telephone, its ring cleaving the world in two, brooding, black. Afternoons and evenings of another place. A dog barks. Interminable waiting. He is waiting for his father to die. His father lingers on. Outside, the railcars rumble.

But he is no longer a child skipping in memory. He is a grown man, reaching the age of crisis. He's waiting for the cold war to begin in his loins. His hair is thinning. When he passes his hands over it his palm sprouts greyish tendrils. The first sign of madness. A child's joke. A harvest of hair. Leaves fall from his head. I don't want to be here, in this world of afternoon sun and yellowing trees, he says. The child, skipping, has yellow hair. Once it was possible to make this hour happy. So he won't go up. She's up there, he thinks, his wife Thérèse, lying on a slab. They want to do tests. If she could speak, she would ask him about his trip. Fine thing, asking him that at a time like this. He'd have to tell her he's free. Like a bird, flying. The nurses will clap. Then he will go *hnnng*, *hnnnng*, and she will know he can't say it. Constipated. Fucked. Unable to write. Then she will smile. He travels to avoid himself. He tells her of his latest successes and excesses. But the truth is that nothing comes, not even from his latest trip, from that old flat shore upon which the waves are pounding, pounding, beyond which it is impossible to go.

There is an open window somewhere. I can feel the draught, and I'm pounding my head on the walls looking for it, and I think: What a damned waste of a life. But what am I saying? Thérèse can't talk. She's been dead for thirty-three years.

Looks kind of funny, strapped to a slanting stainless steel tray
with tubes feeding and sucking and machines making sounds
like submarines on a death dive and everything smells funny.
Sort of sickly. The television I bought her duty-free is by her
side. Already it, too, smells funny. They told me to take it
home, because she won't be watching TV. I'm not so sure . . .
about taking it home I mean. It's got that smell of wounded
flesh. Drips. Here, open a vein; let my life-blood flow out.
Thérèse is dead, they shout at me. Thérèse, your wife, died a
long time ago! They are horrified that I've somehow slipped
into the autopsy room. It's not your wife, they shout, somewhat obscenely. After all, I have a white coat and an identification card clipped over my pocket. I took it off the stand in
the scrub-up room.

Let me tell you about my Grandad. That's my grandfather
on Mother's side.

Grandad was huge. All six feet seven of him. He was tough.
He used to knock his sons around. My Uncle Nicholas has
been deaf all these years in one ear because Grandad cuffed
him a good one. Can't remember what Nicholas had said to
him many, many years ago, a shell to his ear, listening for
eternity. They were competing for the same woman. It was
straight out of *The Brothers Karamazov*. In the end she married
my uncle, who was then promptly disinherited. That was
when Grandad drank himself to death, and lost his memory
on the way.

KATOOMBA

1978

You wake up in a guesthouse in Katoomba. The air is bracing when you open the window. They don't encourage you to open the windows because the heating bill soars. Sometimes, on the rare days when it snows, you open all the windows of your room, simply to defy. Simply to let the dark day drift into yourself. And if it snows you will walk into the bush forever, afraid to be silent you will marry silence, never to be heard of, from, again, in order to understand something, you don't know what, perhaps the beginning, the idea of freedom without hope.

You've been in the Aeneas guesthouse for five years. Mrs Harris, the concierge . . . although concierge is a bit French and pretentious . . . Mrs Harris, the old slut that runs this place, eyes you off in mock flirtatiousness every morning before your walk, eyes you off as she runs her hand lasciviously over the tea cozy. 'Professor Catacomb,' she purrs, 'are you taking your morning constitutional then?' 'Yes,' you say, accompanied regularly with dissonance from your nether end. Then, as though guilt flapped by on batwings, you tell her to call you Artie. You're very regular. You take the morning paper with you . . . just in case.

Yesterday, for the first time in five years, you went into a bookshop. It was a small second-hand bookshop on the main street. A wind so cold it cracked the ironlace on old verandahs. It raced up the street and tore at you. But the shop, so you thought, might have been a refuge. The perfumed past and its seductions. Old phobias. You sighed. The girl at the counter looked suspiciously at you. What she saw you saw too. Grizzled, muffled, you could have passed for any old tramp; alcoholic, mentally deficient. On cold days in Katoomba the

8

tramps stayed tucked up in bed, in guesthouses that were guesthouses in the twenties. Old women emitting clouds of garlic vapour, old women crackling with infirm hips run them now. Not all for profit. Something to be said for old women. That's where you found a home, spending the last of your savings.

Now you finally get up. Put on your greatcoat. You take the top blanket off your bed, fold it neatly in two then fold it in half again. From the pocket of your pyjama coat, from the pocket closest to your heart, you take out a pocket knife. It is a Swiss Army knife which you found in a garbage can a long time ago. The cross on it is no longer visible. It's had cruel usage. But the blades are still sharp. You sharpen them on the step near the back door. Spitting and sharpening, spitting and sharpening. The mind gets honed that way too. It cuts into the years, cuts into the heart, into the blanket. You cut a neat segment from the corner. There. Now put it over your head. A poncho. A priest. *Introibo* . . . never mind. Scratch a bit. Into the fray.

You stand in the small bookshop, studying your double. You can see that the girl wants to kick you out. But she can't quite recognise you from yesterday, and even if she did and said something nasty you might kick up a stink, vomit on the floor, break things, tear books. She cannot make up her mind because you are clean. Spotless. You make a habit of spending at least two hours at your *toilette*. You patch, mend, clean, soak, scrub. This has nothing to do with dignity. You cannot stand filth. Your nose is too sensitive. For example, beneath her perfume the girl smells of stale love-making. She shifts her weight from one foot to another. She knows you aren't going to buy anything. You stamp one foot, then the other. She clears her throat. She sighs. You hawk into your hanky. Clean out filth. She clucks her tongue. These are all the sounds you make as well. Only for real. Involuntary noises from the soul. A kind of anamnesis. And when things get really bad, a howling.

Books. For five years they lay in wait for you, circling, watching, alert to your drifting. You weren't going to keep in step, and the girl knows that too. She, though, is frightened of books, and of people who read. For a brief moment she turns her back. You see her turn down the heater. You might go, experiencing the draught from the glass door, which she leaves lightly ajar, to funnel up the wind. But you have provisioned for this. You have on three jumpers and an old tweed you found at St Vincent de Paul's and on top of all this an old greatcoat with a slit in the chest received in a bayonet charge circa 1915. Then the poncho to add flair. Apart from the greying hair, you're of indeterminate age. She positively hates you now, tapping her nails on the counter. Her buttocks, you can tell, are shimmering, roasted on the heater, which she has to turn on again, because, well, an alcoholic doesn't experience the cold immediately. Somebody should tell her that . . .

You open the cabinet. Finger a book. It's been such a long time. Feel the paper. Feel your heart kicking over, firing and failing, firing and failing. Years ago, your whole life served an apprenticeship to knowledge and then you discovered you were waiting to die. Even wisdom was a wisecrack. Your colleagues played with the notion of death but they could not have known that you smelled it on them, this stink of decay. You smelled everything that came from the abyss, the emptiness, the breath of the void . . . the foetid cesspool stink of grand and abstract notions. But here. You finger the paper. It folds easily. Creases. Doubles under your scaly hands and broken fingernails. Smudges under lickspittle. Scratch it. The hair rises on the back of your neck. The girl edges over. Stands behind you. Outside the glass door Katoomba is roaring.

Have to be secretive. Freud himself specified that this art had to be protected like fire from the gods:

> *You can believe me when I tell you that we do not enjoy giving an impression of being members of a secret society and of practising a mystical science.*

That was in 1933. No wonder the Nazis were suspicious. You didn't let Freud down. You *knew* what he meant.

Kherson
1891

Grandad, or his mother's father, owned one of the largest estates in what was known as the 'breadbasket of Russia'. Breadbasket was right. The afternoon storms rolled in from the Black Sea and the whole region rumbled and was fertilised and produced. Sergei used to crouch by the banks of the Dnieper and watch the black clouds spit and the wheat shooting and hear the black soil shifting and sucking and the land giving off a kind of sigh, like a soft fart. Grandad made that sound when he weighed and stroked his pockets, which he wore outside his peasant's smock. Yes, money made him fart. Maybe it was all the bread and liquor. Now and again, always at the wrong time, when the weather was bad or the crop had already been harvested, Grandad made his sons work twice as hard. While they were expending their energies on the same woman, Grandad made Uncle Nicholas chop up a huge tree that had fallen in a storm.

My uncle complained that he was tired.

'Tired!' Grandad exclaimed. 'You don't get tired until you reach the age of sixty. Maybe seventy. Even then, if you want to survive you've got to keep ahead of the herd. You just don't know what work is. Tired! I'll give you tiredness!'

Maybe it was then that Grandad cuffed him. A flat palm. Ear pressure.

Uncle Nicholas was anaemic. Perhaps that's why he was tired. Grandad made everyone feel guilty because they weren't working hard or fast enough. Work was like a competition. It was its own reward. Grandad always won. He bought new estates. Perhaps that's why when he died he had over a million in the bank. He went from feudalism to capitalism in

11

the short space of a lifetime. That was quite an achievement. Especially as he had lost his memory somewhere in the shift. But then capitalism was based on forgetting, especially of its previous axioms. You see, even though he had over a million he must have realised he would never be successful in the way we would be. You've got to start in front; make the money spurn everything that went on before. This was a *fin-de-siècle* idea. He thought we would just keep expanding, and our sons would conquer the world. So when it came to work he never gave us a chance. History, however, has proven him wrong, because the third generation always lost it or frittered it away, or, worse still, fell victim to a revolution.

It was just as well Uncle Nicholas was cutting that tree that day. I remember that it was very cold. If you did happen to sit around you froze. We had three-thousand acres in the plains near Kherson. Between each section of the estate there were stands of trees. Poplars, I think. Grandad was running to and fro in a stand of trees, marking out the right ones for firewood, going *thunk* into a tree with his axe and then half running to the next one. *Thunk*, in his whaleskin coat because it looked like it was going to snow. I helped to chop with my toy axe and got in the way. Grandad never laid a hand on me. When he wasn't looking I took out his axes from the leather bag he kept in the dray. The bag was stained and gave off a comforting smell. I liked to pull out the sharp axes and run my finger along the oily blades. I left axes stuck into trees and forgot about them. The thin, hard trunks were unforgiving. *Thunk*. I couldn't pull them out. The handles came loose.

It was about lunchtime and Uncle Nicholas took out his bread.

'Not now boy,' Grandad shouted. 'It's going to snow.'

Nicholas resumed chopping. Thick low clouds formed over us. Grandad darted between the trees and appeared behind my uncle. He was wheezing. He was tired. He watched his son, who was handsome and tall and swung an axe like a peasant forester, dressed in his blue smock. Nicholas was almost six feet tall, but he wasn't strong. Mounds of vapour came off his head. Phlegm gurgled in his chest. His anaemic flesh glimmered beside the darkening wood. Chips sprayed into his hair. Nicholas coughed. He swung. It grew dark and quiet. There was a sickness in the day.

Grandad mustn't have seen the wedge of black steel hurtling through the air.

Humble beginnings. Life must have flashed before Grandad's eyes. For a split second he must have thought: What a damned waste of a life. But he wouldn't have believed it. Not after all the hard work. He had drive. He could put ten men in their places. Shamed them all. He had always been a better worker than anyone. Until the accident. Scenes from the past must have run before his eyes.

Vienna
1972

Yellowish, like an old newsreel.

I tell you I'm just crazy about movies. Last night it was *Casablanca* I went to see for the third time. Kiss me again Sham. All this spying and romance. Above all I like the accent . . . like Donald Duck's. Not the kind of English I was taught as a child. My friend Artie and I practise at it.

Goddamit, this is not a hospital at all. What is this? What is going on? The patients lumber around slowly, talking to themselves, smoothing down their hair, looking at themselves in the glass. A doctor comes towards me. I can tell he is a doctor because he's in a crisp grey suit. He's well-off. I used to be like that once, before I encountered manic-depression. But he recognises me, for I'm, well, sort of famous. He smiles, puts out his hand.

'Wolfi!' he yells, and then corrects himself. 'Mr Wespe. Great book,' he says, pumping my hand. 'Great for the profession.' He's eager to say no more and to be off. I know doctors. They pretend to have no time. Small-talk is of course analysis-time. Two hundred an hour, I hear. But I grab him and whisper in his ear:

'What year did my wife die?'

He looks slightly alarmed at first. He hasn't been on a television quiz show for two years. He has tufts of grey hair as eyebrows and these stir like mice on his forehead. He smiles. His teeth are crooked and yellow. He's stalling for time on the sixty-four-thousand-dollar question. He's about to say that he gives up. These Viennese are all the same. In the event of a challenge they settle for an Anschluss.

'Mmm. Thérèse. That was her name. I'm correct there aren't I? Wasn't it '37? Or was it '38? Why, Mr Wespe, you know

14

better than I on that one. *You* wrote your autobiography, or should I say: *This is your life.'* He laughs a sort of two-beat laugh. He winks. From one 'normal' to another. 'Are you sure you aren't dreaming?' the shrink asks me slyly, his eyebrows doing rodent chinups over his spectacles.

It was a dangerous question to ask mental patients. Yet, they do it all the time. I know these sorts of philosophical teasers. It was undergraduate stuff. Descartes must have had sleeping sickness too. It was called meditation in those days. *Corgi a tergo zum*, Descartes said. Dogs do it backwards, moreover. Not a world-shattering observation. Nevertheless, reality is more profound for dogs . . . if it smells, eat it or screw it. Then the shrink astounds me.

'Someone's been slipping you Dopamine,' he said. 'That gets the brain over-excited. I tell you what . . .'

He pushes a bottle of tablets at me, shakes something into my palm. He was feeding me paranoia. I thought maybe he was extending my disabilities. He walks off.

In my hand I find a couple of black jellybeans. He treated me like a child. Just like a child. And like a child I have to confront these lies all over again. Lies. All lies. The fiction of my life.

I catch a passing nurse by the sleeve. She's perfumed. Smells of Chanel 1938. 'What year is it?'

Scarcely looking at me, she replies: '1972'.

KATOOMBA

1978

You must have blacked out for several minutes. You didn't fall on the floor: these things happen without warning or violence, like a trance into which you slip, or a sliding into hypnosis from a completely confused state. Don't think. Don't think too much or you no longer belong to yourself. No identity, no future, or at least very little of it because of the divide, which is nothing dramatic. People think of these things as breakdowns, something sudden, a little tainted with insanity, disturbances you are unable to control. Nothing of the sort. Where you come from, reality is a handicap. When these people think of the imagination, they see an animal hide nailed to a wall.

In Katoomba, in the bookshop, the girl is back at the counter. She is thinking up new ways to be rid of you. You turn around. You stare at her. She tries to be defiant for about a minute, holding your eyes with hers, which are black with hatred and dilated with fear. For a second you find this attractive. But she relents. You see that she has no will for perversity. No stomach for the fight because the weight of popular morality has crushed her. Reading, in a bookshop which only sells second-hand books after all, still exerts a kind of aura that is not purely commercial. She might smile, sidle over and say in a trembling or harsh voice that this is not a library. To which you will smile too, revealing broken yellow teeth, and, shaking your head and wagging your finger under her nose, you will ask her how many minutes she allows for browsing, the number of minutes per book or per shelf, the making up of one's mind, time in terms of money. Could you possibly be hurting these books? Absorbing too much heat? What is it that is transgressing her propriety? You are annoying her. That is the crux of the matter. Worse, other people are being prevented from browsing. But you see no other people. You call her attention to this imaginary opposition. Of course, if you had a gun you would have called her attention to that. Opened your coat a little for her to observe and to decide whether all this is worth it.

Like a bull in a china shop you turn, engulfed in jumpers and greatcoat and blanket, hair held firm by a discoloured beanie, mittens with the fingers out. You are bovine. You browse. She turns. She's not too bad looking really. You put a finger to your chin, a sign of thinking. You would have propped your foot up on some shelving but are wary of the consequences. You could imagine her, sweet in your fouled sheets, her black eyes rolling back. You see her more clearly now. Pale skin reddening from the confrontation with you. Hands fluttering. You know that you are incapable of any anger. Slow to be roused. She picks up the telephone and throws her scarf around her shoulders, obscuring the white neck and the thin necklace of imitation metal. You run your finger along the dusty shelves and smear the glass cabinets with spit. Clear the smudge with your elbow, break the glass. Luckily she doesn't even notice. There is only a slight crack and a sliver, a triangular piece has fallen inside. You open the case. Hello? she says. She is calling for help. Her voice is hostile. She can't read your eyes, milky with love. Sounds like backup from a boyfriend. Let's see. Nietzsche. *Ecce Homo.* Christ, that was good once. Your eye blinks back a tear. By God! Philosophical sentiment! Might be the heating, which she's turning up. You could take this all day. Finger probing along the spines. Dances over Plato. Joined by its stubby cousin. Twin compasses of love. Kant. Too aesthetic. Heidegger. Too Nazi. You're being boring. You see that the old diseases haven't left you. Years of struggle to master all that. To have once professed it. Lectured three hours at a time about the essence and the existence. Dead now. All dead. The mouth was the manufactory of power. When you dug up graves to study decomposition you saw faces which imploded in the sun and in that horror you saw more clearly what was always hidden from you: the true face of the human . . . the point at which God excuses Himself.

17

What is not hidden in Katoomba is disease. It had its heydey in the twenties when valetudinarians wheezed their way up here to take the air and die. Before they kept tuberculosis under control. Before they eliminated Spanish 'flu. Before it was found that pleurisy sufferers should have gone north to Queensland. Even the cancerous came, expecting the air to decrease their lumps and growths. This was a resort, a sanctuary, a refuge and a brothel all rolled into one. The erotic and the neurotic spawned in the cold.

No. Keep all that under. Your observations are jaundiced. You've been too long in the cold and your genitals have shrivelled. Lack of use. Alcohol. An effort of will may have stirred the fires of lust. Something stirs for the girl as her bottom collapses back onto the heater. You pass along the shelves into the psych section. Psychiatry . . . psychology. Been there before. Looking for a lost companion. There he is. *The Wolf-Man by the Wolf-Man*. He was a patient of Freud's. Dog-eared. As you left it last time. Once a year, every June between 1919 and 1926, the Wolf-Man visited Freud. Sigmund gave him money. The Wolf-Man was down and out. The Russian Revolution had made him the recipient of charity from the Viennese Analytical Society.

When you sold this book last time to a second-hand dealer you had made all kinds of annotations in the margins. Corrections. Digressions. Nobody has rubbed them out. Quite possibly nobody has read this book since. You are overjoyed by this. After all, the story is not everybody's. It remains an aside, subsumed by Freud, the case made to underpin a theory. A Russian aristocrat, neurotic and so self-obsessed that historical events apparently had no effect on him, spends half his life in sanatoria and becomes a patient of Freud's. It is really what Freud wrote that makes this his most famous case, a writing which subsequently became the three-cornered cornerstone of psychoanalysis: the proposal of infantile sexuality, the interpretation of dreams, the castration complex. Without Freud, the Wolf-Man's story would never have been told: the story of a man with a predilection for sodomy, self-absorbed, for most sodomites are also sodomees, senders and receivers in a communion of universal love and emptiness. (Ishmael

Liebmann, the famous psychoanalyst who spent some years in general practice, told you about the number of people who came to him with things up their bums. It's a lonely universe out there.)

But what is interesting in the Wolf-Man's story is found in what seems the most unexciting chapter of the book. It covers the longest period in the life of the Wolf-Man, the period from 1919 to 1938. The period between two wars. It is the chapter entitled: 'Everyday Life'. It is three and a half pages long and spans nineteen years. In this chapter of absences and omissions, the Wolf-Man lets slip one important fact. It is the seemingly open secret that he *wrote*.

Primal scenes

She used to give herself injections with a hypodermic she took out of a silver case. Held it between two fingers like a cigarette. Pulled up her dress to the thigh and rested her arm on the bunched up material. She had no underpants on. She'd said she was ill, but Father knew what she was when she leant over him at the piano and whispered: 'You can do anything, you know.'

That was Mother. She was a hypochondriac. She died in 1950, aged eighty-nine.

Father first saw her on a deserted country road near her property. People used to think she was an alcoholic. In those days very little was known about hypochondria.

Father was clattering past in a battered droshky when it was just starting to snow. He reined in the horse to clear some branches from the wheels when he noticed a woman standing on the side of the road. After a few moments he realised that he was watching her urinate, standing beside a pine forest in full view of the road, legs apart, steam rising from her puddle.

He's not blaming her. He played her games. Later he told her he'd seen her breasts, that when he approached, she'd pulled her fur coat quickly around herself.

Father tried to understand everything. He too, was convalescing. He had a bad case of priapism. A drunken serf had emerged from behind some stooks, the last of the harvest, and had lunged at him with a knife. The blade embedded itself in his side. When they sewed him up and pulled the flesh together he had this constant erection. 'That'll go down,' the doctor said, making a long-range forecast.

His mother, beautiful in her long skirts. Now and again he saw

20

the apparel she hid underneath. White lace and camisoles and pantaloons and petticoats. A strange contraption called a bustle. He put these things on when Mother was out, these things she hid. Looked at himself in the mirror. He was disappointed in his grotesque nine-year-old body, without form, without curves, his small but obtrusive erection. His sister Anna came in and saw him all dressed up. She was two years older. She wore trousers and riding boots. She put her hand under his petticoats and said: 'You have a tail just like Misha (the Corgi), only it's in the front.'

He looks in the mirror. He is someone else. He would like to be ill, feverish, in the silken counterpanes of his mother's bed. But he has to be careful. He was allowed to skip the religious service this morning on account of a rattling chest. Anna was to look after him because his old Nanya wouldn't have missed church for anything. He was glad he didn't have to endure the long processions of fearsome priests, chanting and swaying at each corner of the street. He had his own procession. His mother's incense. Too late. Here they are. He hears the carriage downstairs, tears himself out of the stays, hides in his own bed, unable to remove the knot in the satin ribbon Anna tied around his still inflated penis.

Mother had sullenly absolved father from his sense of duty. THERE WILL BE NO MORE, she said.

— It was a long and arduous process, she would tell me one day, years later. And I would hear again his grunting and whimpering, the pleading, coaxing voice of Mother, when I stood at the door with my still-warm chamberpot.

— You are a man, but you don't make love like a man.

Father grunted.

She had a knack for making a travesty of everything, he said.

He couldn't bear to look at her. Father shuffled out of the room in his pyjamas. He was of a melancholy disposition. Thin, tall, sensitive, he preferred to play chess. He was a swine. God cast evil spirits into swine. He looked at me. One day you will understand everything, he said.

21

Then something happened to our sheep. Two hundred thousand lay dead in the fields. I wandered among the bloated carcasses beginning to stink in the heat. Most had already been torn open by the village dogs. Offal lay strewn like twists of fly-paper. A million flies set up a whirring that came in waves. They were inside me, streaming out of my orifices.

Gypsies came and burned the carcasses on the spot. Everywhere there was the smell of decaying and roasted mutton. I saw families eating half-cooked lambs. I was appalled. I feared them, with their campfires and loud talk. In the night I looked out my window and it seemed to me that it was a kind of hell out there, which was both fearful and attractive. The idea of eternal wandering found a place in my heart. Suspected, without a nation, despised but together, gypsies and nomads became for me the truth of a world in retreat, of a backward motion.

It must have been then that I wrung my hands, made a noise like an animal about to be slaughtered. I stayed awake most of the night. I was lucky I had an upper bedroom, and the flickering of their fires had to compete with the South Russian moon. The moon must have won out, because in the morning I awoke with the sun casting detailed shadows of the walnut tree onto the wall beside my bed. The shadows were so fine that I could count the leaves. A wasp landed on one and slowly folded and unfolded its wings.

Vienna

1972

They allowed Sergei to use the Hospital Library ... honorary
patients like him have the same privileges as the sanatorium
staff, who have access to the medical section of the library. He
could look up all the case studies and all the diagnoses. Let's
see now ... wolves. They say you cannot dip your hand into
the same river twice. But every time he comes upon wolves in
a library he stumbles upon the fact that they go backwards
and forwards in the same territory and do not cross their
defined borders.

Of course now that I'm famous anything is possible. Maybe
they'll make movies of me. Oh, the rise and fall of fortune!
And the rise again. My book was a smash hit. Stayed on *The
New York Times* best-seller list three months. Nobody ever
heard of anything like it. I imagined agents parachuting into
my garden, publishers who had rejected me previously jumping from skyscrapers. That was the book trade, I said to
myself. But all that, all the applause, the book signings, the
envy, was worth absolutely nothing when you pissed a thim-
bleful every twenty minutes. My prostate like Caesar's faithful
reminder: thou art only a man. Worse still, the pain that
courses beneath the surface.

Psychiatrists were more cautious about the book. They did
all sorts of tests on me, just to make sure I didn't make things
up. 'Did Freud have a beard?' they asked me. 'Did he ever
shave it off?' Silly questions. Freud was always distant. I could
analyse his body odour. English tweed with a little cigar ash
thrown in. Sort of a cross between a leather-bound edition of
Conan Doyle and a well-worn deer-stalker's cap.

It was Freud who first taught me that parody comes before

23

the paradigm, play before principle. The origin of man was a sort of partying without precedence.

'Listen, Wespe,' he used to say to me, 'to be famous you got to have a double. Some poor schmuck who'll do the straight routine, who sweats, who gets bored, who wants to commit suicide. Call him reason. Then there's you, swinging from the chandelier. You throw in a few setbacks and some professional suffering, powder your face so it looks pale, and then effect a remarkable cure. People have forgotten that life's a game. Play is the essence of thinking. I did my most important thinking in bed, before breakfast. After two cigars and a coffee I've completed a whole volume of ideas. Then I pass everything over to the schmuck while I eat a full breakfast. With luck, the patient's also a disciple hell-bent on hagiography in order to get himself some of the limelight. It's always the patient who makes sense, do you see?'

That was Freud. A good family man who was always passing things over. Transferences; transactions. Knew how to do business with the Other.

Wolves. 'Man is the wolf of science', a prominent philosopher has written. Wolf-boys; Romulus and Remus, lean and hungry; 'beware of false prophets, which come to you in sheep's clothing, but inwardly they are ravening wolves' (*Matthew 15*); Peter and the wolf; 'his sentinel, the wolf' (*Macbeth*); 'a cursed past in which man was wolf to the man'—that last by Bartolomeo Vanzetti, who, with his double Sacco, were executed for treason in 1927.

Wespe's Uncle Peter, one of his father's three brothers, was diagnosed as incurably paranoid. He was institutionalised, but because he had a large estate in the Crimea, he was able to live there as a hermit. He achieved a certain notoriety. A solitary is always regarded with suspicion, as both saint and devil. It was said that his constant companion was a wolf.

Wolves are always two; a pairing that describes a paradox; a prehistoric unconscious which makes civilisation possible.

A wolf is always a double.

Pripet River, White Russia

His father bought this property when he was about two-and-a-half years old. The place went cheaply, part of the land reclamation of the Pripet swamps. Forests abounded, full of wildlife. The leader of the drainage expedition, I.I. Zhilinsky, came to visit. Sergei's father and I.I. went hunting for elk and wild boar.

The family used to come up in the summer when the light stayed low in the sky well past his bedtime. On those nights, in his bedroom at the villa (it was nothing grand, just two storeys and looked after by a family of serfs), he heard the wolves howling in the forests that ringed the estate. At dusk, with the light thinning and the mosquitoes droning, his mother would already be asleep. Sometimes when he woke in the night he heard her walking the corridors in some mysterious vigil. Ever since those days at Pripet River, wolves have been his favourite subject.

I used to talk about them incessantly, after dinner in the servants' quarters below the house, or on long walks with my father, trudging through peat bogs or following forest trails. It was always at dusk, or after night had fallen that my desire to talk about wolves emerged. In my adult years it would always be at dusk that my breakdowns occurred, as if some threshold needed to be crossed, as if, at that time, some carnal desire for life exceeded itself, exceeded my capacity to gather it in. Between dog and wolf I howled, imitating the wolf's loss, howled for that gap between what he knows about the world and an existence that might have been . . . his loss of history.

I was interested in wolves because they scared me.

I used to go downstairs to the servants' quarters after

supper. It was the only time in the day that father allowed my sister and I to go into their 'region'. Father used the word 'region' in order to insist on the specificities of place, in order to impress upon us the difference that privilege had imposed; that it was not equality but decadence to try to erase that boundary. My father was a great liberal. If he hadn't died before 1918 the Bolsheviks would have murdered him.

I used to go downstairs to listen to old Dimitri tell stories. Dimitri looked after the estate. He grew flowers for us each summer. He cut wood for the stove. He took trout from the stream for our meals and sometimes, if his eye was still good, he brought venison or boar home. Once I lingered behind the sheds to watch Dimitri skin an elk. When the blood started to flow onto his hands a kind of ravenous sneer came over his face. His work became less precise; his slashings with the knife at the layer of fat beneath the skin amounted to a frenzied flailing. The animal's legs palpitated to the strokes as though it were alive, while Dimitri stood astride the carcass pumping, pumping with his little knife at the mass of organs which tumbled out at his feet. An animal had turned into matter; naked, undignified, violated. Dimitri said he was 'dressing' the meat. From that day on, I refused to eat flesh of any kind, resulting in long hungry nights and several illnesses. My father stopped beating me over the issue when he saw my poor health, and ordered Dimitri to cover the eighty kilometres into town for maize, grain and vegetables.

During the long winters when we were not there, Dimitri gorged himself on game, grew fat and slightly scurvied, drank and abused his wife. Dimitri came from Minsk. He was a tailor before landing this job. In Minsk he sat in the basement of a shop with his legs crossed, flattened to act as a rest for a sleeve board, for sixteen hours a day. For sixteen hours a day he unpicked the linings of coats and turned them inside out. That was how people got longer wear out of their garments.

'If only,' Dimitri said to my sister Anna and me one day, 'if only we could turn our bodies and souls inside out.' Dimitri was smoking his pipe. He was smoking Turkish tobacco which he cut into shreds with a large pair of sharp scissors. The smoke made my eyes water. Dimitri took this to mean that I was frightened. He enjoyed making me frightened. 'That way,' he continued, 'we could be saints on the outside and wolves inside, and in that way keep renewing ourselves.'

Dimitri told us the story of the time he was tailoring in Minsk when he heard scratching at the window above the basement. 'I thought it was some urchins making mischief. I remember that it was a freezing day. Snow caked the panes, and even though I had a fire going, the cold seemed to funnel down through the walls and crept up my back. I shivered so much I could hardly hold the needle.'

Dimitri paused to re-light his pipe. Sometimes he paused so long he forgot the story. Sometimes he said nothing more and would look up at the ceiling and at the smoke and would fall into reverie. His wife Olga said that on these occasions he became stupid. She said he was infected by Satan. When we looked at his dark and brooding face we would indeed see that the light in him had been extinguished. But when I told father that, he looked hard at me and said: 'Sergei, never believe that Satan is stupid.'

Sometimes, though, after a long pause, Dimitri would brighten up and continue:

'I went to the window. I couldn't see anything out there. The shop was on the edge of town and usually you could see the forest, at least the trunks of the trees, through the snow. But on this afternoon, you could see nothing.'

Dimitri stopped again, and I feared he would lapse into silence for the next two or three days. These silences were not calculated to keep us in suspense. Now, when I look back on it, I understand that he did not really want to tell the story, because even though it may have been an old story, he was inventing it too, making himself the main character. The story gave him life. If he told it too slowly he could lose himself in it. If he told it all at once he would no longer exist. He paused, delayed, recalled in fits and starts.

Dimitri put his hands in front of his eyes. Interlaced his fingers. '*Glazá*,' ('eyes'), he kept repeating. What was he trying to see? He saw, he said, a pair of eyes. He saw a pair of brown eyes looking through the glass over which the snow had melted as though before a great steamy breath. He opened his fingers. He opened the window.

'Before I knew what was happening a big grey wolf, a wolf the size of a small pony, had pushed under the window and had leapt into the room. I was paralysed. I didn't know what to do. I thought of jumping through the window, but at the same moment the fear of exposing my hind-quarters to the fangs of the wolf prevented me. The wolf had a very red tongue. It trotted to the corner where I kept my bread. There was still some soup left in a bowl. When the wolf moved I saw the fur on its back rippling, opening and closing, like gills on a fish. Without taking its eyes off me, it ate all the food. It only took a couple of seconds.'

Canis lupus: the common grey wolf. A large male may grow up to two metres long and weigh fifty kilograms. Its fur was used in trimming clothing.

Once, not so many years ago, I was walking in the Schwarzwald outside Baden Baden. Now, if you told me that wolves could still be seen there, I would have said: Yes, only in hallucinations. You can imagine: a nuclear pall hangs over the European sky; the afternoon darkens dramatically around three o'clock; branches jettison their burden of snow and spring up without warning. It is easy to get lost. I saw a wolf. It was a big wolf, healthy, well-fed. So well-fed indeed that it was burying something in the snow. I walked towards it and it loped away. I searched for what had been buried, but I could find nothing; neither the exact site nor any trace of wolf tracks in the snow. In the human world, a wolf exists and doesn't exist at the same time. For a moment I was completely lost. I panicked, tried to retrace my steps. When I finally found the road I happened to look over my shoulder. I saw the wolf again . . . in the dark, watching me. It had been following me, its tail held high like a flag.

'A wolf never loses his way,' Freud said to me once.

'When it tried to make its way out the window again, I grabbed its tail,' Dimitri said, hanging on to the end of his story. 'And do you know what?'

28

'What?' Anna said, sitting on his knee. She liked doing that, pushing herself up and down on his knee. Dimitri liked it too.

'The tail came off in my hand!' he roared, 'Just like that!'

We looked at him in astonishment.

'What did you do with it?' I asked.

'I made it into the collar of my coat,' Dimitri said, showing us his coat.

We felt the collar. It was wolf fur all right; we nodded to one another.

Dimitri had a tail too. Anna said she felt it on the front of his trousers.

In the summer, when the wind blew strongly and brought the smell of the bogs and the light played upon the forests through broken cloud, on these long afternoons, I used to see the rye sway to and fro and the rippling fields became the sea. The peasants would then say: 'The wolf is coming through the rye.'

Dimitri said: 'I was walking during the summer, along the stand of trees near the rye fields when a pack of wolves appeared beside me and began to chase me. I immediately climbed up a tree. When I looked down I saw the wolves climbing on one another's backs in order to reach me. I noticed that the wolf on the bottom was the one without a tail. Quick as a wink I yelled: "Grab his tail!" '

Dimitri took a long pull on his pipe.

'The wolf was so scared he ran off and the others came toppling after him.'

'Bullshit,' Anna said.

Anna was a great realist.

I was frightened. Then I felt angry. Then I felt sad.

I felt a loss. I must have felt, I told Freud many years later, the loss of myself at the end of every story. My childhood was full of fictions.

Freud said I was experiencing the castration complex.

'Balls!' I said.

He must have felt it too. The loss of a tale when it was funnelled into theory.

29

Odessa
1892

In 1891, when I was five, we moved to Father's estate in Odessa. I was glad to leave Kherson. Once I saw a man hanging from a tree by the banks of the Dnieper. He was swollen and his trousers were bursting and the bough beneath which his body was twisting creaked like father's boots.

They hid the man's body in the ground.

Odessa was, once, beautiful, full of old villas with cream garden walls, large walnut trees, white sea steps. On the cobbled boulevards lined with acacia trees, soldiers in white uniforms and peaked caps used to clatter past on horseback. In 1925 Sergei Eisenstein made *Potemkin* here. In that film you can catch a glimpse of the huge rest homes, the sanatoria by the Black Sea.

There was a violent storm during the journey to Odessa, which was made in a closed carriage. I sat backwards in carriages. It was the way I would always look at my life, from the perspective of the past, which receded before action.

Mother promised me that in Odessa I would have a French governess and the thought of a French governess who smelled of lavender and wore long satin skirts must have aroused my curiosity. I dreamed of sleeping, nestled in her bosom, while she told me long stories in French. Such innocence then. Such lust now, in order to recall this.

Then the betrayal. She didn't tell stories. She was an empiricist. 'Prove everything you say,' was her favourite dictum. Endlessly, she commanded us to address her correctly. 'Call me Mademoiselle', she used to say. A petty tyrant. A Napoleon. She had a pinched face. Her stories had to have a moral. She came from the countryside and not from Paris, as she originally said. A bourgeoise. The worst kind . . . in whose mind money had been equated with preciosity. We regarded her with spite. Freud said to me early on in our acquaintance: 'Herr Wespe,' he was looking over the tops of his spectacles, 'in order to prove something you must have spite and menace. Pure and decent good sense is not enough to prove anything.'

My sister Anna tried to prove to me that female genitalia was not what I had called 'the missing portion'. We had been playing in Mother's room. We took off all our clothing. Where Anna did wee-wee there was a kind of pod, lips that flowered red and moist. Nothing is missing, she said, clambering on top of me, her lips wet and savage, pasting my face with kisses. Kissing is what you like to do to yourself. Do it. I've seen you. She pushed my elbow up to my face and my lips sucked at the flesh inside my arm. Women, she said, have the ability to kiss at both ends, to absorb. Such strangeness, such childhood firsts. These things would never be repeated, not with such carefree delight, not with such ignorance of evil. We were one. She placed her mouth over my penis. The desire never burst. The impulse never became too much. There was no necessity to prolong. There was nothing but the pure and utterly absorbing voluptuousness of infantile sexuality. Anna was right. There was no missing portion. There was no original sin. The Garden of Eden was ours. Anna, double-jointed, supple, athletic, stood on her hands, went down on her elbows, brought her legs over her head, did a crab-walk, positioned herself and pushed her face between her legs. She kissed herself. She was a snake swallowing her tail, a tongue with a new tale. She could roll herself into a ball. When we went to the seaside one day Anna got down and rolled over the sand dunes like a pig, over and over, all the way down to the beach. God cast evil spirits in the form of swine, the priest said. From that day on, spite came into all our games.

'Why don't you fuck me like a man?' Anna mimicked, as Father stood listening, pale and desperate, at the door of our bedroom.

These things have a habit of recurring. Years later, in Munich, in a Schwabing nightclub, Sergei witnessed an act in which the girl, not as boyish as Anna, a little too tall, too thin, proved

31

to him that there was indeed something missing from his experience as he stood entranced by the lights spewing out of the walls, waterfalls of amber vomit, plaster scallops plunging onto the stage, electric fans batting at full blast to clear the foul breath, stood reaching out to touch Anna and feeling himself borne backwards, the cold outside making him gasp, finding himself in the gutter one lonely night in the city, and when he looked up, dazzled by the lights of the *Cabaret de Paris*, he was staring into the muzzle of a pistol going up and down under his nose, the smell of cordite in such a place pure and strange, an S.S. man's scarface oscillating between the spotlights, a smoothly shaven skull looming up like the moon, hearing the man's smile crackle as the butt of the pistol came down on his head.

In the gutter he breathed in the morning air, which had a sea-tinge to the foulness, a rotting smell not unlike seaweed, or a sea-cave at low tide. Out of each doorway he smelled heavy and stale perfume, cigar stubs, urine, beer, vomit, semen, leather coats, cat shit, garlic, mothballs, vaginas, herbs, talcum powder, flowers, sweat, feet, disinfectant, armpits, paint, burnt steak, farts, coffee, bacon, cordite, cigarettes, blood.

Lucky this time, he thought. Usually there was a pane of glass between him and life, between him and death, like the glass lid of a coffin.

Vienna
1972

Vienna, the city of schism. The city of dirty cream and commercial reality. Mozart probably captured it best . . . Amadeus Wolfganger. He knew the top and the bottom. But Vienna is possibly the only city in the world where an octogenarian, wandering in the archives of the National Library, will be interrupted by a young woman with a tray of coffee and *Kipfels* . . . to aid him in his search, during the long morning, for his destiny. When she stoops down, when she squats and then gets on her hands and knees to read the spine of some dusty manuscript, he is filled with the most indescribable lust. Her buttocks swell, and in the dim fluorescence of the library stacks he approaches her from behind, a hasty pilgrimage to a dank grotto in search of apparitions . . . or memories . . . which stop him. Remembering who he is.

In reality though, my private parts are in a cocoon. It is this waiting that astounds me. The way I'm paralysed, the way she waits, her skirt tight around her thighs, the electric snap of her stockings, her faint odour of musk which the perfume cannot mask. Ah! Life in this frieze of books makes words munificent. Lust and dust in these archives. Desire going back and forth trying to pick up a trail. Prolongation of death. Everything remains a promise.

Like my sex I was born in a caul. They told me this was filled with the significance of good fortune. At an early age I was already a budding pornographer. I drew Anna's private parts. But drawing cannot convey sounds or smells. As I grew older you might have called me a phonographer. I recorded sounds and later set them to scenes. Then I replayed them. For instance, I can remember exactly the words I put down in my notebook when I first met Freud:

A grandfather clock was thocking monotonously in a corner of his consultation room.

'I would indeed like to read everything you have written,' he said, smiling in a preoccupied sort of way, downplaying their significance. Perhaps in case I would not want to give the manuscripts to him, believing they were of value to people other than myself. Freud never showed admiration for my writing. At least, he never expressed it to me personally. In his lectures and papers I know that he has more than once used the adjectives 'interesting' and 'imaginative'. In order to please him I've had to become more and more obscene. But Freud was never ecstatic about the manuscripts. He took all of them. That was in 1910. I never saw any of them again. I only have fragments, found, luckily, among my wife's things. Pieces I had written and secreted among her underwear.

The young archivist is clever. She keeps our relationship on an even keel by urging me to go ahead of her along the shelves. I think I'm falling in love with her, although I have to keep looking at her to remember her face. From the back she looks like Lauren Bacall. Low-slung hips. From the front . . . anyone. One day I'm going to follow her with my camera, a new Voigtländer I've just bought, and when she bends over . . . snap!

KATOOMBA
1978

In the bookshop in Katoomba on a windy and grey day you are snug as a bug with the copy of *The Wolf-Man* in your hands. You open it. Before even reading any of the words you come into possession of his peculiar state. It seems only you can see into him, feel the immense grief of which he was the prisoner, of his dilemma, of his nomenclature. He was also a prisoner of writing, which had already proclaimed for him a fame which could never be literary. Everything he wrote would be subject to analysis. No one would want to forget himself in the Wolf-Man's story. And yet he was a writer. A pornographer of the highest standard, for pornography in that time was the preserve of the élite, of writers, theologians, philosophers and men of science. But the chasm has closed in a democratic age. You see it now on the other shelf, vaseline-stained pages caked with dried semen, second-hand, as it were, making it difficult for the reader to turn the pages.

You once had everything. That's why when you first met Sergei you recognised a fellow spirit. He took for granted what you gave him, the apartment, the use of the Mercedes, the nights out at the Opera. But these were mere bagatelles for an aristocrat down on his luck. It could never match his former lifestyle: the luxury hotels, the estates, the Winter Palace, holidays at Bodensee. Imagine the turn-of-the-century splendour, the fur-lined sleighs, glamorous women, laudanum, the *volupté*.

Ah! You see how you've fallen into the old jargon. The years haven't silenced that orifice of production: the oracular predictabilities of research and academe where you once rented one-room apartments in New York, in the Bronx and in Queen's, and brought up predigested lectures beneath

35

incoming flights landing at La Guardia, lectures based on the long afternoons of your inherited melancholia ... yes, the dullness, broken only by having two jobs—lecturer and janitor—the upper and lower orders—day and night—reader of theses and lavatory-wall graffiti—to make ends meet—it was the beginning of your breakdown, backsliding, call it what you will, from action to actor, fishing for bodies in the river and going through wet wallets before the cops arrived. Eager to see your name in print you lingered sometimes for reporters, but they ignored you. Back in the apartment you read the telephone book and took pleasure in seeing only two other Catacombs. Ah! The days grew restless for the hasty after-seminar coupling with Fräulein Wittgenstein who let you fondle her impressive breasts frigidly encased in white cotton cups, nipples an inch long erect like twin penises or snail antennae and the dark unveiling of her taboos, each time you reach the triangle of compromise, a split second in which she put away feminism for the sake of being polymorphous, she shoos you away with theory ('The Russian Formalists', she begins, 'have this thing about real time —the sequence of events as you turn the pages—and story time— the correct series of events in the story itself ... which often have to be read backwards'—Formalism or feminism it had the same effect of detumescence), like she shoos away a dog or cat, ('Did you know the dog is the Oedipal animal par excellence?') and all things considered you have to take the initiative, for she likes it behind after you pull her leather pants all the way down, working backwards like the Russian Formalists, and smelling like a musk ox she always says: I'm too old for these games though she only looks twenty at the most as she pumps into position and your hand holds nothing ... the disappearance of the object of desire ... she knows all this, having studied in Budapest and Paris as she herself disappears in swirls of veils as you both slide into the hollows of New York, the stormwater drains where you get your second wind and slipping beneath her she whispers in your ear: you dirty foreigner ... to re-establish otherness, her racist bad-mouthing, which you love, giving her a vicious and no doubt painful pinch between orifices and you end up calling her a Nazi whore and she sobs, genuinely, sobs and splutters and crawls into a foetal position in one corner of the huge brass bed, shouting and shrieking, leaving scars on your back . . . but you get caught time and again, because she suddenly becomes nice as pie and begins talking of family life and having children and that really is the end of everything.

Primal scenes

Sergei's mother knew nothing about a trip in a rowboat. His father had taken him in a rowboat on the river. It was a cold afternoon as the weather was closing in and the school children were jumping the furrows to run cross-country home (the sky was black). Looking back from the boat he could see the house, three storeys, with turrets, more like a château, on the edge of the woods.

It was the way Sergei's father inhabited his body, the aristocratic bearing, that gave you the impression he belonged in a château. But before his marriage he was poor. Grandfather was a tailor from Minsk.

His mother wanted to leave the estate. She lay in bed thinking: It was already three o'clock and the chimes had sounded in the hall, had kept ringing in her head and she was sick in bed, sick of bed, had spent six months in it waiting for the coughing spasms to pass, the fits, the sour burning in the throat and the fishy taste of blood. She did not know of the trip her son had taken in the rowboat in that afternoon fog which drifted in over the river and which set the bells tolling in her head, counting the way the minutes passed like the beat of her son's heart when he slept with her during the storms and when the air in those febrific rooms turned yellow with powder and humidity, hermetic like the pages of a book or an old photograph, in a time that could not be retrieved.

His mother is young, suffering a passionate disease, made beautiful by it, by the flushed cheeks and pallid forehead, her hair quivering like a seam of gold caught in a segment of light. Or is she instead very thin and somewhat angular and her face too small and not young at all? Perhaps her hair is dark and shines not with oil but with the pathetic sheen of night

38

sweats, her cheeks marked with the flush of her affliction conceal rotting teeth, and her voice issues scornfully from the confines of her room. Yes, and her breath is bad, like that of most people who believe they are ill.

Her son returned ill as well, chilled from the mist, soaked with sweat from a fever. They tucked him into the spare bed in his mother's room. (In the bath his father poured wintergreen over his back and he had screamed and tried to put his head under the water in protest.) The night-light was dimmed. The air was bad. The first onset of malaria.

It must have been about five o'clock when he was wakened by a noise. In his sleep his sweats had begun and the sheets were soaked. He was caught in his cocoon of fever and sleep and turned, marking his presence in the dim light, took his place in the silk lampshade patterned with fauns. Turned again. The fever burned his eyes. Projected onto the wall was his Grandad, his mother's side, related to Tolstoy, the rich one, his forehead spurting blood, white foam at the edges where the axe-head went in. They said it was his brain exposed. Somewhere the howl of a distant wolf. Turned again and this time his mother, playing a game on all fours on her bed, her white satin slip bunched around her waist, her head in a pillow, murmuring oh God! Oh God! Silence. Refused to turn again; he couldn't believe these images and if he closed his eyes it all might change. There. His father crawled on all fours and hid behind sofas and he had a wolf-mask over his face, springing up and terrifying the children, who ran screaming into the garden. Please! his mother cried, please! The child! Opened his eyes. Wanted to be released from this superstition, but oh, the weight of this long night, the fear of its empty spaces. In the forest tree branches sprang up when the snow melted, like giants scaring little children, but oh, in a fever nothing really happens and the imagination runs like hot mercury over the exposed brain. Oh, his mother was saying, and his father was on his knees, praying, kissing alabaster buttocks. Turned again. He could freeze them, prevent their pagan worship. Turned again. They moved and stopped like clockwork toys. But he didn't know until many many years later, this interruption to desire was its very meaning. Stasis. In it he

39

saw his sister Anna, getting into bed with the wolf, a red cap on her head. He could not participate; waited in the expanse, cold now, the arctic winds racing down to the Black Sea. He forced himself to hold still. If he blinked, he was at the window. If he blinked again, he was outside in a park sloping down to the sea, the waves glistening in a patch of sunlight. Transposed, the waves became fauns. If he blinked again his father would come down from the timbered slopes to devour them. Oh, his mother cried. All of a sudden he saw her, the wind blustering now, a calculated brush of wind painting up her folds for him to behold a lavish score of black silken rows while that distinctive perfume of opulence found a passage to his heart. He yearned, he pined. He saw the animal she exposed and wanted to be her, with that softness, loving himself by tracing the route of curiosity, satisfied with the idea of her hiding such a vulnerable creature now exposed, now hidden, himself exposed to his father who slouched along that darkened and seamed passage, powerful, demanding and sadistic in that nightwash of evil and attraction, the glimmer of dancing gypsy fires. He was hiding again. It was something from the past, like a wound closed over, like the black mark in his palm pierced by pencil-lead when he thought of those things on an ancient school day many years later and so many years ago. He pushed that pencil into his palm, still hot and red from the teacher's birch. Plato, his nemesis. When asked to translate he trembled to such an extent his hand drummed on the desk top. Plato, con-artist, authoritarian, said souls went up in a chariot. Tripartite. Two horses and a rider. One white horse of reason, nobility and goodness. One black, presumably inky, lascivious, dragging down moderation. This grave horse, heavy with non-seriousness and homoeroticism was the cause of all the trouble . . . ink . . . Plato's blind spot, and Socrates his blinkered mount. Hidden desire. Excessive force. Turned again. Authority. Father had authority. Three times it happened, until all the fauns were dead and the boy screamed because he had just passed a turd, a hot nugget of disapproval and a gift to win back the image of the fauns which had disappeared, and he was suddenly giving birth to wolves, each emerging from his behind like sheep droppings.

Several nuggets. I gave birth to several wolves. Well, these are fragments. Shards that still cut. Anna came into my room one night and said: 'Sergei, I have been wounded.'

When Freud read the original and complete version, he flew into a rage. It was the only time I had seen him in such a temper.

'By what authority,' he shouted, 'do you take the liberty of misusing this information?'

'What information?'

I was dumbfounded. Did he believe that pornographers rendered something called the 'truth'? (Was this perhaps why they were vilified?) Did he really mean to say that sexuality had firmer foundations than narrative, than a patient construction of scenes? I doubted if this angered him. It was rather that I, a patient of his, *wrote*. Shit. He said as much.

'All you do is complicate matters.' He was now, calming a little.

I could hear someone moving about next door, in the Freud family wing. They too, must have been unused to raised voices. Madmen had never set foot in this house, I thought. Neurotics were generally well-behaved, and they paid well. Then Freud became almost happy. I saw a thought wing its way across his face. Never again would he be so transparent.

'You know,' he smiled, shuffling over to his desk and putting my manuscript on it, (I remember he knocked over a couple of carved figurines) 'psychoanalysis is writing at its greatest desire to *prove*. We mustn't get ahead of ourselves in making up fictions which invade propriety.'

Freud wore thick corduroy trousers and a velvet smoking jacket. I noticed that he had a white bandage on his left hand. He told me later that he had burnt it when he attempted to take some bagels out of the oven. He sat down in front of me (yes, I was lying on the couch. People are wrong when they say he never faced his patients. He did, once in a while, for practicality's sake. He could threaten. But yes, for an intellectual he was quite practical, I mean, in those days only women cooked bagels). He lit the stub of a cigar left in the ashtray and

41

stared into my eyes. His beard was grey and white.

'Look,' he puffed, 'we Jews have an in-built bullshit barometer. That's why we're reputed to be good at business. Anti-semitic nonsense, but we let them think that. It saves time.'

He circled the stub in front of his face. I thought he was trying to hypnotise me, but he was only fanning the cigar lest it burn unevenly.

'What you've written is bullshit, but I find it interesting, because it says something about your personality,' Freud said, dragging on the cigar. 'It gives me a key. You see, I, as the reader, am the detective. You, the . . . ahem! writer, are the criminal . . . irresponsible, confessive, hiding in your text. You have a predilection for wandering. You tell a story without seeming to have a point . . .'

He punctuated this point with his cigar. I noticed some embers falling onto the carpet. Come to think of it the floral-patterned carpet was dotted and smeared with arabesques of soot and burn-holes.

'. . . when you are actually *evading* the point,' he went on.

I was astounded. It was in the hope of his following my trail that led me to him in the first place.

Anna

1883–1905

Anna had one hell of a mouth. Believe you me. She was only two years older than me, but she was encyclopaedic. She could be a cornucopia of curses, a lexicographer of lewdness one minute, and nice as pie the next. Honeyed obscenities flowed and rattled from her. She picked up the latest from the peasants. Father thought she was really something. 'A girl like that,' Father used to say, 'needs no looking after.'

She was always self-confident as a child. To think what I missed out on. I was twisted up inside. Maybe it was on account of my stature. At school the bigger kids picked on me; called me shorty, squirty, runty, you name it. Life was tough, but I rolled with the punches, took in a few black eyes and carried a dagger. I had a private life. No, what worried me was that Anna took to protecting me. For example, she'd enter the school unexpectedly, march straight up to this Frankenstein in the classroom and say: 'Frankie, you're a swell guy. You remind me of . . . of a thermos.' (The Dewar Vessel had just been invented. Anna kept abreast of the latest in science.)

He would stop choking me. He'd think about this, scratching his head. 'A thermos?'

'Yeah. You're kind of a warm character. But essentially you're a fuckin' vacuum.'

The bully would smile at this. Pleased. I think he saw it as a compliment. Then Anna would hit him with her latest 'peasantries'. They rolled off her tongue like sheep pellets. She would go into a frenzy, her face twisted and blotched. The teachers would have to remove her by force.

No, what really worried me was that she used to say the most hurtful things to people she actually liked. E.g. old Alex

Dick, our private Latin tutor, had a coronary in our studyroom. (In his mid-thirties, A.J. Dick wasn't old, but after the heart attack he looked a hundred.) Holding his chest and gasping for air, he stumbled out the door. When we visited him in the hospital the first thing Anna said to him was: 'That was quite a performance.' She meant that the attack was serious, but it didn't come out that way. Dick asked her about the new Latin teacher, and she said: 'He's deadly. Hasn't got his heart in it.'

And so on.

I think the worst things she said without meaning to were to our Uncle Nicholas. When Grandad died, Anna never forgot to remind Uncle Nicholas that he had put an axe through the old man's forehead. Still, Anna remained his favourite niece.

'I didn't kill Father with an axe,' Nicholas would say to me on average three or four times a day. I believed him. The other kids didn't. They called him the Axe-Man. I half expected him to live up to his name . . . slaughter one or two cousins before winter. Nicholas was very depressed. He had no friends, knew no girls. Everyone said he was going to remain a bachelor.

'Don't worry, Uncle,' Anna said. 'You're a real killer in my books.'

Nicholas hunched, would look as though someone had struck him, and he'd slouch away, hands in pockets, condemned by his only supporter.

'What did I say?' Anna would yell. 'What the hell did I say?'

She would hit her head against the wall. Damn. Damn. Damn. The walls boomed. Mother caught her at it.

'What are you doing, Anna?'

'I've changed religion,' she said.

'I mean, to Nicholas?'

'God, Mamo, can't you give him a shot of something? Liven him up?'

Mother's face reddened. Her hypochondria was not a matter for joking. Anna tried to bite her tongue, but it was too late. Besides, that muscle was ferocious. Mother slapped her. Anna wet her pants. (She later filled up Mother's syringes with urine.)

44

Anna went to apologise to Uncle Nicholas.

'God, I need this family like I need a hole in the head,' she exclaimed.

Nicholas went pale. He began to choke.

AAAGH! EEEGH! HO! WHOO! Would she ever learn to keep her mouth shut? For years she was dogged with this. She shouted and yelled and made groaning noises. At nights I heard her moaning and shrieking, repeating the one line in French A.J. Dick ever taught her: '*Je suis un saligaud comme mon père*'. She shouted in a high voice, unable to stop her tongue. She was possessed by such babel. A flame danced above her head. Nothing was taboo.

Onomatomanie: the urge to shout obscenities. Further developments: tics, mannerisms, noises, involuntary compulsions, mimeticism, a sort of cheeky playfulness. Tourette's Syndrome.

Anna loved words. Poor Anna. She was also tormented by them. If only I'd known that then. They were like rats in a maze. She chased them around, ran them together, ( )ed* them up against each other to produce sparks.

Herr Riedel, another tutor, fell in love with her. Anna was fifteen. Herr Riedel tried to teach her Kant. Herr Riedel quoted Kant on laughter: 'a sudden transformation of a strained expectation into nothing'.

What did Anna say?

'A sudden transformation of nothing into strained expectation is the definition of an erection.'

OOOH! EEEGH! AAAAAGH! FUCKINGKANT!

At the age of twenty Anna took poison. An empty mercury bottle was found beside her bed at my aunt Xenia's place in the Caucasus. She was brought back in a lead coffin. I'm glad

---

* *Tieret*, (Russian) *rub*. A word he cannot say. A word made flesh, an image which in turn hides and distorts the word forever. A kind of anamorphosis in reverse. He writes, he sketches, hearing the scratching of the pen forming parentheses. It is both a pleasure and an omission. A pleasurable omission, like a missing footnote or a woman's name into which he could insert his appetite for her full image. Anna shouts *tieret*! all the time, discovering his secret when she saw him flinch.

I didn't have to put up with the long procession of priests, chanting and howling at each corner. They hid her in the earth. Anna is hiding, forever hiding.

The wound and the bow

Nanya is his old nurse. Nanya scolds him a lot. A tick lodges itself in his penis. There it is, its head buried in the folds of the skin, legs waving, combing back against its engorged body, plunging and anchoring deeper. How do you dislodge a tick from your penis with least injury to your flesh? You make your penis swell. Yes, at his age. By ( )ing. That part of him was always precocious. Nanya catches him at it. 'If you do that,' she tells him, 'your thing will drop off and you will have a wound there . . . forever.' Nanya called it his 'thing'. Later on his British nanny called it a John Thomas. 'If you fool around with John Thomas,' she would say, 'we'll have to put Jeyes Fluid on it, and then it will disappear.'

Anna has a wound there forever. Up at Pripet River a few summers later, in the heat and the wet of summer, when the ticks are plentiful, Dimitri tells you another story of a wound.

'Philoctetes,' Dimitri said, 'was given by Apollo a bow that never missed. But on the way to Troy he was bitten on the foot by a snake. It became a wound that never healed. The wound stank. For ten years he was like a leper, isolated on the island of Lemnos. For ten years the Greeks didn't realise that they couldn't win the Trojan war unless they sent for old Philoctetes, with his bow that couldn't miss. How would they get him to come back? Would you come back to defend the Motherland if you were treated like a leper for ten years? If you were old, living in a cave, rotting in your stinking bandages and cursing the waves?' Dimitri asked.

Of course you and your sister didn't know what the hell he was talking about, this Dimitri, who looked after the farm and who appeared so learned and sensible—even when he gave your sister rides on his knee and Anna, who was so experienced, knew how to comport herself, flaunted her wound at him, groaned in exactly the same way as her father had done with his arrow that never missed. The foetid smell afterwards.

We went to ask Father the answer. 'How did they get Philo . . . what's-his-name to come back?'

'Cunning mixed with humanity, that's how they got him to come back,' Father said. 'Young Neoptolemus persuaded him by taking his part, standing together with the old man against the others.'

Sympathy as well as need. The Greeks understood how to be both true and false to themselves. Savagery and civilisation. Crudity and refinement.

Anna grew up warped. Herr Riedel, the tutor who was in love with her, tried to teach Greek tragedy. Anna wouldn't have any part of it. 'You can take your Sophocles and get Philocteted,' she said.

Grusha

1889

When Papa beats the dog it does pee-pee on the floor. When Mama beat Anna she did pee-pee in her pants. I sit in the cupboard and peep out at Grusha, our maid. Grusha is eighteen. Grusha is blonde. Grusha wears silk pants under her skirt. I've seen her putting them on. After she puts them on she sits down and combs her long blonde hair. She combs a long time. When Grusha bends down to pick up her shoes I see a shape that looks like a church. In Odessa there is a church with a dome that looks like Grusha's behind. Grusha cleans, Grusha sweeps. In my cupboard I am snug and warm. I watch Grusha sweeping the kitchen floor. After that she splashes water on it, then she puts soap on the brush. As she sc( )s she shakes. Grusha. Grusha is smooth. Grusha's breasts are white and tilted upwards. When Grusha washes me in the wooden tub she is rough. She makes my skin red. Sometimes she threatens to beat me, but she never does. When she wraps me in a towel afterwards she always says that I am her little cocoon. When my parents are away Grusha has a bath with me. Grusha, white and smooth. Beneath the soapy water there is a church. Where is your temple? I say to Grusha in English. She laughs, points to her head. She doesn't understand English. Grusha bathes in her silk pants and chemise. They cling to her like a second skin. Now Grusha dips the brush into the pail, sc( )s the floorboards more vigorously. She bends forwards on her knees, sways back at each corner, chanting, singing. My view is limited. Without it there is nothing. In the dark, in the cupboard, I can reach across and feel Grusha's things. Her wardrobe is built onto the kitchen cupboard; her room separated only with a curtain. Grusha has nice things; soft things which she wears on Sunday. Grusha has a coat lined with wolf-fur. I touch it to make sure. From there I can always find my way. My hand feels several dresses, leather belts, shoes. At the bottom of the wardrobe I feel Grusha's silk pants. On the washing line her pants are like butterfly wings, for without the ribbons which lace up the sides, the two halves open and close as the wind blows. I hold it against my chest, watching Grusha sliding and singing, the floor almost done, the pants wet, she opens the windows to let it dry, I hold her pants up to my eyes, wait for the light, blood. Blood. A dark stain before my eyes. I drop the pants. Run from the cupboard. Blood. Grusha smooth and white. Blood! I scream. Grusha catches me running over the slippery floor. Her fingers dig into my arm. In her grip I am fainting. I pee-pee on the floor. Grusha has a broom of twigs in her hand. For a moment I can see that she wants to hit me. She is so angry she cannot speak. Her face is very red. Her blonde hair is wet. She pulls down my pants. Holds my little penis tightly. I will cut it off! she yells. Truly, I'm going to cut it off! Grusha. Blood. My sister Anna comes in. She is laughing at me. Wait till I tell Papa, she says. I pretend to be frightened. I want her to tell. Grusha sweeps so hard with the twig broom that sparks fly.

Anna forgets to tell. In the evening the grown-ups have a party. That's why Grusha was sc( )bing and cleaning. My cousins and uncles and aunts are all present. One of my mother's brothers, who's very rich, has travelled the world. In my bed I can hear him talking. He has a booming voice and he frightens me.

'In Australia,' he says, 'in addition to shearing the sheep they have to cut off their tails. That's because of the flies. With the males they also cut off their balls. Just slice the skin and squeeze them out. There's a legend that farmers do it with their teeth, but I didn't see that myself.'

Dream

1890

I have a dream. A dream is always a place, but when you tell it, it becomes a story, which is neither dream nor place. It is about a man trying to climb on his own shoulders. It is ridiculous, I say to myself in the dream. Though he's almost as good a contortionist as Anna, he can't gain more than his own height. Man, basically, makes a monkey of himself. Not so wolves. I go to my desk in my room, on the second storey of our villa. When you look through the photos they've taken of me, you'll see the villa in the background. My room is in the eastern turret which looks like a grandfather clock. I sit down at the desk and try to draw my dream. The window is open. I take father's revolver out of the desk drawer and place it on the paper.

I hear the beginning of rain pitting at the windows. Rain usually brings the awful prescience of disaster. I always feel a kind of power when the rains come, closing the curtain against it, lighting a candle in the darkness and glimpsing in its small flame, the past. Later I will call it a *reaching over*, a movement towards death.

It is the eve of my fourth birthday. The window creaks, then flies open. Outside there is a row of walnut trees. On one of them seven white wolves are sitting quietly. They have huge bushy tails and their ears are pricked. They are staring intently at me.

Grandad said:

Once upon a time, during the Teutonic Wars, there were seven white goats who lived in an old ruined castle. They enjoyed complete safety. Their ability to climb the battlements and their sure-footedness over crumbling buttresses ensured a healthy and long life for each of them. When threatened by

51

force, they simply allowed the walls to crumble and jumped nimbly onto the next parapet, signalling danger or the 'all clear' with their short tails. They had the ability not only to escape, but to be totally unpredictable.

One day a wolf visited the castle. He knocked at the thick wooden doors and presented his paw at the peephole. The goats saw immediately that it was grey and without a word, sprang up onto the highest balconies and rained stones onto the invader. The wolf went away and thought hard about a method of entry. He used reason and cunning. He went to the baker's and covered himself with flour. On his return, he knocked at the castle door. The goats, seeing his white paws and believing that he was a fellow goat, signalled the all-clear with their tails and opened up. Quick as a wink, the wolf swallowed up six of the goats. The seventh hid himself in a grandfather clock.

Freud said to me: 'I'm interested in your writing.'

'No,' I said. 'You couldn't possibly be. I'm flattered.'

Freud showed me his bandaged hand. 'I burned it in the oven,' he explained. 'No, it's not the literary element that interests me, it's the way you jump from one thing to another, which is a form of resistance.'

'You inspire me.'

'Let's not muddy the waters.'

'I'm quenching my thirst for knowledge at your stream.'

'I know you're slandering me in your writings.'

'How could I be? I haven't written anything about you.'

'You will.'

I asked Grandad: 'What about the goat in the grandfather clock?'

'Can't you hear him?' Grandad said. 'He's going tick tock, tick tock, in there.'

'Is the wolf outside?'

'Yes.'

'Then who wins?'

'The goat. Because he has control of time. See his beard?'

But pure reason still has it over time. In time all the great truths crumble. In time interpretations dissolve, but pure reason remains in its wolfishness . . . strength, talion, persever- ance and surprise. There is cunning in the old goat, but it is not enough. The wolf too, makes use of time.

I wrote all my dreams and was dumb enough to go back to him bearing gifts. Yes, I was so taken with his explanations I bought him a present. You know me, poor as a church mouse but always giving people things which I couldn't afford. It's the Russian spirit. I mean, what do you give Freud? A couch? A book of dreams? A box of Havanas? I couldn't get any of those things at the time. But I inherited a little Greek statue. Authentic eighth century B.C. My father gave it to me before he died. It was one of those figures with a huge erect penis, completely out of proportion to its body. It was just balanced enough to stay upright. In homage to Priapus.

Freud was delighted with it. He put it on his desk, with all the other ancient figurines. He had centrepieces there that would have astounded the museums of Europe.

'In time,' Freud said, 'this will become a link between us.'

Photos

1903–1904

The body is also a place, with its own topography. Portraits that are also landscapes, these photos of bodies are sites. If you breathe deeply three times ... Father, Son and Holy Ghost, you can disappear into them. If you breathe three times you can become invisible, and there will be no history, no time, only the rushing of the water and the howling of the wind and the snapping of the trees and the sound of the land being renewed. In a group portrait I will have a new family, each member the product and catalyst of happiness. But there are no group portraits.

Father

He is sitting at the table. He has the eyes of a wolf. He does not need a wolf-mask. His lupine nether regions are not shown in the photo, though he has his legs crossed.

This photo was taken after a particularly ferocious hunt. It is evening. Father is smoking a cigar and drinking tea. The samovar is just out of frame. That afternoon he took me on a hunt for wolves. He carried a shotgun. Even I knew (because Grandad had told me) that you can't hit a wolf with a shotgun. Wolves are so cunning you can never get close enough. Father saw a wolf. He tracked it for miles, but the wolf kept just out of range. In frustration, father fired off both barrels, bringing down a couple of tree branches. Then he grabbed me by the back of the neck and forced my head into the ground. The ground was covered with soft pine needles.

Tribal people have totems. They know that if you kill your totem you also kill yourself. Father didn't know these things because his people had always been city people. Grandad told me this. Grandad was a country man, but his memory was gone, because an axe-head had been buried in his forehead. Forgetting made him very tense and irritable . . . just like Father. When Father was dying in the sanatorium several years later, I was able to say to him: 'I've got it over you now.' But he just looked at me and didn't seem to recognise me. I made the sign of the cross over him and breathed out forcefully. He would no longer inhabit me. I had a farewell gift for him. I had given him, on his last birthday, a new German rifle. It was 1908.

Yours truly

Seventeen years old, in his school uniform. By a stream. Always by water, whence the cure, for fire and fever; for sensuality and sophistry; for his lust for Joan of Arc tied to the stake. The inseparability of water is both passivity and force. Also always by a wood. Wringing his hands, a far-off look in his eyes. Hair heavily oiled.

A big question mark here. What has he just done? What is behind him, in the woods, in the stand of birch trees which are bare, since it is autumn or early winter? Do we not see, in the extremities of the photo, a white stain? A retouching, perhaps, of something that he didn't want displayed? A piece of female undergarment strewn carelessly on a branch?

Anna

Anna, nineteen. Plump, with parasol. Sitting on a . . . stump? Looks as though she might swing from it, upside down. That day I lit a small fire in the garden. I was drunk on my father's port and had pissed on the fire. Anna shouted that she could do that too. 'Impossible,' I said. 'Women can't direct their piss.' 'You wanna bet?' she countered. Then she climbed onto the branch of a tree, spread her legs and let loose a stream which well and truly doused the fire. A year later and she would be dead, poisoned with mercury. Mercury, of course, was also Hermes, the herald. Of what? Of other places. New borders to cross. Which is why I didn't miss her when she died. She sped past me with wings on her feet. Anna! Wait for me!

Most of all Anna wanted to be a servant. Her greatest ambition in life was to run away and hire herself out as a maid. She had a fixation on her nose. She thought it too red and large. One day I overheard her saying to her maid Grusha: WHEN THE MISTRESS IS UGLY AND THE SERVANT BEAUTIFUL, THAT MUST BE TERRIBLE FOR THE MISTRESS.

G.

In front of a huge mansion, standing with the painter G., who appears a lot older than me. Trees again. W., standing there in a sort of military (school) uniform, with peaked cap, no less. The painter looks like a painter.

Who was G.?

G. had been visiting the Caucasus, and had stopped over at the Wespe estate on his way back to Milan. Outside Odessa that day, G. had been caught in a stampede of white cattle. Shaken but unharmed, he was taken by gypsies to some low wooden houses, where the people fed him and warmed him with cups of tea. During this act of kindness he had witnessed, through a torn curtain which served as a partition between rooms, a sexual act between a man and a child of no more than twelve. On his way to Odessa, he had stopped in a forest in order to make some rough sketches of the countryside. There he found a wolf's head. Out of the eye sockets and earholes streamed an army of maggots. The head, when he kicked at it, was quite hollow.

Dogged by sex and death, it was rumoured that after a long trail of amorous adventures G. was killed in Trieste in 1915, having been suspected of being an Austrian agent. I, however, maintain that G. died of cancer of the larynx in a Munich hospital.

G. was incurably romantic. Narrowly romantic. With a strong leaning towards degeneration. Anna loved him passionately; perhaps too passionately. For a while we were a *ménage à trois*. Then she became disturbingly silent. She no longer

56

cursed. Her voice softened. She turned into a lady, and like most well-bred young ladies of the time, language became a kind of preciosity. However, she could only pretend for so long, for then the mercury must have burst from her thermometer of boredom. More and more often we found Anna swinging from branches, alone, smelling unmistakably of urine.

G. was rotund, red-faced, full lips like Oscar Wilde's, totalitarian, wore waistcoats and cravats, smoked cigars, drank of course, (though I've seen him *run*, by God, fully drunk, when an irate woman, an injured party, chased him along a railway platform), and he was a genius at the piano. I don't use that word lightly. Yes, G. was a born genius. For one thing he read music better than he did words. For another, he only had to listen to a piece once, at times a whole concerto, to play it better than any virtuoso. So why wasn't he on the concert platform? Drink, of course. Oh, and a certain predilection for voyeurism . . . and photography, which meant he hated to be looked at, found out, spied upon, because, as he said, *there was nothing there*.

We'd just had a few bottles after G. had carved his initial in the trunk of the tree from which Anna was swinging, when this kid from the next estate, Alexander, I think his name was, rushed up to show off his latest possession; a camera, for God's sake. G. was immediately interested.

Of course when one drinks a good wine there is a loneliness about it at first . . . all the pasts added up . . . a settling of accounts . . . heavy grey clouds scudding over treetops . . . the threat of snow . . . the recuperation of innocence. There would soon be other places . . . Munich, Berlin, the long Vienna nights . . . which would all come later but which I thought I knew already, from G.'s talk. And then there was evil. There is no greater evil than a good wine. Dry. Like the leaves on the trees. Dry like the residue of cremated jealousy. Sometimes I forget why I'm walking, where I'm walking to, why and whereto am I driving, et cetera. Perhaps it's not forgetting, but desire, desire for Anna and G . . . for a life in three dimensions . . . a burning.

I didn't like the way G. was busying himself with Alexander.

Of course the boy had a way with the camera, a mystical apparatus which captured reality in a way words couldn't . . . extracted the juice out of explanation.

'It's good. It's inspired,' I said lamely, when I saw the daguerreotypes.

'Good? Inspired?' G. scoffed. 'You know what the boy lacks?'

I looked at the prints.

'Failure. The boy lacks a sense of failure,' G. said.

I didn't understand. I shrugged. Alexander was standing just a few feet away, with a pained look on his face.

'He's too clear; too defined. I know him. He thinks he's classical.' G.'s eyes suddenly became clear, as though he'd sobered up. I had noticed this before. The immense will when it came to judging what was fine.

'It's like walking into someone's private library,' G. continued, 'and pulling out somebody else's books. He's using everything.'

'What should you do?'

'You read the spines. Keep your hands in your pockets, dear boy . . . a sense of failure; holding back.'

'I thought it was a sense of respect.'

'No. Respect is bourgeois love. Not so initiation. After that you understand failure like a purifying shaft of light. You recover from love.'

I understand all too well now that had I that sense of failure before, things would have been better for me. I had no one to judge myself against. In a privileged upbringing you never failed.

'He's going straight for death,' G. indicated Alexei with a toss of his head.

At the far end of the garden I caught a glimpse of Anna, levering herself up onto a branch. I really didn't know what she was trying to achieve with these exercises. Was it bladder control? Larger pectorals? G.'s eyes drooped. He smoothed back his black hair with beringed fingers. I remember hearing the clack of those rings on the ivory keyboard when he played.

'Detours,' he sighed. 'The way of failure is along detours.' He twirled his fingers around the top of his glass and drew intricate patterns on the frosted sides. 'That's the way to go, because the present is one long pathology.'

Vienna

1972

Five fifty-eight. I'm eighty-five. The library has turned grey and people are leaving for dinner. I have to get home. Tonight it is *The Maltese Falcon*. Haven't seen that one for maybe three years.

Shiny cars pulling out. I'm in a borrowed Mercedes. You'd think I could have afforded one myself, especially after the sales of my last book, *Broken Dreams*. You see it everywhere. A blue cover with red lettering. Little emblem on the side—silhouette of a wolf's head with a hat pulled low over the eyes. Another psychoanalytical thriller by 'The Wolf-Man'. A real potboiler. Need to boil underwear afterwards for twenty minutes at least; get all that excitement off. Human discharge. Kill the little buggers. A great toil. All this human perseverance. The imagination useless for books like that. You just try purple prose and see if you don't come up with a laugh. Yes, laughter is the supreme antidote to the cobra. Knew a woman once who laughed every time we did it. Laughed her head off. She would've stopped most men. Not me. She was my wife.

Broken dreams. The reality is I'm still poor. People read me for the wrong reasons. Most of the royalties go to institutions. I've always had bad agents and lawyers. But this next book I'm writing will save me. It's something more than mere fiction.

Father used to say to us that he had nothing but he dreamt of everything. On our million rouble estate we ate boiled potatoes and drank milk if we were lucky. Went about with toes out of our boots. My own dreams fouled in a rat's nest of anxiety and paranoia, even self-mutilation.

There are friendly sounds and there are hostile sounds. Outside my building, someone has smashed into a wall. In the

city, this would be a hostile sound, but in this expensive
Viennese quarter, in the secluded, upper reaches of the Prater
in which I live, the sound of a car smashing into a wall is a
comforting sound, like a muffled insurance premium. This is
the fifth time my neighbour has done it. Backing his car . . .
the car I just borrowed and left outside, into a tiny garage. Or
is it the sixth time? I can't remember.

I'm strapped in a caul.

Morning. A beautiful sunny summer morning. I need to go to
the lavatory. I'm anal retentive. Holding back. The lavatory is
where I write best. In my four-storey house overlooking the
Prater I have an IBM typewriter on a shelf bolted to the
lavatory wall. They say Jack Kerouac typed on unending rolls
of lavatory paper.

'No shit, Sergy,' my American friend, Art Catacomb, used to
say.

KATOOMBA
1978

You are chewing bubblegum to keep alcoholic desires at bay. In Katoomba, in the bookshop where you've rediscovered a copy of the Wolf-Man's autobiography, the girl's boyfriend has suddenly appeared. He's about six foot five, wears a net tee-shirt though it's howling and about to snow. You don't like aggravation yet in the past these things have passed over you like the Angel of Death whispering to someone else. You just batten down the hatches and turn out the lights. Yes, you're subterranean. Nuclear proof. Like the Wolf-Man, you were born in a caul. You were destined. You blow a bubble like an embryonic sac. The boyfriend says something to you but you pretend you cannot understand. You pretend to be a foreigner. You speak a bit of Russian. You have an accent. Monuments, these moments, to another life. Perhaps you will challenge him to a duel. You will stand at ten paces, in the snow at Narrow Neck, and listen to the silence before the muffled report of pistols. You will be hot and then cold. But enough of these fantasies. It is sleeting now. Dirty gobbets of mush begin to cake the cars outside.

In the winter of 1910 the Wolf-Man was tirelessly tracking down his childhood wolf book in second-hand stores so that he could help Freud establish fact, be responsible for the evidence. The connection between the wolf book and the dream brought about a massive side-track: it made the connection between fairy tales and childhood trauma and gave to the imagination the benediction of innocence. A familiar modus operandi. He accepted Freud's theory that the wolf dream was explained by the scene of parental intercourse. Many years later he said that it was his seduction by Anna that was the cause of his neurosis. Continuous supplementing. If dream is equivalent to memory, as Freud first insisted, then fiction is equivalent to history. One looks for wolves without any tracks. For the Wolf-Man, it is a simple matter of shifting his desires between innocence and responsibility.

The boyfriend puts a hand on your shoulder. It is heavy, big as a shovel, like a policeman's hand when he arrests you. It is symbolic of the law, this laying on of hands, but it has all the weight of brutality behind it.

Introversion

Or: Two halves don't make a whole

When G. left and Anna committed suicide, one taking a detour and the other a short cut, I simply refused reality. Facing reality was a peculiarly human enslavement. Animals didn't have such an imposition. They were programmed into a trance mapped out of phenomena. I lingered by the tree upon which he had carved the letter G., smelled the honeysuckle trapped in the warmth of an early spring, and waited for time to evaporate. When I heard later that G. had died, it was that letter, upon the very moment between pleasure and pain, that seemed to open (the tree had grown) a fragrant wound.

For days after Anna's suicide, I immersed myself in writing. I drew a vertical line down the page. On one side I wrote down what I was inclined to, my desires. On the other side I wrote down what my potentials were, my possibilities. Both sides were equally weighted. The line dissected neatly the past and the future; fullness and hunger, passivity and devourment. The line dissected the page like an incision down the body, where it takes its fixed point and moving along the *levator ani* muscle, reaches the margin of the anus. Detours and action didn't appeal to me. I felt that they were only ways of giving into authority. Detours and action meant, in one sense, progress and forgetting, the twin axioms of the bourgeoisie. G. did not turn away from a goal, but progressed towards it while swerving from a linear path. Anna did not kill herself, but momentarily forgot the deathly hollow of existence.

Who are the introverts? They are the dunces and the dreamers. They are the readers who don't understand a word, because the words get in the way of euphoria. They do not face another's reality, but bare their backsides to it. They are ruminants not carnivores, goats not wolves, bullocks not bears, collectors not consumers. They scramble onto ideas and browse there for days. They are nimble, and they very easily cross the line from dry speculation into carnal experience.

I am a ruminant. I've been chewing on an idea for days. I have also been devoured by it. I've been thinking that two halves never make a whole because there's always a gap in between. The world and the word. The devil is in between. In between there's a hollow, an abyss into which desire falls. The in-between is represented by a pair of brackets: ( ) thus. A pair of buttocks. Yoked bullocks delivering an infinite aside. If you penetrate the aside, you discover the apostrophe of truth, which is empty. The problem with me, at the tender age of seventeen, was that I hadn't learned how to devour truth and to live on its emptiness . . . to bullshit, like everybody else.

The teachers, however, had got it wrong. I wasn't an introvert in the way that they defined it. I wasn't turned inwards, making a detour into death like a fatalistic Pharaoh. No, I could be sociable: at least, what's more to the point, I could be vulgarly social . . . which is the way of ruminants and the epitome of aristocratic breeding, at least on my mother's side. Father's side was pure parsimony. All this probably accounted for Anna's obscenity and my masochism. At school I cherished punishment, which would be delivered by the prefects in the quartermaster store. These punishments took various forms. They ranged from the purely physical: a caning on the rump (which I preferred); kneeling on the ground with a rifle over one's head; running ten miles over ploughed ground; to the psychological: the continuous scraping of one's fingernails over a blackboard; being forced to lie in a tunnel under the building while rats scampered over one's face. I was particularly partial to holding a chair over my back while a prefect dressed as a Cossack made repeated charges and plunged his sabre into the wood. The sensation of the sword thrusts and the blood-curdling cries filled me with the happiness of battle, of historical experience, which I felt I lacked, and which came upon me from the back . . . *a tergo*. At these moments the past reeled out before me as though the Angel of History had unfolded his wings and bore me aloft upon his buttocks, and we were flying backwards into the face of events. Once I

65

fainted and the prefect was himself punished, for exceeding the punishment. Tempted to be a mitigating witness for him, I saw in time that he was enjoying his punishment as much as I had. He, of course, had discovered his better half.

It was inconceivable, then, that I was an introvert in the ordinary sense. I enjoyed too much this social game, this acting out, this drama of power. If anything, I was a retrovert. I was continuously being borne back, enlarging the wilderness of the past. Retroversion had its apex, its flowering achievement, at the height of the conditional past, the *would haves* and the *could haves*, balancing its side of the page by recovering lost opportunities, against the proclivities of being to the future, to death. Without this balancing, this androgynous doubling outside of time, there could only be catastrophe.

An example of retroversion:

What caught your eye? What has been disturbing you these last pages like the fluttering of something white, female apparel, bloomers, twisted around a branch beside the stream? You could have overlooked it. (Could it have been W., who was walking down the path to the stream in his school uniform? Could it have been a servant girl called Matrona who was washing by the stream on this heavy autumn morning, bending on her knees as she pressed her sodden and soiled underwear against the rock worn smooth and round by the water? Could it have been her buttocks which attracted him, the way she presented them to him, the way she pulled down her pants and lifted up her skirt and he was able to kneel on her just-washed pantaloons and make repeated charges, yelling like a Cossack, riding her immense brackets in a huge aside?)

Recapitulation. Without it he would discover emptiness. G. had told him so.

Fire. All is fire and pus. I tell no one. I have a tick in me. The Cossack rides limply through the field of dead trailing a mangy bearskin. The snow crusted with blood. I sink into a deep depression. They send me to Dr Anton in Berlin, but I go only on the condition Anna comes with me. But in Berlin all is grey. The rain filters down from the sky without energy or force. In the grey courtyard framed by skeletal trees I see Father giving Anna money. Less than a month later, Anna commits suicide.

The past is the repressed. In 1910, Freud kept the door of the past open to me. I thought him the kindest and most wonderful man. I remember saying to him: *What did civilisation think of the wolf, which had emerged so recently out of the Dark Ages?*

Of course, the original context of that question is now lost for all time. What made me think of the occasion was that while I asked that question he had accidentally knocked over the little priapic Greek statue I had given him. Part of the penis broke off. Freud picked up the pieces and muttered an irritable apology to me. Then, as he so often did, he smiled after a brief frown, and handed me the piece of broken penis with his bandaged hand.

'In ancient Greece,' Freud said, putting a boot up on the couch, 'the owner of a house would break off a piece of pottery or tile upon the departure of a guest and give it to the visitor. That would ensure he returned, so that the pieces could be fitted back together.'

I was impressed. 'That's real hospitality,' I said. 'Imagine knocking apart a priceless antique for a pal.'

I wasn't churlish enough to remind him he was giving me back my own present, damaged, what's more, and that I paid handsomely for these sessions. Such forgetting had reverse effects: it kept the visitor from your door. It was civilisation's answer to the wolf. Besides, what really kept me coming back wasn't friendship but fetish. If I stopped, there could be catastrophe on a grand scale.

Freud wasn't listening to me anyway. He went off on a private reverie and then began to speak in Classical Greek.

'In Plato's *Symposium* we are told that humans were originally spheroids, both masculine and feminine, until Zeus, in a moment of rage over human striving, cut them apart. Originally we were androgynous. In love-making, we resume that conjunction.'

AND . . . I was thinking. A copula. It makes us whole, we who have been cut in half by our transgressions. It also makes us multifarious *and* whole. Hot diggety, a thousand and one nights; a thousand and one personalities.

But I said to Freud: 'Herr Professor . . . ' I said, loath as I was to pay homage to a fancy title, 'two halves may make us friends, but does it make me whole?'

Vienna
1972

Artie got me this apartment when he saw the slum I was living in. I now spend my time perusing the city with binoculars. Put the heating up a notch. Getting fogged up. Cloud building up downtown. The weather returns the past to me. Over at the Steinhof rain is beginning to glaze the sanatorium windows. When I move around I must be like a goldfish in a bowl. Look at me now. Here I am. I have a huge glass pane instead of those mean frosted lavatory windows. It stops about waist level of course. I'm not entirely an exhibitionist. No, moderation is my motto. But some are more moderate than others. If you focus on my plate-glass window with your telescope you would think I was working hard at my desk. A reconnaissance plane used to buzz around out there till I took a shot at it with my Mauser. Turned out they were working for the historical mapping authority. This house is built smack on top of eighteenth-century foundations. Rises four storeys up with a view over the entire gardens. Top floor built around a courtyard and pool. No curtains anywhere. This is a mark of my self-confidence. Haven't had a real anxiety attack for maybe twenty years. I still believe in Brutal Modernism as a solution to neurosis. If you get rid of the Romantic, you get rid of the neurotic. No more desire for death. Nobody bothers me much on that score now . . . about being cured, I mean, except old Catacomb. Professor Art Catacomb, who rents the place next door. Artie baby. He's sort of a psychoanalyst, born in Australia. He came from a place resonant of caves and cataracts. Kedumba, he called it. It was Aboriginal. He concealed this behind a Yankee burr, perhaps even changed his name like some people in Newark, which is where he says he spent some time. Nobody in Newark wants to be Jewish these days, he says. Artie had this unplumbed sense of sadness. With his turned down mouth and drooping eye sockets, you'd swear he was in perpetual mourning. Why, I asked myself, should he regret his origins?

I had never heard of Catacomb. Wouldn't have known him from a bar of soap if he hadn't knocked on my door one morning and asked if he could use my shower because he'd backed his Mercedes into the water main. Had nothing else but a soap-on-a-string around his neck.

That's how he appeared at my door, all covered in white hair, with a long white beard. He looked like an albino mole that had discovered sunlight . . . or Walt Whitman on the make in Central Park. When I come to think of it, with a shorter beard he would look remarkably like Freud.

We got to talking. He was very interested in what I wrote. He said he might do a paper on it.

'Your wild claims do nothing for your reputation . . . after all the great man had done for you,' he used to say, puffing on his half-Corona. He was always reprimanding me for playing tricks on Freud. Playing in the background was a record of Beethoven's Fifth.

'What do you expect me to do?' I asked. 'Tell lies? Invent fictions?'

'There was no doubt,' said Artie, 'that Freud covered his tracks to placate his critics. He didn't want to appear authoritarian. He was a civilised man.'

Artie was referring to Freud's ambivalence over what was primal, fact or fantasy. But I was thinking of something else. I was thinking that Freud had displayed the ruminant's rump, cast his backside to the wind in an apparently passive gesture, when I knew that somewhere there was the memory of the wolf. He hated open spaces. He didn't care for America and Americans. He would have disliked Artie, who blew terrible noises on his saxophone from the next apartment by way of greeting.

'Say, can't you turn that confounded racket off?' Catacomb yelled.

Catacomb heard beneath everything I said a multiplicity of

70

voices. If you really want to know, I think he's a split personality.

Professor Art Catacomb and I used to argue, sitting around the pool in the slightly embedded top storey of my apartment. That was when Catacomb wasn't lecturing or giving papers or appearing on Italian television. The two of us would sit around the pool in the early evenings burping over Pouget and Brie. As an old Marxist he tried very hard to be abstemious. Torn between the choice of cars he wanted to buy, he settled for the more proletarian Mercedes instead of a Rolls or Porsche.

There's old Catacomb mending his wall. It's amazing that he's out in daylight. Half of the wall got taken off together with the water main, which had sent water shooting up like a geyser, and for a few hours Vienna looked like Geneva. *Something there is that doesn't love a wall*. Catacomb loves walls, though he occasionally knocks them down, loves caves and tunnels as well, loves structures, mortar, brico something or other, which is his hobby, staying in touch with the grassroots of life. He's also fond of using words like 'closure' or 'always already', and despite his name I have a strong suspicion he's Jewish. One day he handed me some keys and told me to use his car when he was away.

But he's watching me. I know. He's watching me like they all watch me, through a one-way glass. That's because I'm a classic. They write books and articles about me. They send pretty female journalists with impressive buttocks to interview me with tape-recorders. They all wear long dresses. Each time they come they present me with orchids. I don't know why they insist on this obscene flower, which belongs in a hothouse, not in my freezing Viennese apartment which I keep artificially cold in the summers. The cold helps me think. The cold helps me figure out one move ahead of what they are planning to do with me. They allow me to stay in this luxurious town house. But I'm trapped. Trapped like an animal in the zoo. I pace up and down, wag my heavy head backwards and forwards at the windows. They publish my books, but there are no reviews; not a smidgen of notice in the literary pages. I'm a curiosity. A museum-piece. A displaced person. I don't fit in. Nobody acknowledges the fact that, without me, Freud would never have gained the recognition he did. Nobody notices that my nomenclature, which they all take for granted as representing a passive terror of wolves, in fact signifies the Other, their own ravenous bellies, the open vault of their being. We carry around a frightening propensity for other people's deaths. I hear jackboots in the street.

Take Catacomb. He wasn't even born when I began my sessions with Freud. Now he talks as if he knows me inside out ... everything he knows, he's read from journals and books. But the logic of course is this: the logic is that to stop myself from being the observed, the subject, the patient, I have only to come out into the open. To usurp the authority of the story. To legitimise for myself what has for so long been the territory of others; to re-appropriate the ground. But there's also an inverse to this logic: one can become the observer, without a sound, without the slightest stirring of branches, by being folded back into the forest, without scent, without spoor, invisible, inertia being the last resort of instinct.

The Caucasus

1906

My father suggested I take a trip to the Caucasus, to pay homage to my obsession at the time: the poet Lermontov. It was a year or so after we buried Anna. Father grew distant, distracted and was seeking every opportunity to vent his irritability.

'Go and visit his shrine,' Father said sarcastically, 'since you care so little for your own sister's.'

It was true. I didn't mourn Anna. It is the same with animals. They sniff, they prod the dead in anticipation and they keep coming upon a wall which they do not see . . . again and again, finding death both alien and familiar.

I departed for Novorossysk with Monsieur Weinstein who was a friend of the family and who was to be my travelling companion. It was 1907. Weinstein was a pretentious bastard. He wore white suits and affected a white fedora. He pranced around Kislovodsk and Bermamut (where we had a grand view of Elbrus, the highest mountain in the Caucasus) and spouted his theories on socialism. I think his problem was that he wasn't rich. At Pyatigorsk we stayed in a mountain hut rented from a peasant family.

Photo

Pyatigorsk. Mountains in all directions. Little vegetation. Boulders strewn like an abandoned game of marbles. The day they set out to visit the Lermontov Grotto the clouds roll in and soon there is a thick mist. They bathe in the sulphur springs and engage a local girl in conversation. She speaks with that patois that distinguishes her from the two of them. You can see Weinstein, naked, brutal in the Russian tradition caressing her haunches with a hand. When in Pyatigorsk, do as the tourists do. Pay her of course. Who? Weinstein? No. Weinstein is green with jealousy because the girl prefers Sergei, who breaks off suddenly and looks away and tries to articulate a principle. Weinstein gets dressed, picks up a sliver of rock and scratches on Lermontov's monument the lame inscription: *La propriété c'est le vol.*

But let's be literary for a moment. What obsessed Sergei about Lermontov? Romanticism? There was possibly an element of that. After all, he had brought with him a copy of *Geroy nashego vremeni* (*A Hero Of Our Time*). Perhaps it was a horror of, and a fascination with duelling. After all, Lermontov was obsessed with Pushkin's death by duelling, and Lermontov himself died in a duel with a fellow officer at this very spot. No, none of these. Sergei was obsessed with the demon of oppression. With serfdom. With the passivity of the enslaved. He felt his whole being infused with love, with the passion to subjugate, to wound this gypsy when he stood beside the monument on a windswept hillside and gathered up the girl's skirts behind her, perched on boulders like mountain goats. At that moment he was transgressing and doubling Weinstein's inscription by stealing back his birthright—not his inheritance but his freedom to kill the human by entering this place, becoming this emptiness, driven by the mechanical nature of motion and rhythm. And he was immensely relieved, reborn, thinking of the way Anna moved, back and forth, the way her name ran, against him, an eternal motion machine. His father said he almost called her Anastasia, ('God, I need this family like I need a hole in the head,' Anna had said) and it wouldn't have been such a misnomer, anastasis.

KATOOMBA

1978

In Katoomba, on the main street. They have just thrown you out of the shop for talking so much. Not quite literally. The girl took you by the elbow and the boyfriend by the neck and they propelled you out onto the street in this fashion though it was difficult to get through the door all together. You suppose the girl must have stood back a little while the muscular boyfriend pushed you out, saying: 'This ain't a reading-room eh?' Or: 'Piss orf or I'll fuckin' make mincemeat outta yer face wiv me own 'ands.' He might have been more polite and said: 'This is not a charity organisation.' Which is what a priest said to you once when you lingered near the Virgin Mary in the vestibule of a church warming your hands over the paschal flame.

All you did was to pinch her bottom. The girl's, that is. Passed your hand over the leather skirt stretched tight over her buttocks as she leant forward in front of you replacing a copy of the *Guide To Good Sex*. An act which wouldn't hold up in a court of law. Have you ever tried to pinch leather?

Well, in all their haste they've forgotten you have it in your hands. The book, that is.

You stand in front of the Aeneas guesthouse. It is a large old building which is neither here nor there. Set against a perpetually grey sky it looks mottled and overgrown with ivy and moss. It isn't exactly geometrical. A wing sticks out like an afterthought, a decaying building hemmed in by more modern, uglier structures. A tree is growing from the flat roof, an unhealthy bristly tree which has clung tenaciously to the cornices. It grows out of a giant pot and it has cracked the base and the roof and one of its roots has punctured the ceiling and has crept along the mouldings in search of water. Around the building are cropped plane trees. There is a low wall which surrounds the place and which contributes to the rubble forming at its base. Thorny bushes, rocks, slabs of granite tumble down into the courtyard. An old streetlight, a gas jet in a glass trapezoid stands like a silent sentinel at one corner. The shutters are tilted, slats missing. On the second storey, which is slightly embedded because the foundations on one side of the building have sunk, are your rooms. The decay is palpable. It takes a certain kind of corrupt and pickled air to preserve this. Restoration, alas, the kind that takes place too often in homage to history, the making new that results in kitsch, is threatening the Aeneas . . . and you. Lately members of the Council have been uttering words like *bulldozers*.

This is the guestroom where he will spend a few nights. You've had Mrs Harris fix it up with new sheets on the bed, flowers in the vase— dried—you couldn't get orchids this time of year. You put down some checked lino you found rolled and discarded at the back of the hospital. A tree-root has forced its way down one corner of the room. You are asking yourself if this rhizome with its tiny tendrils will one day spread all over the building and constrict its decaying heart. Your heart, at the same time, slows. You breathe in and out according to the creakings of the building. You know it so well. When you open the window you know that a silent sleet has infiltrated the courtyard along whose crumbling wall the water mains would have frozen. A goat ninnies beyond, clattering over loose rocks in search of dank grass. Late afternoon. The streetlights are on. A heavy sky. A tea-kettle whines. You dredge up sadness, heavy and trailing seaweed. A film of water forms over your bifocals. There is a loss of poetry in such deep melancholia. Which place? Which story will you tell? You block one nostril, sniff in. Block the other. Sniff out. Reverse the process. For balance.

Vienna
1972

Vienna nights I do the nightclubs. It's an old habit. Not the innocuous nightclubs the young go to. Not the jazz cellars and retro cabarets where they breathe powder and exchange LSD tabs and talk about the avant-garde and the fashion system. I am reminded of Paris, 1923. But that's another story. No. I do the nightclubs for dirty old men. The *Wolfsschanze* clubs. These are the real clubs, the seedy leftovers from pre-war Vienna, the hard-core stuff and not the pretentious cafés. These are the clubs where you can still get a drink, an old-fashioned schnapps or straight whisky; where men come and go with raincoats over their arms and cigarette smoke is heavy like cyanide gas and somewhere in the walls you can hear camp victims scratching; because behind these barmen and bouncers are Nazis. Yes, you can see it in the eyes. Bright blue. They pick them for racial purity. Because most of the audience, if you look around, and if you do a bit of checking, are old S.S. men and stormtroopers waiting for the next Reich when the physically strong and the mentally weak will come together again. They are all big men in braces and you can hear them creaking as they age. They won't go quietly. At the special table which is reserved for me I have a side of boar and a bottle of schnapps. Somebody sent me an invitation once and now they all know me as Herr Wolf. On the stage the girls are doing their routine. They are all too thin. I eat heartily, slurping gravy and spilling it over my suit. In the last couple of years I've put on fifty pounds. Twenty bare bums. They dance, they bend down, stick out their bottoms for the applause. I wave my fork for some wine. Soon we will begin singing. After a few more circumspect acts they will turn down the lights. There will be a minute's silence. Many of the men will remove their hats, which they have kept on up till then so they can specially remove them. Lest they forget.

The lights come on. The girls circulate. One comes over and sits on my lap.

'You're the Wolf-Man aren't you?'

'That's what they call me.'

'Why do they call you the Wolf-Man?'

'I like to sink my teeth into buttocks.'

'You like them?'

'Delicious.'

'Pity. Mine are thin.'

'You're still young.'

'You know what they call me?'

'No.'

'Little Red Riding Hood.'

'You got a hood?'

'I got all kinds of things.'

'I'm eighty-six in two days' time.'

She wiggles. Once only peasant girls offered their bums. Now everyone does it.

'You got good teeth.'

As I said. Sordid. I look across at Kurt. Kurt von Pfaff is seventy-two and weighs two hundred and fifty pounds. He has a long scar across his face. A ceremonial sabre cut. Kurt is also ex-S.S., one of the few S.S. men to have had an aristocratic upbringing. He bows theatrically and I tilt my glass at him. Kurt has sent the girl across. His face has that awful ironic sneer on it. As usual, we play these charades with ambiguity and emptiness. Kurt wants something from me.

Vienna mornings I haunt the cafés. Have breakfast at a Balkan place on the Franzjosefskai. Change seats when some pair of warm buttocks has vacated a chair to nestle in the imprint, like a sampling of blood.

Petersburg
1906

I am twenty. I don't have a passport. There are no such things as passports, though Czarist Russia required some proof of identification upon entry. G. (the painter) was very upset by this. I tried to explain to him that all Russians were neurotic. To which he smiled sadly and nodded.

I don't have what is called *identification*. Am I a Russian? What is my identity? It is death. I am death. All mimicry is death. A wasp flies into an orchid, changes colour, imitates it. It is soon pasted to it with nectar and it dies. Yes, nectar. The Russian nectar glues me to death.

Upon my return from the Caucasus I fell into a deep emptiness from which I have never been entirely cured. It began with Weinstein talking to me, berating me about the necessity of *identity* on the boat back from the Caucasus. We were grumbling from lack of sleep, moving along the Georgian coast on a shuddering steamer. The sea was heavy and the sky was black. In our cabin was a coiled hose in a cabinet behind a pane of glass. 'In case of fire break glass' was printed above in Cyrillic alphabet.

'It is in *classification*,' Weinstein was trying to impress upon me so loudly, 'that we can make sense of the world.'

Whose classification? Whose sense? Power, control, sense: I had none of it. I was directed by destiny, the caul, the hood which protected me but which endowed me with visions . . . of a jellied mass of humanity overflowing borders, of flesh sliced by broken glass, pregnant women disembowelled, umbilicals uncoiled like a firehose . . . this was classification. This was the future. But this was also Weinstein's reason and sense, already demonstrated by the suffering of animals in the abbatoirs we saw in Tbilisi, buttocks cleaved and torn into hindquarters, smears of excrement, blood, placental liquid swelling the membrane of the world. Descartes' reason, the animal as machine in the service of men . . . to be devoured. And this was my destiny . . . to be devoured, in turn to devour myself, and to withdraw, to accompany reason like a shadow . . . destiny . . . to be farted out into the world in a bubble, endowed with the retroversion of inactivity, passivity, incompetence, divine neglect, *but to reason as well*, oh glorious! To shit pure form, that was my desire. Blood runs down the screen. That was me being born. I looked up and saw the light. Through the membrane I saw my father dancing around. He held up Anna for me to see. Anna was like a frozen turkey in his big hands. His face was dark with worry. But with the dark came a kind of insane and gluey light of satisfaction. My father may have wanted me mummified forever. Then they burst my bubble . . . enlightenment . . . and I felt the first shock of reality: my mother's nipples.

My mother couldn't suckle me. Do you think that accounts for my lack of identity?

You try to blur all distinctions, Weinstein said.

Of course ruminants blur all distinctions. Ruminants were definitely pre-passport. That really angered Weinstein and he left the ship at Simferopol. I never saw him again. He would be killed years later, trying to prove his identity to the Bolsheviks.

What was this passivity of mine, this neglect, this trust in destiny, this stoic abstraction? It was, of course, something *Oriental* . . . inscrutable . . . incapable of being discovered. Perhaps it was precisely the lack of a necessity to do battle with Western reason.

If you look at a map of South Russia, you will see that it is possible to draw a vertical line almost directly from Odessa through the Bosphorus along the 30° longitude. To the left is the Occident, (which Freud understood better than anyone else to be in need of analysis). To the right is the Levant, the Orient, the trope in which the sun turns from progress to regress, from a bright concern to glaring neglect. Freud had little time for the Orient, understandably. It wasn't his bread and butter. Though he once said he yearned for the East. But what was this turning away while rising? This elaborate figure of the East? It was the arabesque. The feminine principle. It was a swerve away from the straight line, from voracious action, from the brutality of the willed result, from instrumental reason. It was a curlicue, this *naskhi* script, doing without the Christian gamble of heaven or hell and the spiritual quantifiers of St Cyril and his alphabet. It was pure movement, force without power, mystery without cipher, a movement *away, never to return while repeating itself.*

I dwelt on the node between East and West. When Father suggested I study law in Petersburg, I went westward with an eastern soul. Petersburg's petulance, its bustling crowds, forced a solitary like me into the narcosis of the past. They had a riot here last year. Bloody Sunday. Last year was the bloody future. Nevertheless in 1906 you might have seen me in any droshky, making for lectures with a face as long as Rasputin's, behind the glass darkly. Like a lamb to the slaughter. They crucified me in the seminars, the professors made a laughing stock of me. I brought a duelling pistol into the classroom, pointed it at the lecturer. 'How easy it is,' I said to him, 'for the law to become an abstraction.' The law couldn't put up with much eccentricity, though I explained it was a fundamental mimetic experience . . . the *theatre* of the law. I admit I caused quite a stir. I had grown my hair long. Took a hundred potions to calm my nerves while the professor waited in front of the class, clearing his throat. I was expelled. Divorced from learning. Decree nisi. Nights while the students studied, drank or whored, I made my way along the Nevsky Prospect to a street off Znamenskaya Square, where a distant cousin, Doctor S., gave me enemas. Ah! Sweet decadence! The stench of corruption was in my nostrils as I sampled the height of Russian literary and artistic life. I was richer than the rest . . . I had my own box at the opera and ballet; attended the salons in disguise and said not a word but coughed lightly into my handkerchief, not feigning, but *professing* illness. Even with my mask on, someone invariably recognised my hero. 'Why, it's Lermontov!' they exclaimed, jokingly. It was no joke. Why did they say that, even though I had on a wolf-mask? They were provocative but I didn't challenge them to a duel. I was an aesthete. Neurasthenic, tubercular, passionate for what was dark, forbidden. Nights along the windy, icy English Embankment, I followed servant girls with alluring buttocks to their quarters. Paid them for their bleating. Oh decay! Oh sacrilege! Once I found myself in the Peter and Paul Cathedral, clouded in incense, and was so overcome by eroticism I fainted in the pews. Days I grazed in my special carriage with windows of one-way glass and was filled with disgust, depression, guilt, as I studied the crisp backsides of boys and girls running home. In my overheated rooms rented from my Uncle Basil, I read Huysmans and Proust and sucked on lozenges of laudanum. Once, in a dream, I met Proust. He said to me: 'I was the only one to write "I" without shame in a century of boring, classical bums.' Then he faded into his own writing.

Petersburg, too, was a dream. I skipped lectures and failed exams. I began to paint. I painted sadness. They thought I had some talent— the Russians were a depressed people, especially after their defeat by the Japanese. I painted sadness and knew it was a special sadness, different from ordinary melancholy. It was what the medieval monks used to call *Acedia*. It was far from despair. It was the ability to steady oneself up against despair. It was pain. It was suffering. It was a scholarly sadness and a necessary initiation into the human condition. Call it a sociable sadness. I made it into an individual pathology.

It became fashionable to consult psychiatrists. I went to visit Dr B., who was a friend of the family. (Father was by now in a sanatorium in Germany.) But all B. wanted was a donation to the neurological institute. Then I decided to go to Munich, on the advice of Dr H.

It was snowing at the railway station. I felt very good. It was 1908 and I was manic with joy at having found a path for my wandering.

KATOOMBA

1978

They began to say, as you promoted yourself in your middle years, that you were an opportunist. Perhaps they didn't notice that danger was your inspiration. Something familiar you've tried to repress . . . the scimitar slash and intricacy of the arabesque . . . the same writing, the same heartbeat, like a domesticated wolf who still hears on cold, still nights the creak of a man's boot, the snap of twigs, knowing here was danger and opportunity, damp fur leaking blood between steel traps, the moaning labours of the imagination in virgin birth, the savage bolt of jaws, the real and the resonant in concert . . . Moving further eastward: in Chinese, to be in a crisis is to face both good and bad. It can go either forwards or backwards, into danger or opportunity, containing both destiny and fate. A double path which eventually forks. You were in continual crisis. You straddled both.

Vienna

1972

Here I am again in the library archives. I'm discovering more and more of my notes, jottings, clippings, half-written chapters. He must have been as busy as a squirrel, secreting away my writing. He knew the value of hiding them. Must have crammed whole suitcases with it on his departure for London. Would have had a lot of hangers-on, I guess, people who claimed to have known him gathering all this stuff. Imagine him saying Moses was an Egyptian! The Nazis made a bit of mileage out of that, I can tell you. *Totem and Taboo*. Sounds like a script for a Hollywood movie. Totem and taboo. Tomtoms in the jungle. Weismuller strutting his stuff in his leopard skin shorts. I took personal offence when he published *Totem and Taboo* in 1913. You know what the subtitle was? *Some Points of Agreement between the Mental Lives of Savages and Neurotics*. That was a real low blow. Way below the belt of civilisation's discontents. Man, in one fell swoop he'd turned me from an aesthete into a cannibal.

Didn't see the archive assistant today. Must be her day off. I prowl the stack aisles. I've got my own fan-club too. I'm the man who was Freud's outstanding success. I exist only as a pseudonym, but they all come to see me. Yes, I'm a freak show and a conduit to the great man all rolled into one. Come to think of it, I look like a giant apple strudel. At my age, when everybody who's still alive is starting to shrink, I'm laying on the fat. Sure, I've had my lean years. I wouldn't mind dying now, amongst my books. They are my real friends. They always have been, though at one time I couldn't read. I don't mean couldn't as in the case of an illiterate. I was blocked, that's all. I used to work in a library like this once. Not as big. A municipal library, you might say. I was poor. Lost everything in the Revolution. Reduced to begging from Freud. I'll say this for him . . . he was kind. Slipped me a few English pounds now and again. Made it look invisible. He left the notes as though they were bookmarks in the volumes he lent me from his own library. For a long time I didn't tumble. You see, I couldn't read books. I sent them back to him unopened. He finally gave up and stuffed the notes in my pockets . . . to my not very vociferous protestations.

Well, better go and get some lunch.

So here I am almost half a century later cruising this expensive city in Cardin slacks and Italian shoes and a sweatshirt given to me by Teddy Kennedy's cousin (who is a shrink) which says on the front 'Chappa-what?' and on the back there is this big L sign in fluorescent yellow. I walk on into the suburbs. Two-storey buildings, rhododendron gardens, villas, churches, schools. Religion once owned the best land around here. Imperious old ladies left gigantic estates. Now it's episcopal capitalism. The Catholics hold their own. 'There's the wankers and the marketeers,' the Bishop once said to me out of the side of his mouth about his priests, 'and the wankers don't know blood from wine . . . totally deluded, but you got to have 'em at the coalface'.

Self-help. It took me a long time to live by that rubric. Life was no charity bazaar. Grandad was right. The third generation either lost the family fortune or squandered it. The Bolsheviks saved me the trouble and the guilt.

I worked by day in a city library, pushing around trolleys of books, sorting items, snagging the odd thief who needed to possess books rather than read them. I understood the fetish of the collector. I understood his neurosis, his whimsicality. I knew that wars were begun in his head because of obsessions, and that when he opened the book finally, he would be unable to read. The absence of a real text was his true desire. Domination, the will to civilise, the ambition to write the book of books and put an end to all books. I'd ring bells, summon security, give him a dressing down. You'd be surprised at the types I caught; bankers, politicians, bishops. They bribed me with vintage scotch. When I became famous they came to call on me like a procession of old friends.

Artie Catacomb said he was a friend and not an analyst. He used to spend three months of the year in New York, three months in Paris. The rest here. He wrote articles for *Libération*, trying to connect Freud to Mao. Everywhere he went he carried a rucksack on his back, as if he were on the march. He was a fanatical devotee of both men. When I published my third book, a Freudian thriller, he turned up like a bad pfennig. The book was a shocker. Nothing to do with Freud. Plenty to do with sex. I intended it as an appendix to Sade, but Sade had no need for that organ. People wanted to sue, left, right and centre right. All kinds of moralists came out of the woodwork. Artie knocked on my door and invited me to dinner along with several women doctors, all shaped, by God, like decanters. They took notes, swayed to and fro and lounged at doorways. I went mad with grief and desire. But I, too, played the moralist. I slugged them with a story Freud once told *me*. He wasn't very good at stories. It was more of a parable. It had some kind of serious intent: 'There once was a man who told stories,' Freud began. 'People came to listen. Then the man went away. The stories were passed on from one village to another and from one generation to the next. The man was trusted as a giver of knowledge.

'Then someone appeared who made signs. These signs were curious things. They didn't particularly tell you anything about the world. They were a little threatening. The people made up names for the two men. They called the storyteller "Herr Truth", and they called the writer of signs "Herr Cunning". However, they soon realised that these signs were at odds with what the storyteller had said about the world. For one thing, the significance of the signs was missing. There were so many significances that they were empty of meaning. The people soon began to make supplementary signs themselves. They believed that they no longer had any need for Herr Truth. But without Truth the villages broke up. With signs alone, the people wandered in a maze, fighting and killing each other.

'Then, one day, a man appeared among the wandering people and claimed he was the original storyteller *and* sign-maker. He told them the point of his signs, that it was . . . well, the truth about human nature and that they were living proof of it. *You had to be initiated into the truth*, he said. The people were so angry at having been thus betrayed, that they stoned him to death and made him into a sign. It was a warning to apostates, to the silver-tongued, the forked-tongued.

'Then a strange thing happened. The villagers suddenly discovered that they had come back together, entranced by what they had done.'

'That's a hell of a story, Herr Professor,' I said, totally nonplussed.

Freud took a deep breath, fixed me with a hypnotic stare and asked:

'What was the man's error?'

I shrugged. I was hopeless at riddles.

Freud looked at me in a kindly, though, when I come to think of it now, mocking way.

'His concern for community.'

Later he would say to me: 'The community . . . the collective unconscious . . . wishwash!'

Herr Truth and Herr Cunninglingus. Freud, the *artiste manqué*, had had a vision. '*En masse*, truth is cunning and trust is fear,' he said. 'Think of yourself.'

When he spoke of his 'grave philosophy' and his tentativeness in reaching further into cosmic mysteries, he was expressing to me something more than his bitterness with Jung. 'Each of us is another,' he said. 'It's a symbiotic dependency especially when you're in the dark. But never at any time, in any circumstance, endeavour to defend me.'

Now, all this came as a shock to Maoist Artie, though he recovered quickly, and in that charming way of his which I found extremely naïve, said that Freud always identified with victims.

I am afraid of telling too much of this. I am anxious about possible misunderstanding of that blessed release from obligation that Freud bestowed upon me. 'Just think of your own body . . . ' he said to me, ' . . . what a *mess*, Goddamn.'

I emitted a little turd that night, a hard, shiny little nugget . . . without using an enema.

KATOOMBA
1978

In the German newspapers in 1938 it was often reported that
Jews were using more gas than anyone else . . . for the purpose
of suicide. The camp commanders later employed this
malicious joke to the full. Jews were given (last) suppers and
told to take showers. Ordinary communicative routines were
bound by the most illicit of relationships: the symmetry of
trust and fear.

Confessions, anxieties, omissions. You didn't want to push
Sergei too far. He was seldom lucid. You told him you were a
friend, not an analyst. Sergei may have omitted the fact that in
1938 his wife Thérèse committed suicide by gassing herself.

Munich

1908

To present one's back to the world may be either passivity or anarchy, and maybe both.

In Munich I presented my back to my childhood, signing myself in with the initials S.W.—(Sergei Wespe. My name, unless you forgot, means 'wasp', and has a sting in the tail)—a serpent and a double-wolf, under the care of Professor Kraepelin. Professor Crap, as I called him, fussed over a pair of long moustaches and wore a clown's mask pushed up onto the top of his bald head. It was Kussnacht. It was my twenty-first year.

'So. What you have leaking in your life is lurv.'

'Leaking?'

'Lecking.'

'Crap.'

'Call me Professor, if you please.'

I went for seven days and stayed seven weeks. Nothing magic about it. Nothing really medical either. Hydrotherapy, they called it. Suspended in baths of brine which women in nun-like garb poured on top of me from wooden buckets, these women looking Egyptian, their veils starched like pharaohs descending upon me from the Nile, blue and white habits . . . you had to call them *Sister*, with such strong hands, oh, strong hands kneading your buttocks on the after-bath massage table so you feel something close to God, an elevation to the inner sanctum of this primordial holiness, this laying on of hands under the auspices of health . . . *mens sana in corpore sano*; yes, this was pre-war stuff, before they divided the mental and the physical illnesses among the wealthy, before the physicals went up into the mountains and the mentals into the military;

so why was I cold? The crowd left me cold, that's why. You
don't have to guess. Take Colonel S. from the Peter and Paul
Fortress. He's got a heart murmur you can hear. When you
pass him in the corridors there's this *hnnng, hnnng, hnnnng,
hnnng*, because inside there the organ is creaky, pumping
blood with leaking bellows. Because the Colonel was a physical fanatic. Used to run up and down the steps at the P & P,
did push-ups in the office and was the proud father of three
orgasms a night. Till the heart complained and rumours were
circulated. Death, death, the pipes wheezed. Your body is
telling you something, Dr Crap said to him. What? the Colonel
shouted. Tell me! Tell me! The Professor studied him with a
listening trumpet. You are lecking lurv, the Professor said. The
Colonel regarded himself in the mirror after his bath. I walked
past his half-opened door. He flexed his pectorals, went up to
the mirror, gave his reflection a kiss.

Gonorrhoea. A legacy from dear Matrona, my Mary
Magdalene who crowned me with thorns. Professor Kraepelin
thought he was treating me for that . . . leaking, lacking, the
absence of desire. It was something else. I was bored. Dinner
times were worst. I had to go downstairs to face these refugees
from service, whole armies of uninspiring autodidacts and
casualties of once-promising careers. The accountant from
Tiflis who had bad breath, whose stomach must have
harboured whole factories of anxiety, spoke unceasingly of
refurbishments. I can hear him now: 'Ha! If we moved the
furniture into Mama's room, then we can paint Papa's study
. . . we could have green paint, or maybe yellow . . . but no,
yellow makes me a little ill . . . Ha!' A wave of sourness cruised
the table. An ill wind. A burp from the collective cesspits of
the Ottoman Empire. I replied by farting. Oh, yes. I let my
trained sphincter do the talking. Whole bars of Beethoven too.
Ordinary civilised life couldn't continue in this cocktail of
smells, but the accountant, used to a lifetime of siege,
remained steadfast. Other people moved away. His wife, thin,
insipid, said not a word. There was a space of smells between
us. It was supreme idiocy to try to dissipate the self in this
community. There were so many alter-egos in the room we
could have played musical chairs with impunity, never caught

out. There was a woman from Odessa with a skin affliction. It must have prevented her from talking. She rolled her eyes and studied the ceiling and she rocked up and down. I thought of kissing her sandpaper cheeks, pare down speech, curb excesses. When I tried she slapped me. That's what you get when pity worms its way into affection. There was an Italian baroness. There was a famous professor with a very young wife . . . you could tell she wasn't enjoying this. I ogled her unceasingly. All this wealth; new and old money, and achievement. The cigar I was practising on, waiting for my inheritance (yes, my father would die soon, by the look of him), didn't taste so good.

Nights I read debilitating novels: Huysmans, Proust, Daudet. The French understood illness. Alone, among all this brocade and carpet, with the exquisite pleasure of hating their muffled laughter downstairs over their game of cards, I festered exquisitely. Rain batted on the shutters. The night trams made slits of light on the ceilings. I felt nothing. I was dead. And there was all this time to kill.

I lie perfectly still all night. In the morning I do not rise even though they come along the corridors ringing bells for breakfast. I lie mummified in my quilts and wait for death. On the table they have put a vase of fresh dandelions. Maybe dandelions is all they can get in Munich at this time of the year. At nine they send someone round to look up those who have not appeared.

'Herr Wespe, please. You will have to get up.'

I am dead. I am nothing. It is a wonderful state to be in.

'Are you hearing me?'

The ward sister is fat, her features bulbous. She wears a longer veil than the rest of them. She shakes me. I can't bear her touch. No experience at all is to be God, isn't that it? Can't be touched by the cesspit of sentiment. The morning light pales into the oblivion of the day when she opens the shutters. Another grey one.

'You will have a wash then downstairs then breakfast which you will find is too late, Herr Wespe. Then all that on one condition: that you be a good boy for your examination with Herr Professor this afternoon.'

This gives me no joy, I tell you. Not the examination but this motherly figure who pinches my foot. In my prime I would have embedded her but I'm not in form at all. I examine her pinch on my foot and the sensation is receding, becoming a distant memory of once great pleasure when Anna and I used to caress each other's feet, tickle the soles, ( ) them up and down our genital areas ... oh, sublime, sublime. But this woman has the backside of a barnyard door after the horse has bolted, yawing and swaying on one hinge under her uniform. She's lopsided. Asymmetrical. No sensation. Nothing. I'm dead, I tell you. Not a tremble in the nether regions. This, as the Greeks said, was the state of pure detachment. It is supposed to nourish.

Goddamn Eduardo. Eduardo comes in, minces across the room and pulls down the shades again. Eduardo is my man servant. He knows I hate the light and what's more he has power over the Valkyrie. 'I'll take over now,' he says softly and the nurse pulls a face and stomps out. Oh, I tell you, I'm tired of Eduardo, who turns me over roughly and administers an enema.

'You're full of shit, Eduardo,' I say.

'I think you mean that the other way round,' he says, smartarse that he is.

I don't argue. Eduardo is the Italian bare-knuckle champion of Milan who's as camp as a battalion of Romans on a ten-year bivouac. I tolerate him because of my innate passivity. He takes advantage. With the enema-gun. I only let him entertain himself as far as the metaphor. I may be listless, but inside I'm boiling ... the words seethe. One day I'm going to write the truth. Turn and turn about. Five years old and I have a fever and it's five o'clock because the grandfather clock, the one with the goat in it, strikes five and Father is screwing mother backwards, three times it happened, everything in threes: Father, Son and Holy Ghost and Father steps over to my cot with his huge and frightening member (the only one in this club, buddy) which is still erect, and this is the greatest terror of my life because he no longer looks like a wolf but is a man: totally out of place in the schema of nature. When I tell Grandad about it he guffaws. The next day I was up a tree and Grandad was underneath, urinating onto the trunk, when they said Uncle Nicholas let him have it with the axe-head, right in the frontal eminence.

Eduardo goes to the phone and makes the appointment with the Professor. He holds the ear piece like a cigarette and prances around while he talks. In the ring, I'm told, this prancing is deadly. I send him away. I wish I had a maid in a short black dress and white lace apron whom I can spank on the behind while she sc( )s the floor, the soles of her feet nicely soiled in my service, and I, perversely aristocratic and superior in suffering, would be afraid of her when she turns around to vent her wrath upon me. I am writing a manual on these things. There are rules, not to restrict, but to constrict desire.

But none of this can be spoken. It is only wrong when it is explained. By wrong I mean incorrect.

The world is hidden in a veil, and the veil is torn only when, after an enema, the contents of the bowel pass through the anus. Then I feel well again for a very short time and I see the world clearly.

That's what I wrote to Freud when I was on holidays. Subsequent analysts have identified this veil with the phallus. The faeces is the rebirth of the penis . . . et cetera. But do they not know about the startling evacuation of the self? The scream that says: 'I was buried alive, but now the sun streams in and nothing is as light as this desire to fertilise the world, rhythmic, uniform, and which, at the moment of knowledge, disappears'?

At one o'clock I got up, got dressed and went downstairs. In the dark corridor near the dining room I saw a maid, on her hands and knees, sc( )bing the wooden floor. Her black dress was pulled up around her haunches. She had on a white veil, just like the nurses had. Below all, she waggled her buttocks in a most impressive manner. I felt the shock of recognition, the shape of an aside presented itself. As I passed, she looked up and smiled, and wonder of wonders, I saw the most beautiful woman I had ever seen in my twenty-two years of life. On her hands and knees. Browsing over my feet, boots, once spit-and-polished objects of veneration, great mounds of white mould now, from endless walking in the snow-slush streets larded with urine, dog shit, come-what-may, shuffling under her nose, making to move away as she begins to wipe them . . . I don't feel at all good about this, the merest pressure on my instep, oh stop! Oh, pity! This is care, love, concern. She turns, arse-side once more. I dislike myself, but there is something incremental here, lust, life again, presenting itself, no longer a deadshit. Myself? All right. It's the picture of myself I hate. All those selves, the mob, howling at the door.

KATOOMBA
1978

You are sort of skating and slipping down Katoomba Street. The snow is settling and the cars cruise very slowly down the main street because of the gradient. Most of the cars are four-wheel-drive vehicles and they belong to tourists who have come up for the experience of driving in snow. The locals slide. You are elated. You have a book in the pocket of your great-coat. The cars are making slalom tracks on the road, which shows up black. A friendly crust of snow forms on your beard. You make your way down the street to a little tea house which is still dirty and non-respectable and which is run by a greasy old woman who caters for the lower end of the market: families who can't afford holidays in summer and who can't go further than this uplifted plateau over which explorers almost killed themselves. Fornicating with the ridges, you would have said, in order to smell the rich plains below. You never go below. In fact you never go too far. You go back and forth within a square mile spinning a web and making a nuisance of yourself. What else can you expect from age? Wisdom? Refinement?

You know that you are onto something important about the Wolf-Man. It is the 'circumstantial evidence' that troubles you. That same 'circumstantial evidence' that Freud took such delight in—thus inscribing his interest in Conan Doyle. You know it because of something that will happen here, in Katoomba, New South Wales, Australia, which the world knows nothing about. For many years you have called it your Big Secret, which is not so big and not so secret.

A few years ago you walked ten miles to visit your cousin and his wife. You knew where they lived because they had been sending you letters. Letters to which you hadn't replied.

They asked time and again if you were all right. They tried to speak about themselves in modest ways, not wanting to pry into your life. Without notifying them, you turned up on the doorstep. They were just bringing your cousin's coffin out. You had brought a basket of fruit which you picked from an orchard at Blackheath. You stood there in an old St Vinny's wide lapelled suit with the fruit in your hands while your cousin's wife burst into tears. Later she brought out his shoes. There were at least a hundred pairs of fine leather shoes, hardly worn. Here, she said, you are the same size. You can make use of them. Perhaps she saw your down-at-heels boots, caked with mud. The shoes fit well. She paid for a taxi to take you and the two garbage bags full of shoes home. You never thought people noticed shoes. But that is the first thing they notice. Their gazes work up from the bottom. You tell yourself you're not suffering from paranoia. But with your new shiny shoes people stopped staring at you after the first glance at the booties. You came up a grade from tramp to eccentric. You went to a few more cheap restaurants. Nobody bothered to kick you out, even when you lingered until closing time.

Your cousin was a crim who died peacefully in his sleep. He called on you once, many many years ago, with two cases of beer under his arm. He drove a white Bugatti. 'Dead men don't shuffle.' That had been his favourite expression in those days, while doing a soft-shoe on your decaying linoleum. Your cousin worked the racetracks while you went to University. He was always good for a rigging. When you wanted to drop out he turned up at the door with a hundred pounds in cash. 'For your schooling,' he had said, like an older brother.

You were born poor so you didn't know any different when you lived in a rat-hole in Forest Lodge in a bare room with a single light bulb and a mattress and where the plywood back of a wardrobe formed a common wall. Nights you curled up in the lowboy to avoid the slurry of rain and dirt creeping across the lino from the paneless window, and you listened to your neighbours making love, the girl screaming, the smell of semen and cigarette smoke. One day, you said to yourself, you would study these primal scenes in earnest.

You did just that, but now you've ended up where you

began, cursed by an aspiration for refinement but hamstrung by crudity—that's mental health at least—and here you are, an old man sitting in a cheap eatery studying your cousin's shoes, still trying to learn the footwork.

Vienna

1972

Artie Catacomb has taken to having noisy parties next door. He always makes it a point to invite me, but I never go. There they are. In and out. They are young. Athletic. They balance glasses on the balcony railing. I catch snippets of their conversation:

'So. I live in this one-room apartment and work in the local bar.'

'Is it good work?'

'No. It smells and the boss is a bastard. Feels me up inside my sweater, a teat-pincher.'

'But you don't say anything out of place.'

'Of course not. I make it a point to maintain discipline.'

'And you practise?'

'Yes. I practise three afternoons a week.'

Artie's house guests wear denim jackets and and come on motorcycles. They aren't students, though I'm not too sure about this. I met one or two in the stairwell. They were too intense to be students. Most were women who never smiled. They had long mousy coloured hair. Under their jackets they wore thick woollen jumpers which covered their backsides. They were attractive in a sullen sort of way. They were not the sort who would have brought me orchids.

Once when Artie was away one of them knocked on my door and left a book she had borrowed from the Professor. I thanked her. She didn't smile. She spoke very correct German, as though she had learnt it out of a primer. I asked her for her name. Gudrun, she said. I took the book. When she left I began to read it. But I couldn't get past the first few pages. It has been a long time since I had actually read a book. From

99

cover to cover. After a certain age I couldn't read without writing. I wrote and read in snippets. I re-read. Re-wrote. Nothing progressed. Nothing was finished. The past and the present intermarried. I could no longer speak correctly like the girl. I became more foreign than I had ever been before.

It is the afternoon. Here comes Artie. He will come to my door, knock three times, ask me out for a walk. I am like a dog who sees his master reaching for the leash.

'So, Sergy. This new book you've just finished. You gonna give a launch speech?' Artie asked as we walked down the Prater, his curbside eye jaundiced from a bad liver and focussed independently on buttocks. A girl stopped us, asked Artie if he was Jean-Paul Sartre. Artie smiled, gave her his autograph.

'I should probably say something,' I said.

'Oh yes,' Artie said, 'you have to say something. And don't, for God's sake, make any statement about psychoanalysts. You want to be thought of as a writer, not as a case.'

I should have taken his advice last time. I'd given this talk in Paris to a group of students entitled: *I was a Teenage Wolf-Man*. It didn't go down too well. They expected to be shocked. I was offering them culture. Neurosis was out of date. Beyond the panelled windows of the Sorbonne the plane trees wept and the tourist buses churned over the leaves. I had gone into a trance, having brought such poor offerings. The lecturer fidgeted. A couple of girls smiled and twirled their hair. So many worlds. To think that more than half a century had passed since I had shambled up the Berggasse to prove a theory for Freud. There were leaves on the pavement, then Swastikas, then squatting photographers. I haven't looked forward since. I think the students expected werewolves. They who saw themselves as the future, the girls' hair turning golden and white now in the sun. Leaves of fall. Bus. It ran down somebody. I was talking about a dream and right at that moment, staring out through the window at the Sorbonne I saw a bus run down somebody.

'Oh,' Artie said again, 'you have to be careful of ASPS.'

It was, perhaps, a society for the protection of snakes?

'The American Society for the Protection of Sigmund,' Artie rasped, staring at the clouds in Whitmanesque ecstasy . . . 'The Association of Psychoanalysts.'

'I was just telling it like it was, Artie. Freud's not God, you know.'

Catacomb sighed.

'Maybe you should just read something from it. You have to think of posterity.'

'Hot damn, Artie,' I say. '*That's* never far away.'

Buttocks were buzzing past on summer Vespas . . . wasp-waisted. Come into my vespiary. We were reaching the city limits.

'Be serious. Don't be retrograde.'

'What's that? A Russian city?'

They've never thought of me particularly as a writer. I was the source of deviance, invented by others; oh yes, I was everybody's Other, a true friend to be reckoned with, like the voice of conscience, or the silent laughter of Jesus . . . I'm always there, an inspiration shooting about, flying faster than the Holy Ghost or any other carrier pigeon . . . let me take a breath here. I'm asthmatic. Inhalation. Howl. There. Mustn't let it get away on me.

I had wolf dreams. Old Sigmund tried to slot me. *The Wolf-Man*, he called me. Nights he must have shuffled out in slippers and secreted into Greek tear-jars. Remorse for misreading. This was the end of art, I tell you. Sealed my fate. Pasted up the caul with fragments of my writing to preserve his own conscience. Uncanny huh? That reminds me, some writer once said: 'Art cannot rescue anybody from anything'.

I know. Art's hopeless: wouldn't know a lifebuoy from soap; couldn't tell shit from cucumber. But anything can be salvaged by anybody. Freud was a collector too. Among his statuettes, my fragments of loss. I had dreams. I wrote them down as poetry. 'Stick to pulp,' Freud said when he read them, 'unless you want to be a pauper.' Freud was prophetic. He was good on alliteration. He also had something wrong with his mouth. From the head of the couch his plosive consonants baptised my head with saliva.

Artie was even worse. Artie sprayed cognac. My twenty-year-old Napoleon. Civilisation was wasted on him.

Catacomb was snorting as we walked. Then he began to cough. Artiechoking. There was something important he wanted to get off his chest.

'I have to take a piss, Artie.'

We had walked further than I thought, for we found ourselves outside the Psychiatric Hospital.

Artie grunted and undid his fly. I don't know why he wanted to join me. With some people, taking a piss is like having a drink. You couldn't do it alone. We stood there, anointing the wall of the Steinhof. A nurse appeared at the window wearing a starched veil.

'Of course,' Artie said, 'if you offered an opinion it would immediately become a paradigm, a dominant which would determine your direction. Make the whole thing a Fascist authorising of the text. It would prescribe spheres . . . ontologies . . . worlds . . .'

'Balls,' I said.

'Where you are coming from, I mean, what position you take,' Artie insisted.

'I come in all directions,' I said, spouting, geysering, sputtering like a Roman candle. Sixty years younger and I would've done cartwheels.

But the sky was lowering. I thought about books. Intellectual orgasms, as Anna once said. Her priorities were elsewhere. Not in seriousness and sobriety, fear and trembling. In amongst all those books in my room, a handful of humour and lubricity. True. The two go together. Run your finger down the alphabet. If you listen closely, they more or less say the same thing . . . that in becoming, we make the strangest noises sounding like laughter.

'I worked in a library once. They gave me the sack after three months.'

This non sequitur startled Artie. It took him a while to recover.

'When did you work in a library?'

'1933.'

Clouds were coming in from the mountains. A cuckoo sang from the woods. Thank you, thank you, it said. Time Artie took his leave. A good analyst always knows when to leave. End of session. He got something from me to put in his book. I bowed. Thank you, thank you, goodnight, goodnight, and made my way to find some sustenance in the next bowl of broth, next brothel, next bottle, next book . . .

Munich
1908–1909

It was important not to know anybody. I fired Eduardo that evening.

There was no doubt in my mind that the only satisfactory way of pursuing an amorous relationship was to write letters, to remain unknown, distant, absent. It wasn't to Eduardo I was referring. There you go again. But to the maid who made so bold as to try to pass her rag over my shoes. I can refer you to Proust, to Cervantes, Lermontov, even to Kafka. But one at a time. Which is all at once. Take Swann's adoration of Odette in *Remembrance of Things Past* ... Odette as depicted by Boticelli as the Zephoror, Odette as the Circassian Dulcinea, Odette as curvilinear arabesque, of whom stories must be woven to keep reality at bay, to keep marriage at arm's length, hands off, keep turning the pages ... or take Kafka's Félice ... the denied ... or Thérèse the inscribed, with a tattoo on her buttocks ... no more. I am hamstrung by refinement. Maybe Proust didn't feel the urgency of it. Yes, Thérèse was the maid's name, dark as Leonardo's 'Belle Ferronière' and, if you can suffer a little anachronism, just four years later Kafka would write *The Judgment* (and whom do you think the Russian friend was in that story? The friend who perhaps didn't exist, the Petersburg friend who was nothing but a *letter*, which puts off the hero's marriage?). Me of course. I get in the way of plot, action, consummation ... a French letter preventing the routinisation of ecstasy. Bliss if you prefer. Freud called me the superego. I inhabited mountain tops. A self-censor. But in Munich, 1908, I was snowblind with love. Dark Thérèse was dazzling in her white silk. (Thérèse. She was all the women in culture. Tieret. ( ). Her name was taboo.) The marriage of figuration ... a literary beauty ... extraordinarily

even-featured, blue-black hair parted in the middle, southern
eyes, slightly sad, cheeks sculpted by a cruel sirocco, lips
welded to a mysterious past . . . Oriental, to say the least. Least
said the better. Here, a photo:

Photo

Thérèse: She could be a Spanish dancer. Firm bosom. Thin top
lip. Slightly ironic, teasing eyes. Loud voice. Good little
worker, you could tell . . . but also strong willed.

He began a letter and fear entered his heart and he wanted to
die, to become a spirit, to follow her around twenty-four hours
a day. Then again you didn't need great hearing to sonar in on
Thérèse . . . she really did have a foghorn. You can just
imagine her saying: 'So. What the fuck's all these unsigned
letters? All this literary beating the bush? I bet some prick's
stuck it up himself again.' And that was that. She dealt with
some hard cases at the sanatorium.

I wrote her unsigned letters and pushed them under her door.
All day and all night I walked around Munich. I was restless,
disturbed. I wore out paths in the forests. I almost had no time
to write, I was that busy being in motion. But I also wrote
because I had no time. I wrote on the run. It was my only
escape into hope. To bring time to a standstill. At night in the
sanatorium a chamber group played sonatas. I detected insanity in them. This was the ultimate in voluntary urbanity . . .
some called it life. I called it fear. I couldn't stay at the sanatorium, and was only at peace when I knew Thérèse had
finished her shift and had gone home. When she was on night
shift I tramped in the cold, sleeping under a bandstand at the
English gardens. To relieve myself I cruised the red-light dis-
tricts, all the time reassuring myself that Thérèse was pure,
unsullied, ready to receive me. Then I found out that she was
married to a doctor and had a daughter. Misery of miseries!
Why then was she a maid?
I found Eduardo at a bar with two women who spoke in

deep voices. Eduardo didn't hold a grudge against me for firing him. He told me instead that Thérèse was divorced. That she was a Sister and not a maid. (Nursing Sisters, of course, did maids' jobs as well. Having been brought up in a sheltered environment, I was unfamiliar with this overlap, which struck me as peculiar at the time. But it wasn't that which formed part of Thérèse's attraction for me. It was the indescribable clarity she represented, the whiteness of her veil, the blackness of her dress. Years later in Vienna I would see a film called *The White Sister*.) I felt so happy I bought everyone a drink. They mistook my intentions. I had to let them down gently. They were puzzled when I kept saying to them: 'Sister is really a maid! It is really a short step from sister to servant!'

When I escaped it was very dark and I walked for hours. I must have taken the wrong street, because suddenly I found myself back at the bar and was able just to step back into the shadows as Eduardo and his friends trooped out, joking, shouting, taking pleasure in language, in their worldliness, in their defiance, while I ran in a maze of my own imaginings, without even the courage to identify myself to the one I loved. I followed them, hoping that they would lead me from the area, but after about fifteen minutes they took a turning and I lost them. I thought I was on a familiar street then, and walked more briskly. At about midnight (I know this from the clock on top of a building which again looked very familiar to me), I found myself back in the same place, opposite the bar where I had met Eduardo. What is lost is also what is familiar. I squatted down in primitive fashion to resume my sense of direction. Quite involuntarily, I burst into a silent laughter which provided a strange warmth, an animal heartiness that drew in the mist, my shoulders moving up and down.

Vienna

1972

We came, Artie and I, upon a sort of square, which had an
Italian feel about it, with the late afternoon sun slanting in on
one side, warming the flags in the corner towards which we
walked. Squares are like puzzles. You never know which
corner to make for because everything seems identical. You
look for a clock, a sign. These are essential for the idle stroller
. . . a shop sign that reads: *Herren Mode*, or *Fotos*, or a blue
clock . . . familiar things from the past.

Of course Freud had said that hysterics lied. I am too old to
lie. My memories are as clear as that warm patch of sunlight
caressing the corner of the square. Freud had said to me: 'Herr
Wespe, you just keep writing me your books.' He implanted
the thought. I wrote everything to him. Just like he wrote
everything to Wilhelm Fliess, the ear, nose and throat special-
ist who bungled his operations. (Fliess left half a metre of
iodoform gauze in Emma Eckstein's nose. It smelt bad to
everyone but her. Was it supposed to curb her masturbation? I
don't know. Sometimes smells set people off.) Freud had a
quack on one side and a con-man on the other. I never pre-
sumed. Fliess didn't either. It was all one-way traffic. Sigmund
was a mover, I tell you, of everyone's ideas. He listened and he
needed a listener. Then he went a step further.

'I grant you reciprocal fame.' He may have said that. That's
if I stuck by him. He made out like he was a good agent, you
know, unassuming, in a waistcoat, books under his arm and a
pencil behind his ear. He flattered everyone and took a hefty
commission. He never wrote anything down of course. He
hated writers. (Ferenczi's diary: May 1, 1932: *I remember certain remarks Freud made in my presence, evidently counting on my
discretion: 'Patients are riffraff'.*) He loved Plato though. Plato

107

hated writers too. Then one day, *bazoom*! Freud's the most famous man in the world. I still had faith in him but I'd wasted a lot of years. Most of my best phrases got submerged. He told me that was life. Sort of shrugged. Told me to become better friends with failure. 'The logical end of writing is to be written out. It's like sex. What else do you want? Fame? Children? I got all that, and I tell you, it's a damned struggle. And it's perpetual. That's why I do a bit of cocaine now and again. Money, money. Always the same.' Then he started leaving banknotes in books he lent me. He had style. He pushed me onto another analyst when I threatened to publish. He grew irritated. 'Don't even presume,' he said, wagging his finger under my nose. 'You're crazy. You and I know that. Do you want for the whole world to know also?'

Crazily, I bit the hand that fed me.

Artie and I found ourselves on the Walfischgasse where there are a few brothels. This was familiar territory.

We walked across the street. Pressed the doorbell. The heavy door was unlatched. We walked up two flights of stairs. A couple of balding men came down, doing up their flies. Crudity, Artie once said, was a great cure. It made neurosis about as serious as the common cold.

Madam Luise was at the desk. Her painted eyes lit up when she saw us. 'You boys,' she said, 'have been so long in coming.'

Then Kurt came out. You remember Kurt. He was an S.S. officer in the war. He now weighs two hundred and fifty pounds. Now and again Kurt used to come up to my apartment and urge me to go to his reunions . . . crowded affairs in country inns where everybody remembered everybody and at nine o'clock the lights went out and standing sombrely in the incandescence of a red flame they would all sing very softly 'Deutschland, Deutschland über alles . . .'. They were preparing for elections. Kurt jabbed me in the ribs and said: 'You're an old wolf, Wespe. I didn't think you had it in you.' He smelt strongly of semen and garlic. He was eyeing Artie in a disapproving way. 'Who's your friend? Have I seen him at the *Wolfsschanze* before?'

'No. He's an American . . . psychiatrist.'

Kurt snorted.

'He looks Jewish to me.'

His eyes clouded. He took a deep breath and went back inside the room, preparing for his second coming. Artie pretended he heard nothing.

I sit outside and listen to noises from a kingdom that was once open to me, that had once ruled, possessed me. But now it's all different. There's no mock courtship, no talk, no *illicitness*. The same old routine. Artie said this was therapy. Your only hope is lycanthropy . . . *become* what you have been called, he said. You must be running up a hell of an expense account selling that to me, I said.

Listen. I can hear moans. Now these are echoes of a generic curiosity: noises from phantom caverns wherein Freud and I had shaped infantile neurosis, had carved the paradigms of perversity. The noises haven't changed.

Helplessness. I send Morpheus into my bloodstream. I am what I see. Enter a servant. The woman sits on top of me. She is Grusha. Grusha wears a yellow orchid. Grusha has a coat lined with wolf-fur. I touch it to make sure. From there I can always find my way. My hand feels several dresses, leather belts, shoes. At the bottom of the wardrobe I feel Grusha's silk pants. On the washing line her pants are like butterfly wings, for without the ribbons which lace up the sides, the two halves open and close as the wind blows. Suddenly I have the impossible but powerful sensation of enclosing her buttocks. Grusha presents her orchid to me. I hold it against my chest, watching her sliding and singing, the floor almost done, the pants wet, enclosing an orchid, she opens the windows to let it dry, I hold her pants up to my eyes, wait for the light, blood. Blood. A dark stain before my eyes. A blood orchid. I drop the pants. Run from the cupboard. Blood. Grusha smooth and yellow. Blood! I scream. Grusha catches me running over the slippery floor. Her fingers dig into my arm. I pee-pee on the floor. Grusha has a broom of twigs in her hand. Her face is very red. Her blonde hair is wet. She pulls down my pants.

Holds my little penis tightly. She yells. I am reborn.

Artie paid and we walked back through the dark streets. Only by following the lights of the main thoroughfares would we be able to find our way. Quite inexplicably, our wanderings brought us again to the square we had passed earlier that day. The clock was lit now, as were the signs: *Herren Mode. Fotos.* We walked on. Found ourselves back on the Walfischgasse. Turned a corner. Back in the square. Took a diagonal path opposite the shops, towards the unlit alcove bordering one corner. Walked down a tree-lined avenue. Passed the Atrium disco on the Schwarzenbergplatz. Found ourselves in the little square again. Maybe there were several of these little squares, Artie said. He was confused. The Oriental way of crossing a square, I read somewhere, was to go along the sides of it. In this way the walk is not vulgarly diagonal and the 'crossing' is not linear but experiential and leisurely. There is no feeling of being lost. Freud once lost his way in an Italian provincial town. He returned involuntarily, again and again, to the same street. Painted prostitutes leaned out of the windows, beckoning to him. He finally regained his direction by coming to a familiar piazza. The square, its comforting symmetry, gave Freud an idea.

The lost and the familiar; what is familiar is also what is lost. We repress all the other paths, all the detours, paths not taken, crossroads of life. The recognition comes out of the long dead past, an atavistic sign leading nowhere, accompanied by a fear as familiar as home.

And do we not flee from home the moment we are born, escaping from life to welcome death?

So, for instance, when, caught in a mist perhaps, one has lost one's way in a mountain forest, every attempt to find the marked or familiar path may bring one back again and again to one and the same spot, which one can identify by some particular landmark.

Freud, *The Uncanny*
standard edition, vol. 17

Munich

1908–1909

What came first then, the chicken or the egg? My love for art or for Thérèse? Did she exist first, or did I invent her first? Did I walk around with this *potential* to fall in love, this predisposition for Spanish-looking women, or predisposition for love, passion, a vulnerability at which I never really had to practise, or did Thérèse, who looked Spanish, appear before me, striking me like a bolt of lightning? You can see now how Freud had trouble with primal scenes. I could have written it either way, or I could have taken another route altogether.

I felt passive. Helpless. This wasn't what I was accustomed to . . . it used to be all thrust and parry with servant girls. But now I wanted to throw myself at her feet, run my tongue through her toes, tickle her instep arch, advance like a snail up her leg, lecherous and leech-like, wet, make sucking noises, enter the tender caverns of hypnotic night to watch the shadows cast by the fire of ancient recall, have primitive erections, totems and taboos of prehistoric instincts, to be sat upon, perhaps to sit *a tergo*, listening to the rumble of rhetorical ovulation, speleological peculiarities unaccustomed to such laxatives, scratching genetic graffiti on the walls of hell, retrospective curiosities played out in faecal renewals . . . but wait a minute. 'Put up your swords,' Othello said, and saw himself as jealousy, a monster 'Begot upon itself, born on itself,' devouring itself, a Uroborus. She didn't even know me, and she said I was up myself. But I couldn't rid myself of the thought that she once had a husband. Was she practised? Did her vulva vibrate to another man's baton? Perhaps I had to make myself known. To insinuate myself. Stop this self-delusion, this effete predisposition to *eikasia*, as Plato said, the lowest and most irrational kind of awareness. These thoughts are snakes that

111

dart up your bum. You have to cut them up.

Positive action. I rush into Thérèse's room, and declare my love. (These are most unpleasant states. The point at which you have to find out about someone outside of yourself is the most difficult threshold to cross. It isn't embarrassment. It isn't fear of being rejected. It is the absolutely unshakeable belief that the other will not prolong desire, but will satisfy, crush, kill all expectation.) She is totally under control. She does just that, with a faint smile on her lips, like the Mona Lisa. It is a smile that robs men of their masculinity, Freud said. He was referring to the article he was writing on Leonardo da Vinci. 'Vinci was vanquished as a man. It was the smile of the revenge of woman.' Thérèse is showing her superiority. I want to strangle her. But she agrees to meet me in the park of the *Nymphenburg Palace* . . . near the sanatorium.

She was so tentative, so shy. I understood she had left her husband, and so it was a delicate situation. She had a young daughter. She flushed when I declared my love for her.

She failed to turn up. I was wracked with despair, walking in and out of the Baroque pavilions. People stared. I pretended to be a painter. Indeed, I carried a brush for this purpose. I held it up against the sky, measured off the perspective, swirled it in the fountain.

I have a second attack of love. I am unable to breathe. I want to be everywhere at once. I am overcome by an immense sadness, which manifests itself in an unquenchable thirst for Spanish guitar music. Doctor Drones, my private physician, is alarmed. He cancels my baths and recommends three-hourly enemas. This weakens me so much I barely have the strength to walk down the corridor. Thérèse is there, polishing. She apologises for not having met me. She is scarcely convincing, but this makes me bold. I tell her I can't live without her. This flatters her and she smiles that mysterious smile. She offers to meet me in front of the Palace of Justice. Things are getting serious.

We walk, we talk. I am animated. Just to be with a woman again! To feel her nearness, her wish to be beside you. I am beside you, she says. Isn't that enough? Our hands touch slightly now and again. But there is an immense gulf. I want both to enter and enclose her, but she doesn't see it that way. In other words, she does not want to possess herself, does not see my gaze as I cast it. Does not become me.

We were real people, after all, walking in a park, but I saw everything on a screen, slightly yellowed, perhaps with jaundiced eyes. My liver was playing up. The next day, I quit the sanatorium and rented some rooms in the Kaufingerstrasse. When I was packing my suitcase a letter slid under my door. It was from Thérèse, calling it all off. I was devastated. I swallowed a bottle of sleeping tablets, and was just gaining the threshold of death's sweet serenity when they discovered me and revived me. A nasty stomach pumping. I was full of tubes and pipes. I was a grand neurotic organ in a cathedral of dreams. Christ ministered to me, while outside I heard horses' hooves on the cobblestones. I refused to speak in German. When the doctors spoke to me I answered in English, French and Russian. It was an *entente* I invented myself.

The doctors here are second-rate. All doctors should be initiated into disease. Just as an analyst undergoes analysis, a doctor should be injected with diseases which force him to cure himself. A case of physician heal thyself first. Personal experience does wonders for motivation. It is fashionable, of course, in these times to go for cures: bath cures, spring cures, mountain cures, lake cures, manure cures, sanatorium cures. Cure is the fashionable word. I refer you to three definitions: medicinal healing, spiritual restoration, preservation of meat and fish. The word is most appropriately defined in terms of the last.

There's a Russian colonel here with terrible sores all over his body. When I sit next to him in the dining room I can *hear* them suppurating. It doesn't put me off my dinner. Why? The doctors suspect he cannot tolerate the iodine treatment, which is prescribed for his cure. (Of what? For what?) In the same clinical way they told me that Thérèse was not the sort of woman I could, any man could, get on with. 'She's too unpredictable,' they said. 'She has too many ideas. She's morally insane.' They wagged their fingers at me. I'm an aristocrat. A woman with too many ideas would be completely out of line. I observe the colonel's sores. Why don't I bring up my dinner? Because the colonel has nothing more serious than a dose of gonorrhoea. Personal experience like that appeared in strange places. The body was a miraculous thing. Like the fact that I knew how many sleeping tablets to take before I would sleep forever. I took one less. I am full of shame. I have to leave this place.

Thérèse agrees to take a car ride with me. I've hired a Daimler with a canopy. I can drive in fits and starts. We take the road to Dachau. I've hired a room for the afternoon. I get the key from the woman behind the desk. She doesn't smile and looks Thérèse up and down and studies the ring and appears disapproving. This is all part of the reception. In an immoral establishment the highest priority is morality. Her look said she was comfortable in crying wolf too many times. We go up. It isn't too bad. There are lace curtains and the bedclothes are turned back. I have a bottle of Bavarian schnapps in my pocket. Thérèse removes her hat. She goes to the bathroom. When she comes out she is still fully dressed. I go to the bathroom. In the porcelain toilet bowl a giagantic turd is floating. I flush it away. The doctors were right at least in one thing: Thérèse was totally unpredictable. I am consumed with an inexplicable passion for her.

Everyone dreams about wolves. It is the current tradition. Every child's nightmare. If you go to the Bavarian Hunting Museum in Munich you will see life-sized wolves in glass cages. They are incredibly huge. Some primal instinct in human observers says that nature was once much larger than men's minds. We have dominated it now, grown bigger ourselves. Thérèse sits on me, her face flushed, her hair down, her breathing rapid. She raises her arms, plunges her hands into her long dark hair, moans, screams. The aureoles of her nipples grow dark. A vulture beats its tail against my face. Night

swamps the wilderness with swirling clouds, hair, engorging
the streams with fish. We reverse. A black orchid flowers
before me, unfolds part of what had been inaccessible, its dark
taboos, its scents, its hidden wastes, and a stranger is crossing
the border in sweet transgression. But ... the museum is
frightening in the way it closes off the present. A bear stands
guard. In the drifting moonlight there are howls, unearthly
sounds, the din and clatter of unexplored nature. Time to go.
Outside the air is fresh, dissatisfying because of the extreme
cold and the way it takes one's breath and sense of smell away.
A fountain has frozen, a gargoyle spews ice and grows a
glassy beard. I ( ) my fingers along it nevertheless. Dissatisfying. They say powder is the best. My inability to reach orgasm.
The whole thing has been a dismal failure. Thérèse looks
wonderful. The episode has freshened her cheeks. I hail a
passing photographer who looks dismal enough for a few
cheap shots. In the Daimler she has never looked more beautiful. In fits and starts we arrive back at the sanatorium. I shall
have to leave this place. The doctors are obsessed with the
modernity of the cure. They do not believe in nature. They are
preserving me for the museum.

Photo: Thérèse

Winter in Munich, 1909

Hey, look at me, my hands in a fur muffler. Sister Thérèse. Nobody knows what I had to go through, working in that greasy sanatorium as a glorified maid, cleaning up their puke and spittle and urine and blood, washing down the bannisters and stairwells where they shook turds out of their trousers, hey, hot rolling turds still steaming because there's no heating on the stairs, some of them would pause to look up my skirt, others crawl on all fours like dogs to sniff and lick my shoes, the General from Petersburg the worst of the lot, hey, jabbing his fingers into my shoe and sniffing, something that always brought him to climax. They expect too much. Where I came from dogs knew their place. Hey. One day they brought in a woman. Obsessive-compulsive, they called her. She had dung-phobia. Bathed at least sixteen times a day. We couldn't get her out of the bath. Her skin withered and wrinkled. We told her that if she stayed there any longer her flesh would flake off her bones. She never ate because she didn't want to crap. So. Maybe she thought she was the Virgin Mary, who never crapped and who gave birth through her earhole. We had to force-feed her like a goose. They ordered me to accompany her everywhere, in case she drowned. I carried a portable basin of soap and water for her and she dipped her fingers like the priest at Mass (maybe she washes them in lemon tea, at home—aristocrats do this because they eat with their fingers, and have their maids wipe their bottoms. So what's new?) and had to watch her bathe, not a pretty sight as she was pale like a fish and flesh hung off her in folds and she squeaked in the bath like when you wring out a wet mop. They made me walk her around the streets. Hey. That was an advance. At first she wanted to run back for a bath. Little by little she seemed

116

happy enough with the basin I carried. After a few months she was able to walk quite close to horse manure. Then they made her take off her shoes. Hey, we walked her around Munich, looking for fresh dung. That was last summer. By autumn she was able to put her foot in it. I put my foot in it. I said to the doctors: Hey, I said, she doesn't have to go outside to step in shit. They took me off her case. Last thing I heard she was bathing in it. Not just horse manure, but human too. An excrement bath, the doctors said. That was her graduation present. Then along came Wespe. Hey, he was one sorry sonofabitch. Couldn't get it off without a great deal of mental energy. Wrote it all down, I was told. Maybe he needed a shit-shower too. A thorough gentleman though. Antiseptic, refined, harmless. Tells me sweet things when I stand in front of the mirror ... hey, like I'm the Mona Lisa or 'La Belle Ferronière', whatever that means. When I come he covers his ears. I know I've got a megaphone mouth but he really annoys me when he does that. Takes the edge off. I like to leap over that edge, fly. You hear me? He takes too many enemas. He wants to try it on me. Hey, I said, if I needed that I'd take a laxative. If you wanna do it doggy-style, why doncha say so? But keep that damned hypodermic to yourself. First time we did it he howled like a wolf ... Heigh-ho.

KATOOMBA
1978

You ever notice it gets warmer when it snows? Fire and ice are not that far apart. Only a matter of degrees. A few summers ago, when you returned from Europe and were still in charge of your wits, you gave a lecture to the Australian Psychoanalytic Society and Friends. You were going to talk about the Wolf-Man. Three old women turned up in the large hall you rented in Katoomba. One of them spat at you and cursed. You took this to be a good sign. But then the others started to leave. You stopped them by threatening to start a fire. The hall was tinder-dry. Eucalyptus resin and the peculiar stink of burnt undergrowth made it hard to breathe. You lit your handkerchief, which was soaked with the most expensive cognac. A gift from the Wolf-Man, you said, the cognac, not the hanky, who had been a loyal friend. More than you can say for your own colleagues . . . who wanted to burn you at the stake. After the lecture an American tourist entered the hall. He was about sixty, wearing a terribly passé cravat. He said he was lost. He said he was from Michigan. You said you was from Newark. He frowned at the down-market grammar. He asked where was the best place to go on a bushwalk. You said the best place was Perry's Lookdown. You didn't tell him that it was so steep one look down and you would never look down again. On anyone. You said you had to go down through a granite chimney, with a chain railing. Two days later you read in the local newspaper that an American psychoanalyst had to be lifted out by helicopter near Perry's Lookdown. You were getting edgy. ASPS were snooping around.

You drank a few more glasses of whisky at the Carrington, watching the smoke haze drift into the valleys. You were responsible for his fall. But in what way? You remembered

118

again that your conscience was alien, has been for many years like a weight that was once familiar, all it does now is to leave its imprint on your shoulder. In the wrong place. It's true. You've lost your symmetry. You're lopsided. Not exactly like the Hunchback of Notre Dame, but close. They ushered you out at six. They wanted to clear the ballroom for a wedding reception. You vomited on the drive. A gift, you said, for the newlyweds . . . a confetti of peas and rice and blood-specks.

Blood. The nights used to swim in blood long before you went to Vienna. Blood was a reminder you had always been alone. In Katoomba, on summer nights when it was hot below on the plains, you could see the redness seeping through your blinds, through your eyelids. When the bushfires roared like jet engines along the gullies, smoke hanging, a pall over the blue skies and the wind screamed and made the whole world brittle, you saw blood, red along the ridges, the lick and curl of yellow plasma at the edges just like the time you had that fight when you were seventeen, at the fringes of university life, when a drunk slashed you across the chest in the pub in Chippendale and you broke his head with a lead pipe. You never graduated. You just managed to keep out of jail, and because you read . . . because you read and had a knack for making deals and not too bad a memory, you were able to work in an insurance company, training first to get your foot in the door . . . honesty is the worst policy . . . going house to house asking for the man of the house . . . women never opened up . . . that was one policy they had . . . thinking you were a rapist . . . and then signing up customers using the Socratic method of only eliciting 'yes' answers, you made quite a living using Plato and the subject of death. Of course you encouraged them to bail out before dying, thus saving the company thousands of pounds . . . you moved on to public relations but you still had this thing about education and you became truly self-taught, sitting in on university lectures in the evenings, making the professors nervous by raising your hand and asking *questions*.

Then when the war came you joined the airforce and while

stationed in New Guinea with a Yankee squadron you collected some shrapnel in the knee during one of those lazy afternoon haphazard bombings, a droning Mitsubishi high in the sky, so familiar like a mail-run or Saturday afternoon joy flight, when they first threw bottles which sounded like the whistling of bombs and then dropped the real thing which always missed and went far out to sea and one afternoon you didn't bother to move . . . you were fishing off a half submerged barge, fishing in the American way, throwing grenades into shoals of whiting and collecting the stunned silvery bodies . . . when you heard the drone in the sky and really, nobody moved because the myth was that the Japs all wore glasses and couldn't see the wood for the trees, but you weren't wood . . . that was the thing everyone overlooked . . . and the Japs dropped one bomb, which was unusual because they always dropped two or three bottles first, and three of you disintegrated, three regular guys who were sitting near their tent smoking some concoction rolled up in palm leaf, three flyboys who were waiting for the airstrip to be laid, just sitting there without even looking up, swapping stories of home, something about this Hoosier getting caught in the wheat with his pants down and flag up by a giant harvester . . . shredded him, just as this two hundred pound bomb drops right in the middle of his story . . . didn't whistle neither . . . and the three guys went up in a fraction of a second without noise then your eardrum on that side was perforated and suddenly an arm without fingers, a forearm with a snake tattoo lands near your feet trailing a cloud of pink water like some exotic squid and still you don't move, because this time you're stunned and the plane is making a second run, engines silenced for a moment as it turned, sort of a Döppler Effect, you were thinking, then it revs up and comes in low this time, to get a better look at the bull's eye and a whistling spews out of it, spirals down . . . a bottle, which lands smack on the side of your knee and then on the gunwale of the submerged barge, splintering into a million pieces, shattering your knee and severing an artery and for a moment arm and fish and knee are joined by a crimson thread, a narratorial fascination with the illogic of trauma stitching through your brain, numb-

ing you, the slow grammar of displacement, and you are sinking, you are sinking into reasoning what is cause and what
effect and none of it matched up with the way you were
taught to prepare for war . . . to expect the unexpected, which
always trailed events in its wake like a pink cloud, but you
didn't for one moment think how something could be so
neatly reversed as your knee, which compared with the shin
and foot faces backwards, reversed like the bomb before the
whistle, death before lightning-strike, mutilation before pain,
reversed so that everything flows backwards in the same haphazard way as most people breast-stroke into chance, mis-
chance, death and life, the whiting recovering now, flicking off
like sperm into the bloody amniotic sea to begin a new life,
and recovering back in Sydney white like a fish though you
were three months in the jungle, you decided to reverse your
life a little, re-determine it, remould it like they were doing
with your knee and you told them you had a degree in this
and that and they said they lacked philosophy instructors
'cause they went to the front first to prove God didn't exist,
and with a few forged papers it wasn't too hard nor too long
before you were publishing and lecturing on a new refutation
of time, and then you went down the alphabet to psychoanalysis, which was logical if you messed with time and there
you were finally, high and mighty, in black gown and slight
limp and chalk smudges, *arriving*, through sheer chance, feeling as legitimate as horse shit in a mews.

Munich/Odessa

My mother came to Munich. She told me Father was very ill. We went to see him at his sanatorium. He was lying in his bed with a porcelain pot beneath him filled with blood. None of the doctors could say definitely what was wrong with him. He looked very bad. I went out onto the terrace for some air. My father's sanatorium was perched on a hill overlooking the city. I smelled Thérèse on my fingers. When we left my father looked at me with fading eyes. Will you be back this afternoon? he asked. Yes, I said. We walked out the door. My mother was crying softly into her handkerchief. Out of the corner of my eye I could see that my father wanted to say something more. He was indicating something with his hand. I pretended I didn't see him. That afternoon, to cheer my mother up, I took her to the best restaurant in Munich. We wined and dined and forgot the time. Neither of us mentioned going back to the sanatorium. For the first time in many years I ate meat: minced liver, spleen wurst, calf's feet, pig's trotters, pork and liver cheese. Father died that afternoon at four. The doctors took me aside that evening and told me it could have been suicide. It looked as though he had been taking veronal for quite some time. They found the empty jars in his desk.

Family money. It was an expression I would never really get used to during those heady days in Munich. It came about in two ways. I was the official heir, but Mother had control over half the property. After the age of twenty-eight I would be free to do as I wished with all of it. About eight months after Father's death my uncle died. He was the hermit who lived, they said, with wolves. His name was Peter. He left me a third of a considerable fortune.

Thérèse wrote me a letter calling our affair off. She sent me a clipping of Uncle Peter's death, which was reported widely in German newspapers. *Wolf-Man Dies Leaving Vast Fortune*, was the headline in one of them. I could never understand the common people's obsession with money. Perhaps Thérèse thought I suspected her of being a gold-digger. My mother read the letter. This woman cannot be trusted, she said, and made arrangements for returning to Russia.

My mother and I returned to Odessa. I spent a few weeks on the estate and then took a baronial manor in the woods. I could stand it no more, living so closely with my mother, she who fed herself pills constantly. She wrung her hands, saying she had caused Father's death. I was no better off in the woods. I expected privacy, but was visited by a cousin of the Czarina's. I'm sure my mother arranged it. She must have been advised by the doctors not to leave me alone.

I could not refuse Anastasia when she sent word that she and her entourage were arriving for a holiday in the woods. That was a royal decree. I had the servants refurbish the place. We stocked the cellars with wine and caviar and pork. I expected a party of fifty or sixty. Instead she arrived alone, in a droshky. She brought with her a basket of preserved fruit and a box of aubergines. She cut each of the latter in half. 'These arabesques,' she said, pointing to the centre of the eggplant, 'tell me you are my destiny.' This simple act concealed multiple layers of madness. I should have suspected it at first, when she cavorted through the rooms wringing her hands and whispering. Stooped, thin, suspicious. She looked under the beds. She said she had visions: conspirators who would shoot them all, the whole royal family, while they stood in the snow. I had to support Rasputin, she said. I thought to myself he didn't need much support . . . rumours said his prick acted as a prop. She went down on her knees, implored me to eat the preserves. When I put one to my lips she snatched it out of my hand. No! she screamed. She said they were poisoned. She was testing me.

I didn't know what to do with her. I pretended to be preoccupied with my studies. I hunted. I slept in till very late in the day. There was no avoiding her at dinner though. She became very drunk. She said I looked ill. 'A little constipation,' I said. 'That's all.'

She invited me to her room. I refused. At first. It was lese-majestie to flirt with one's superiors. She provoked me. When I went to my room after my port she trapped me in the corridor. Danced around me in a flimsy gown. Put my hand to her breast. She was consumptive. I knew that from experience. Doctor Drones, my personal physician, had taught me in Munich how to press ribs. I was not attracted by wealth. I was not attracted by power. Still less by illness. She fainted in my arms. I carried her to her bed. Anastasia, I whispered in her ear, if only you would become my servant!

Hoooo! The night shifts uncomfortably from moment to moment. A wolf howls, sends the break in its voice across the empty spaces. Icicles drip steadily as the night warms, the pen nib spreads like fork tines. I who could never be alone, forbidden to be alone, listen to the locomotive straining on a distant hill, *hoooo!* spreading, no doubt, the conspirators over the icy wastes. Intrigue and counter-intrigue. And out here the almost-tundra squeaks beneath the immense night in continuous motion. As usual, I polish my father's revolver. As usual, I insert a cartridge. Things could end any time. Think of Dostoevski's Stavrogin. I do something in order to prove I can do it. I stand before the mirror. *Hoooo! Hoooo!* Anastasia! Swelling.

KATOOMBA

1978

Of course after the war you had more than glass in your knee; you had a chip on your shoulder. You came on too strong, made people suspicious, used your height to advantage. When you leant over someone you left a strong impression. One thing about being a fraud, you've got to believe in yourself. Real fakes never interrogate their fakery, never reveal the illusion behind the illusion, not like real psychopaths who know that lunacy is simulation and act accordingly. Laid back, that was the way to go, but you were nevertheless too ambitious for a conservative country. Indeed, in Sydney in the fifties, nothing happened.

You went to New York and enrolled in graduate school. You were a lot older than many of the other students, but you had this experience behind you, this experience of being both a sort of hero and a fake. So you made sure you didn't fail. No sir. You lived in a cold-water flat and howled at the moon. You wrote a book. You came to the attention of a well-known Freudian by the name of Ishmael Liebmann. He introduced you to others. You drove coast to coast in a convertible, making love in the Californian sunshine to two girls at once, in the back seat, in the water. You learned to be amphibious. But you never let it slip too far away, this idea that somewhere, inside, you were ready to become a hermit, to give it all up, to melt into someone else who inhabited the wilderness, distinguishable only by your handwriting, to be nothing more than an annotation, a note, a mark of such purity and yet of such insignificance that your life would be relished as a mere post-script, an afterword . . . this is the vanity of the repression of self . . . a social consequence . . . the pack gives birth to the outsider. But there is only the outside: you are a ghost-writer.

125

Berlin/Vienna
1909–1910

I took up the rest of my winter quarters in the sanatorium at Schlachtensee. This was after Thérèse had written an hysterical letter to me. Else, her daughter, was ill with tuberculosis. Then Thérèse wrote a strange thing. 'I am so concerned with my pores', she wrote. Once when we made love in Munich, I'm sure she had said to me: 'A woman's body is completely covered with vaginal pores.' Thérèse had trouble expressing herself. I thought she was joking at the time. I replied that I had psoriasis. We could maybe complement one another.

I am probably not sticking closely enough to the script. She was a notoriously poor speller. She may have written 'I am so concerned with my pore Else', which was surely closer to reality because Else died a few years later and when Thérèse came to the Wintergarten to see me she was sullen and jealous. I lost interest. As soon as a woman gets jealous I lose interest. Freud was right when he kept me from her for a year. During that time he revived my interest. He said things like: 'My dear Wespe, imagine your Thérèse humping your close friend Wilhelm Drones. There they are, the good Doctor and your lover, going *nnng, nnng*, in some seedy hotel in Munich, making fun of you. Hear their laughter. When she comes she screams 'Wilhelm . . . Wilhelm, Meister!' like a Gott-damned slavish bucherworm that she's trying to be. Ach, she will never be like your sister Anna. She's of a different class. So be a man, Wespe. Manliness is conviction. Testimony. Feel the jealousies of a man. Don't you want to strangle her? Mmm? Maybe just halfway, to give her a scare?'

Drones had of course accompanied me to Vienna. With his brilliantined hair and waxed moustache he had become my *maître de plaisir*. In between whoring, duelling and gambling,

126

he introduced me to Freud at 19 Berggasse. At the time Freud was well-known, but you wouldn't say famous. He had very bright eyes. A very big Alsatian dog came to the door with him. It began to nuzzle my genitals. 'Wolf!' Freud ordered. 'This is no time for that! Heh, heh,' Freud went, 'that dog knows more psychoanalysis than me.'

It was one helluva welcome. I didn't trust this Freud, whose name, Drones was telling me in the car, meant *joy*, or *jouissance*. He didn't look joyful to me. How was he going to cure my depressions? He was civilised, but discontented. Oh yes.

Vienna

1910

Freud's consulting rooms are on the upper ground floor at Berggasse 19. One goes up three stairs, then six more. On the landing there's a filigreed iron railing with an old gas lamp. One could impale oneself on the curlicues of iron. I test it out on my palm. A dog barks.

As I am about to knock a woman comes out and stares at me in quite an agitated manner. She clumps down the steps into a waiting carriage. I feel hostility around me. A little maid comes to the door. 'Mr Wespe,' she says sweetly, 'come in.' I follow her. I like uniforms. She's in a black dress with a white apron. At the entrance hall engraved glass doors open out onto a courtyard. I imagine the maid's dress made of engraved glass. Freud is standing at the door of his room with a cigar in his mouth, watching me watching the back of the maid.

'Good morning, Wespe,' he says heartily, taking my hand and thumping me on the back with his other hand. 'Let's see if we can't get you out of this bloody mess. When did you last move your bowels?'

This is where it all begins.

KATOOMBA
1978

You thought that perhaps you'd lost your trail, scooting down the street here in Katoomba, snowdrifts piling up now and you can smell hot chocolate from the milkbars and perfume and expensive leather when they open car doors to marvel at the weather . . . you could have had all that if you hadn't taken the path of regret, lost fortunes, failed ambitions and masturbation. Aye, the last was first, though the memories are dim. Blindness and insight. You went for the insight and became blind to esteem, success, confidence, respect. Now you wish you had them. Well, now and again. Would have produced a good whisky, maybe even a cigar or two. You were unable to get out of bed . . . did your best work between the first sip and the cool watershed, the deep, the motionless, wherein you heard the birdcalls of an inner life, the pulsing, tender sanctity of that human leap of idea become the dying plunge of the word. Ah! Honeyed words! There could have been a national career. Received as a favourite son, a living treasure. But instead: scission. Into your heart, alcohol, false ideals, stubborness, perverse humility. Salve the wound. The aftertaste of a former life, a life delayed, resurfacing, hoping to be reborn, was useless for you. You had lost all memory of it, until the Wolf-Man, who had reminded you of extinction.

Wolves are almost extinct. The neurotic is extinct. The end of the wilderness is the end also of the aristocracy of suffering for perfection. Nietzsche knew it. Philoctetes knew it . . . ten years as madman was nothing compared with one year as conformist. The death of the nobility of the self. When the pressure of time was brought to bear on the imagination, the disease of rationality ensued. It was the great common denominator. Freud knew it. But he went along with it nevertheless. After all, the Wolf-Man was trying to be more than himself. Freud said:

> *I resorted to the heroic measure of fixing a time-limit for the analysis . . . once he was convinced that I was in deadly earnest, the desired change set in.* ('Analysis Terminable and Interminable', standard edition vol. 23).

The lion springs only once. Freud as hero. Freud as writer. You turn the pages and things change. You turn the pages and things dissolve, re-appear, return, depart. When there are fewer pages to turn things get anxious. It is the duration that brings about the metamorphosis. But everybody's wish is to be overtaken by events: *to reach the end.* The Wolf-Man's sessions with Freud lasted exactly an hour. (Indeed, he took over somebody else's hour, a woman's.) In the space of an hour dozens of events took place. In the space of that hour numerous pages were turned. Such perfection always came to an end. Freud effectively sealed off the magic and the secret to effect a different kind of change . . . the veering towards death.

The hero, though, is always tragic. In 1925, informed of the hopelessness of his cancer, Freud wrote: *in those days I had unlimited time before me, 'oceans of time' . . . now everything has changed. The time before me is limited.*

In the late sixties you were on top of your game. A tenured post at Harvard, a visiting lectureship in Europe for six months of the year. You wrote a book— *Fellow Traveller: In Praise of Freud.** Oh, yes. Liebmann was so pleased with you he offered you a post as curator of the Sigmund Freud Memorial Library in upstate New York. You would receive $60,000 a year for doing practically nothing . . . a few conferences here and there, a successful 'cure' now and again, an outstanding research paper written by a graduate student undergoing analysis. You took it. Bought a Mercedes. You were in control of your destiny and had all the time in the world to think about managing it.

Now though, there is no time.

---

* Catacomb, Arthur S. *Fellow-Traveller: In Praise of Freud* New York International Universities Press, 1970

Once on the banks of the Garonne—can't remember why, perhaps a literary-psychoanalytic conference at the University of Toulouse—the Garonne not in flood yet, the banks fortified with huge concrete dikes peppered with storm drains, a maze of tunnels in which whole familes lived—gypsies, drunks, the old and mentally inflamed still festering against the Vichy collaboration—you saw something, while walking there one night, looking into the fires in the caves, so near the Pont Neuf and the rushing river and you heard a wild cry and then a kind of speech and the sound of the gnashing of teeth and inside a drain, gesticulating, beckoning, the bearded visage of a stinking clochard, his face red with fire and alcohol, his eyes shot in both directions like yours, the result of forking paths taken, wrong directions, you don't know, and he offered wine in supermarket bags and knocked the top off a bottle, the way aristocrats opened champagne, and you drank watching the river which was swollen with rain while he told you this story:

'I once had a friend who thought he was a clock,' he said. 'All day long he went: tick tock, tick tock. When you met him in the street that's all he said, rocking from one foot to another: tick tock, tick tock. I recommended a psychoanalyst. His name was Gérard Périgeaux, a good Swiss analyst. He fiddled around, massaging my friend's chest. Périgeaux had also trained as a magician. Suddenly, he pulled out a small clock. It was one of those miniature grandfather clocks. "You see," Périgeaux says to my friend, "you had a clock in there. I have cured you now."

'My friend *was* cured.

'Two years later we were all at a dinner party given by Princess Marie Bonaparte when suddenly who should be announced but Gérard Périgeaux. The famous analyst had almost forgotten my friend—he had so many patients—but it was I who came up to him and re-introduced my friend to him. Périgeaux made a big deal about the cure. He announced to everyone present the importance of sleight-of-hand in psychoanalysis. "Sometimes reason takes on the guise of magic," he said. "But it is reason that always prevails . . . this is the essence of the new science and the victory of reason over time."

131

'I cannot begin to describe the look on my friend's face when Périgeaux said that. My friend muttered some apologies to the hostess and excused himself. He went home, and according to the account of his housekeeper, he sat in front of his mirror and began to start all over again: tick tock, tick tock.

'This was the victory of time over reason.'

'What was your friend's name?'

'His name was Sergei.'

You pursued that drunken thought to its end. There is a new species of wolf out there. It is called man. It will never become extinct. You can say this because if it happened there would be no record of it. Freud discovered this species, which obeyed neither the laws of nature nor the laws of reason. *Homo astutus*. The artful man, who has it over time and reason, but is totally confused by the body.

In the Basilique in Toulouse they were restoring the foundations. You had a rendezvous with Gudrun there, tailed her as she listened rapturously to the guide in the semi-darkness while the rain cascaded down the walls and puddles formed in the excavations. Behind the altar, as you listened to the guide's sonorous voice you made love, Gudrun turning warm and moist and soft through her thin skirt with her back to the damp wall, and you on your knees pleading with her, mouthing absurdities, yes, illogicalities, as she tried to keep her attention on the guided lecture, and she, lighting Gauloises with unsustainable matches, was transfixed like a Visigoth entranced with terror. She was always more eager for direct action. It was the bone of contention between you.

In Rouen, temporary home of both the National Front and *Action Directe*, the two of you met again, and again it was raining and she was looking lovely in her fur coat, her conventional disguise, and there was only a short glimpse of her, lithe and willowy with a parcel under her arm while you stood in the dark afternoon, at the site of Joan of Arc's burning, the air choking with rain and the chrysanthemums bursting into colour and the medieval firewall shining black while the flags whipped and smacked against the poles outside your hotel room . . . tick tock, tick tock . . . and later, precisely when you climaxed, Gudrun heaving and murmuring under you, (*ja, oui!*), the bomb exploded . . .

Kherson

'Dear Freud, is it 1891 or 1910?'
   'Does it matter?'
   'You're damned right it matters.'
   'Why?'
   'You want the facts, don't you?'
   'Coming from you, it doesn't matter.'
   All right. I am climbing up a very tall tree. I am a good climber, even though I am very little. No tree was too difficult, that is, no fir tree. I am reaching through the branches, parting them to see the ground below. Two dogs across the field are sniffing and howling. One dog gets onto the back of the other, pumping his hindquarters. They are stuck. They spin round and round like the horses in a merry-go-round. I've seen goats do this. Uncle Nicholas said you had to separate them with an axe. I hack at a branch up in the tree. The axe-head slips and I hit my finger instead. After a while the blood comes. If I hold my breath God will save me.

I asked Grandad: 'What about the goat in the grandfather clock?'
   'Can't you hear him?' Grandad said. 'He's going tick tock, tick tock, in there.'
   'Is the wolf outside?'
   'Yes.'
   'Then who wins?'
   'The goat. Because he has control of time. See his beard?'

Grandad, who is my mother's father, not grandfather, who is my father's father, used to slap my Uncle Nicholas around. Uncle Nicholas went deaf. Grandad and Uncle Nicholas were

134

cutting trees that day on the outlying estates. It was cold and it was just starting to snow. If you found time to sit around you froze. Grandad was running to and fro in the stand of trees, marking out the right ones for firewood, going 'thunk' into a tree with his axe and then half running to the next one. The story was that while Uncle Nicholas was chopping at a trunk the axe-head flew from its shaft and implanted itself in Grandad's forehead.

It is extremely cold now and my hand is covered in blood. My heart is beating like a clock and I can feel it in my throat, then in my head. Both a wolf and a goat, I reason that if I dropped the axe I will be able to climb higher. Uncle Nicholas is chopping wood. Grandad is shouting. In the next stand Father is laughing. All the peasants are standing up from behind their bundles of faggots and are talking to themselves. Far away I hear the sound of my first locomotive. Riders are thundering across the plain. Wolves are howling. Gypsies are lighting fires. And above all this my sister Anna moans from her window and all the women in the world who are clever and rich are stroking me, saying: 'What lovely hair the child has!' My whole body is vibrating to these sounds, to these touches. An axe-head flies past beneath me. Grandad urinates against the tree and hearing it fizzing past, looks up at the sky. 'It's time . . . ' he mutters, and I let the axe drop, cutting him off in mid-sentence . . .

Vienna

1914

The summer of 1914 turned out to be hot at first. Then it
turned out to be the balmiest on record. Wespe hated the heat.
In Odessa he had to powder his neck, had to run his hand
over the prickly-heat, the powder tickling and scalding. Above
twenty-six degrees and he breaks out into sweat and all inspiration is gone. Endurance was all he thought about. What
could he accomplish in sweat? Nothing. Perspiration solved
nothing. There was only one thing sweat was good for: it
made some women horny.

They are calling it 'Venice in Vienna'. In the Prater the
restaurants and cafés are doing a roaring trade. Three theatres
have sprung up since the start of the summer. The parklands
are filled with flâneurs, lovers, exhibitionists. Every day is a
carnival. The murder rate has gone up, chiefly crimes of
passion, for the summer brings out breasts, jealousies, hatred
among the righteous. Uniforms are everywhere. The gold
braid, the swords, the buttons are all blinding.

I walk in the park looking for washerwomen. None can be
found. People are starting to call this the 'Vienna Summer', as
though there was something special in the air. Cholera perhaps. I argued with Drones. I said that 'Vienna Summer'
didn't sound right. It didn't sound as resonant as 'Autumn in
Budapest' or 'Paris Spring'. I was feeling particularly
depressed amongst all this excitement. It was the dance of
death as far as I was concerned. On top of it all I had begun to
read stories by a chap called Kafka. He's got it down pat.
Families are the source of all evil.

I attend balls, go on hunts, get drunk on fabulous country
estates, frequent the brothels and the smart set of highbrow
prostitutes negotiable only through special procuresses. You

136

find the latter gliding up and down the paths in the Prater with syphilitic faces. I also pay Freud handsomely. He encouraged me to forget Thérèse, but this I could not do since I had just given her a thousand crowns for a pension in Munich that she wanted to buy. Poor Thérèse looks thin and run-down. Her indebtedness to me is like a ball and chain around my leg. I cannot breathe without sighing. She writes me letters every week. She is so jealous she says she is coming to Vienna.

On the 28th there was some commotion. Fans fluttered nervously in the Prater. In the botanical section of the park I saw a wasp fly into an orchid and disappear. Out of another emerged a butterfly. I remember that two years ago Freud had focussed on my obsession with butterflies. Yellow, striped butterflies. I loathed them. In Odessa, every summer, they swarmed out of the forests, powdery, sticky, clumsy in flight, never quite getting out of the way. I used to choke on butterflies, dying in their powder, squashing them beneath my feet. Dead wings. Veined wings, batting in the wind. No more movement now. No body. In my trances I floated with them, took on their colours, began to transform myself. Grusha. Poor dead Grusha. Butterfly wings. I was light. I floated upon her.

'What,' Freud asked me, 'do you understand by *morphology*?'

'It's the science of form, of course,' I replied.

'Of course,' Freud said behind me. 'Now, smartypants, what's the root?' he chuckled, maliciously, I thought.

'*Morphe*,' I stammered, unsure.

'Correct. *Morpheus*. The god of dreams,' Freud said.

In the twenties I would become dependent on him, pressing him into my veins. Pity they missed out on morphine in the Great War, so much pain for nothing.

'You want to float away from consequences?' Freud inquired, 'make light . . . of the heavy moment . . . that maybe is erotic for you?'

I didn't know what he meant . . . making light of the heavy moment indeed. Sometimes Freud got on my nerves.

The cavalry had been mobilised. In our room over the Danube Thérèse and I made love unsatisfactorily to hoofbeats and a

137

dull booming in the mountains . . . summer thunder unrequited by rain. Love had won out over passion. Thérèse had softened, grown quiet and fretful. What was the difference between lust and love? I asked myself. The answer, riding upon the sudden gusts of wind, said that love makes lust impossible. And vice versa. Something was ( )ed out. The ill wind decapitated the orchids. Did more than a blow-job on them. That was lust: beauty allowing itself to be brutalised; sensibility allowing itself to be possessed by the lower orders. Russia was rumbling with thoughts like these. Anna had said as much. Anna's great ambition was to be a servant. I told Freud that. He liked Thérèse when he met her. 'She's not . . . ' he said to me, 'how would you put it delicately . . .' he laughed, 'so *common*. In fact, she looks like the Czarina and not a servant.'

He must have had a reason for saying that. He could have fooled me. I didn't think he had noble Russian sentiments.

I fell in love. Thérèse became more and more passive, and more tubercular. When we made love she put on flannel night-gowns and coughed repeatedly.

A good family man was Freud. But I saw the glimmer in his eye. I saw the lust he tried to kill in me. The pleasure he took in advising me. By the way, he said, tapping me on the arm with a rolled newspaper, the Austrian Crown Prince has been assassinated. That makes you, as a Russian, a sort of *persona non grata*.

Make light of the heavy moment. I was sick of the room, sick of the bronze pots and Empire furniture and the brass Gypsy ashtrays Thérèse filled with red-ringed butts from her Camels, sick of the icons my mother brought from Odessa, sick of all the books and the aridity of a semi-intellect, sick of the smell of romanticism without romance on humid afternoons. Outside, the cavalry, the procuresses, the accoutrements of war.

So. 'So,' Thérèse said to me, 'if he's so much in love with her, why doesn't he marry her and redeem her life?'

She meant me. She spoke in the third person quite a lot of the time. Said she might be a writer one day. That was the way she practised, getting the distance right, making soap-opera out of daily events. I refused to let her smoke at the Imperial Opera. She said that a revolution was on its way. I said that was a hell of a way to make a revolution. She could have set fire to the box. So? she said. So what? I have to go back to Russia, I said. She lit a cigarette in the middle of the 'Tosca' aria. There was some whispering in the audience.

Two nights later and she was gone and I missed her terribly. I lit a Camel and walked a block or so to the Mariahilfer-strasse. It was drizzling and the buildings were black and slimy and I walked slowly, believing I would see Thérèse in her fur coat on the corners, waiting for my apologies, pleading with her to return, along the Mariahilferstrasse chrysanthe-mums with a strange perfume like those I saw in the crypt in the Panthéon where they keep the tombs of the famous . . . Zola's for instance, behind barred doors where it was always cold, at least ten degrees cooler, and the smells of chrysanthe-mum, a flower with a mild scent so as not to be too over-powering in these depths of death, enveloping within its myriad petals the secrets of that awful silence, when I discov-ered the flowers were dried, and the metaphor disappeared, and I realised immediately that these bodies and the bodies of work, the corpus and the text were one and the same, dry ashes, neither fact nor fiction, neither of any consequence in that great arena of death, *death*, the password for posterity, death, the unspoken key that had worked its way into their writing long before the real event, the end of their intention a kind of dying, an addiction of no great pleasure, a numbing deferral of tedium, dry ashes without continuity . . . what good our admiration now? When all of a sudden . . . when turning a corner, I saw the eruption of torches, naked flames in sombre battle with the rain and someone whispered that the remains of the Archduke and his wife were passing through on the way to the crypt in the Artstetten Schloss and it wasn't long before a carriage came clattering out of the mist, the horses' hooves striking sparks on the cobbles and the iron wheels of the gun-carriage making a low rumble, soldiers sitting fore and aft, protecting the dead, protecting the corpse from people as well as from death, all our forgetting and all our memory encoded and entombed within this instant within the night, within the rain, within the flickering torches, a symbolic procession of rotting flesh . . . lest we forget, our memories are placed into sepulchres, to preserve the gap between us and nature, from which we had come . . . it was highly unnatural, this forward movement into stasis, preventing nature, the body, from its due processes . . . that is, to be devoured, decoded back into wilderness . . . then at a distance the second carriage carrying the body of his wife, since they were of unequal birth . . . stranger still this double-murder of unequal gravity . . . no gun-carriage this, but a common hearse . . . the deadly pleasure of the assassin's shout 'I am History', when he fired off his salvo as a monument to catastrophe, drunk on the History Train, which was fucking *terminal* . . . but wait . . . wait.

I found myself on the road, in the path of the oncoming carriage and the soldiers were shouting at me, waving me aside . . . one actually threw his torch and the oily flames licked at my heels . . . this was what it must have been like, stepping over that threshold between my life and my times, for nothing could affect me . . . I merely passed beyond it and was privately coursing alongside it now, several horsemen urging their mounts in a spray of rain and mud cursing, all helmet and cape in this austere procession of an accomplished fate.

I was splashed. I stood aside breathing hard, some unaccountable sadness creeping upon me, though not for the Archduke and his wife. Some strong desire had been aroused, must have connected with disappointment that my father and sister were both suicides. I could have fired, killed them both with my Monte Christo rifle while hunting woodcock, it would have been more natural, Freud said to me—he couldn't abide suicides—Anna saying to me 'You have to put it into me like Father does', straddling, grunting, moving backwards and forwards like her name, falling, falling into a palindrome of death read backwards as life.

KATOOMBA
1978

Photo: Freud

Here is the man thought by many to have opened the doors to
sexuality. You read Freud now with rubber gloves. Sanitised
distance . . . also in case you infect the sacred text with hyper-
bole, which you can't help — it's a disease of emulation.
Ernest Jones was another slaverer . . . you understand perfectly
such mendicant devotion. You wear a gauze mask when you
discuss the Wolf-Man and the way he wanted to open himself
to Freud . . . which of course preserved the sepulchre of his
secret within him, the pleasurable anality of collecting all the
desirable deaths coded within dirty postcards, photos, writings
about his uncle, grandfather, father, sister, wife . . . family . . .
the stillborn turds for which he needed no enema. So close. So
close to Freud's own life. Freud wisely sat at the head of the
couch. Once a woman tried to seduce him, pulling up her skirt
and opening her legs to him, flapped them at his beard, her
thighs an expanding V opening and closing like butterfly
wings, wasp wings, orchid petals. It made Freud dizzy. He
tried to fight it, keeping the distance between theory and
arousal. Float like a butterfly, sting like a bee, he may have
been thinking. The entrance of a servant saved him from
embarrassment. (This was routine staging. Enter left, a servant. A good prop for the career-conscious.) They were
Freudian women before Freud even met them. *Carpe Diem*. He
was going to be the heavyweight champion analyst of the
world. As he said himself: It is either 'all a piece of nonsense
or *reality*'. He kept his mind on the job. Lightness and weight.
Move and jab.

Take a look at this photo of Freud. The eyes, the eyes. They

141

always say look at his eyes. They shine with percipience and kindly rebuke. What manner of photographer are you? he is asking. Why don't you come out from under that hood and get some of that blinding flash-powder in your own eyes? Voyeurism, he's muttering to himself. Has me upside-down on his plate.

But it isn't the eyes that have it. If you look at all the published photographs of Freud you will see that most of them show something between the fingers of his left hand. A half-Corona. It never appears to be alight. A cigar, as they say, is a woman. There is no lingering ash, no untidy, obvious symbol. Its presence between those fingers reinterprets the locus of pleasure. He was not an ascetic. There was work and there was more work. Work and desire were the same. In the last photos of him, outside his house in Hampstead, there is no more cigar. Looking irritable and suffering terrible pain, Freud does not know what to do with his hands. He puts them behind his back. He clasps them together. He is missing his prosthesis.

If you draw a vertical line from the top of his hat through to the space between his feet, you can see how his clothes are decentred. The waistcoat is skewed over to his right side. The fly of his trousers is against his left thigh. The knot of his tie is in line with his right leg. If you draw several horizontal lines across Freud's overcoat you can see that the buttons do not line up with the buttonholes. His long overcoat is wrenched to the left as if an errant hand, tugging at symmetry, has failed to adjust for the loss of balance, failed to command the old skill of making things fit. Freud has been extremely adept at hiding from his right hand what his left hand is doing. He waits impatiently at the point before which everything fails . . . the closure of the lens . . . the revelation perhaps, of a sleight of hand. The camera's shutter reminds him of it.

He waits, and nothing happens. Does he exist still? At this point near the end of his life, hardly speaking, Freud knows more than anyone else that the body does not lie. He is abstracted into the photograph, but he is already the body of his work.

Odessa

1914

Here I am again, this place which is no place for me. Freud proclaimed that I was cured. Cured? Of what? I simply went to him depressed and wanted some advice on whether I should marry Thérèse, and now I'm some sort of psychological curiosity. The moral is: don't seek and ye shall find. Writing in *The Torch*, the famous aphorist Karl Kraus defined psychoanalysis thus: *Psychoanalysis: a rabbit that was swallowed by a boa constrictor just wanted to see what it was like in there.*

Kraus was a one-man show with a pocketful of one-liners. When he wasn't pulling out rabbits he was pulling out snakes.

He also knew he couldn't count on anyone but himself:

I and my public understand each other very well: it does not hear what I say, and I don't say what it wants to hear.

A wise man, Charlie Kraus. Freud read him too.

Back at the ranch. (That appeared in an American movie, in filigreed letters, between scenes. Some of the longer lines you can't read at all.) Mother's going a bit hysterical, trying to read the letters that arrive every day from Thérèse. She tried boiling them open, but all the ink ran. Then she tried reading them though the envelope, backwards, staring up at the sun. But it is autumn and the sun is weak in the sky and Mother's eyes are not what they used to be. I line the letters up in my room, unread. My cousin Sascha came to stay. He's in the army, and has just been promoted. As an only son, I am exempt from the army. Thank goodness. I think I would have passed the physical. Sascha wants to marry Lola, his ash-blonde girlfriend. We have a very large country house here in Odessa. There is a huge park. Every day Sascha rides his horse in the park, which borders on a lake. Lola traps me in one of the dark

143

rooms in the east wing. She plants a kiss on my lips, forces my mouth open with her tongue. A sort of tickle goes up and down my spine, as this organ explores my oral cavity. When I touch her breasts she screams as though in pain. Leaves gust past the window. Autumn has its share of anxieties. Mother yells from an upstairs room: 'Lola? Is everything all right?' A few years later, Lola would divorce Sascha and die of breast cancer. When I touched her, the cells had already begun their revolt. In 1917 everything came to a crisis.

Thérèse came to Odessa. It was inevitable that we would get married. It was also inevitable that Thérèse and Lola would quarrel. 'I didn't come all the way here to take shit from a fake-blonde slut,' she said. Her voice had lost none of its volume. Even Mother, who pretended to be deaf most of the time, was shocked. Mother must have been a little scared of Thérèse after that. Now and again Mother came out with her jewellery box and gave Thérèse some bits and pieces. Now and again she said things about Thérèse to Lola in a voice like Thérèse's. When you're as deaf as I am, Mother said, honesty is the best policy. Oh yeah? Thérèse challenged, overhearing. How do you *know* when you're being honest?

We got hitched in a civic ceremony and spent our honeymoon in Moscow. In the snow and ice, Thérèse's bronchitis got better. Funny that. Maybe because she became quiet for a while. Kept her face to the pillow. I got on with my law exams. Torts. I thought of cakes.

When we got back to Odessa in 1917, fighting had already broken out. It was unsafe for Thérèse, being a foreign national. It was unsafe for me, being an aristocrat. They summoned me to the Town Hall. They told me they wanted to collectivise the estate, but I said to them: wait a minute. My father was a liberal. He put out pamphlets. Lucky for us the Revolution respected intellectuals . . . for the moment. They conceded that Father was indeed okay. I said to them: any time you want to make use of the printing press at the estate you're welcome. They thought about that and decided it was too complicated to print anything at the moment. The French and Austrians were at the border. And, they warned, don't be too much of a smartarse.

I walked back to the estate. It was a fine afternoon, and the almond trees gave off a wonderful odour. Birds were dipping along the avenues and in the distance someone was letting off fireworks. I imagined I could have been in China. Just little ol' me, a modest Mandarin making for home while the peasants were at play . . . a bird dipped past my ear . . . maybe it was a wasp. Voices. People were noisy this afternoon. A car. An explosion. Backfiring. A horse at full gallop. Now, that was the way to go. Progress is a fake, you know, especially when there's a war on. Shit, the bastard's coming at me with his sabre. Fuck, duck. Whew. He sliced the air just above my head. What's going on here? Squeeze into a shopfront. Here they come. A whole platoon. A swarm of something. Bullets are flying. The wall is chipped to my left. I'm running, dropping, weaving. Haven't been so athletic since the Czarina's cousin and I did the Mazurka. I make it to a café. Could do with a cognac, but they've boarded up the door. I can smell tobacco. I look down. There's a chap there making gurgling sounds with his throat. He offers me a cigarette. Thanks pal. What's the fighting about? Landlords and tenants? The same old thing? The guy looks glassy. Slumps forward. There's blood coming out of his back. I get the hell out of there. I run to the next street. A machine-gun opens up. You wouldn't believe it, but the afternoon has clouded over. Bullets are splitting the roof tiles. A branch falls from an almond tree. Lead's flying around like a whole lot of angry gnats. Bullets smack into the walls and then you hear the shot, everything out of sync. A carriage rolls slowly down the street, horseless, wheels spinning slowly. The whole back of it is splintered off. If you ever get caught in a firefight remember this: they can't hit a neurotic. Nerves keep you alive, unpredictably energetic. No time for depressions here. I'm running as though I'm a psychotic though, I can tell you . . . zigzagging, spinning, screaming like a crazy man. It's a wonderful feeling to be in control of your destiny. I edge along a wall, find a door but suddenly a great big hairy priest pushes it against me. It's not time, he pants. I push back. You mean God has visiting hours? I shout at him. He pushes again. He's stronger, more inspired. The door slams in my face. I see the priest's cassock caught in the crack. He's pulling it

145

back. Little by little it disappears. A bullet kicks near my feet. I turn, run along the other side of the street. The church bells have suddenly started ringing. Why the hell would they want to add to the commotion? Priests are like that . . . celebrate everything. There's a tremendous explosion. What I'm smelling ain't incense. Intestines spilling out of a fallen horse. I run backwards. I figure this posture would make them think twice before shooting. I get a split second of indecision on the shooter's part. Freud put me up to this. Don't reflect, he said. Let me do all the reflection. Doubt is what kills you. Give the man a cigar, I say. Shit, I would have made a good soldier. I'm at the end of the wall, or the wall has run out on me. There's a door, a sort of garden gate. It's open. I step inside, make my way among the flowerbeds, then into a greenhouse sweating with tropical perfume, out again, find a path among some trees and discover that I'm in my own estate. I'll have to give the gardener a raise. Pure genius, this labyrinth of orchids and chrysanthemums, these English gardens melting into ponds and lakes. You could have been anywhere.

Thérèse was fuming when I got back. I thought you were dead, she shouted. She informed me she was going to Freiburg. I've had enough of the Russian temperament, she exclaimed. First your mother, now you. I want peace. *You* want peace? I asked. There's a world war going on and you want peace? Thérèse grew depressed and used the silent treatment for a week. Now, *that* was really something.

The Catacomb Diaries[*] I

Where id was, there ego shall be. It is the work of culture—not unlike draining the Zuider Zee.

Where id was, there ego shall be. It is the work of culture—not unlike draining the Zuider Zee.

Freud wrote that in his *New Introductory Lectures* in 1933. He saw his work as that of building dykes to hold back the sea of chaos.

He saw the id as wolf, pleasure principle, sex, devourment, desire. It tried to debouch out of the world of culture while the ego, the hunter, the voice of reason, held its finger in the dyke.

Sergei Wespe said to me the other day: *writing is being animal*.

Like Plato, the ego hates writing that is without reason. In fairy tales the hunter appears out of nowhere, has no social continuity and beheads the wolf or disembowels it while it is asleep . . . in order to restore the status quo. Self-justifying meaning. That bit about the work of culture, which is little quoted, harbours the open secret at work in culture . . . not the repression of desire, but the ruthless restoration of the status quo. The accommodation to tradition. Oh Plato! Oh Freud! Oh irrational reason! You weren't the first to howl at the moon.

So here I am.

The ego has landed.

I'm no longer in the margins.

Let me explain myself.

I studied for five years in order to become an analyst. My colleagues said: Catacomb, you're a fool to embark on a pseudo-science. My lover, the beautiful logical-positivist

* Wittgenstein, Ludmilla. (ed.) *The Catacomb Diaries* University of Minnesota Press, Minneapolis, revised edition, 1978

Ludmilla Wittgenstein (yes, the grand-daughter of one of the famous clan) left me and went mad. I felt bad about that, but New York was New York and when lovers parted madness was mandatory. She would return. And return. Psychoanalysis was like an itch. (I could have said I started from scratch.) Making bad puns, I read Freud in the original German and got myself analysed. Okay, I treated it as a joke at first, but things soon got serious. I took that bit about analysts being like a secret society very seriously indeed. A few threats were made over the phone, late at night, a gravelly voice crackling from the ear piece: look, Catacomb, we can really mess up your mind.

I was in awe of the great names: Papa Freud of course, Klein, Eissler, Abraham, et cetera. I tried to meet the living, worship the dead. After that ... after that it was as if I was seeing all my past life through the bottom of a glass. At the end of five years I was invited into the select Society of Psychoanalysts. Liebmann, my supervisor, treated me like a rediscovered son. At my début conference, he said to me: 'Artie, don't be afraid of them. They will ask difficult questions ... but take my advice: when under fire, any hole will do.' Liebmann was a schizoanalyst. He had just written a book on orifices.

I did as I was told and survived. Some of them even warmed to me. Liebmann's second piece of advice was to prove more difficult to follow.

About a year after I was made curator of the Sigmund Freud Memorial Library, Liebmann suggested I go to Paris. He said I would be 'closer to the action'. I couldn't find out why he wanted me shifted, but I did as I was told, probably because I made sure I was to keep the same salary. At the annual Paris conference he asked me to give out a pamphlet he had printed. He puffed into my hotel room on the rue du Bac with a cardboard carton full of pink paper. I looked at the sheets.

Freudianism In Dire Straits

What was written under this impressive title was psychoanalytic garble the kind of which I had never read before. It may have been a code for those in the inner sanctum of the Society. I mused over the connections. I could not quite see Liebmann in the role of a Messiah. He was more of a fossil. Playfulness eluded him. When I wrote my thesis, he originally wanted it in German. That, he said, was the pure language of psychoanalysis. He relented later when I said the others would never understand it. He said what others? But he relented. Anyway, from what I could deduce, this pamphlet had nothing to do with psychoanalysis. What was being conducted was a private war to win minds and money. It made the Mafia look like the Secret Seven. Liebmann, who was four feet ten inches in height, put the box on the floor and made me kneel to read the sheets. He liked this kind of thing. The humiliation of a man who stood at six four.

'I vant you to give these out at the conference.'

'Sure,' I said, eager to please.

'In the gentlemen's toilet.'

'Okay,' I said. 'Only in the men's?'

'Oh yes,' he stuck out a remarkably long index finger.

I supposed at the time that it was another form of initiation. Liebmann and his friends in the inner sanctum were testing me out again. It was one of the hazards of being at the top. But I knew it would be one of many trials to come.

I knew they knew about my women patients. Ludmilla Wittgenstein was one of them. When I first became curator she barged into my office without an appointment, wearing a sort of Muslim-type outfit, a black cloth shroud which revealed only her face and tightly-wound leggings. I thought she might have had a terrible disease. 'I know,' she panted, 'that all you want to do in the end is look at my body, not my mind.'

She was right. I immediately thought of her in a transparent raincoat and lacy underwear. But even behind the shroud Ludmilla had that kind of athlete's body that was difficult to forget. I used to watch her walking fast to her lectures. She did everything at speed, well-muscled, up on her toes. I was watching women's tennis on the TV before she threw open the door. Ludmilla had a tennis player's body, buttocks made for short skirts. Only that day she didn't have on a skirt. I needed no invitation. These bandages, I said, were constricting her

149

mind. We made love on my desk, the umpire calling the shots. Thirty love. Thirty all. Juice. Four games, five games. We made it past a set. Ludmilla whispered, 'not so fast, not so fast,' in her heavy Austrian-American accent. She offered propositions. I countered them. Hypothetical syllogisms. *Reductio ad absurdum*. She was a logical-positivist. In the end I opted for *Modus Ponens*, the simplest type of position, though she wasn't entirely pleased. In many ways, I'm a simple man.

She though, found complexity in the most basic statement. Her ears were specially tuned to grammar. She had perfect pitch, she told me, and could detect psychiatric illness from the smallest clause or phrase. She had dumb-bells in her bag. She asked me to get them out. She did exercises after sex. I scrabbled around under the bed. 'Got him,' I wheezed. I was already puffing when I got them onto her belly. I lit a cigarette and strained a back muscle. 'Some men,' she explained, 'use the pronoun "her" with inanimate objects. "Got her," they say, when extracting an awkward load. Other men naturally tend to say "him". Why? It's insecurity about gender,' she said. 'In uninflected languages the stress on objectivity leads to neurosis because language is naturally feminine.'

She was a philosophy professor, and quite twisted. When I took up the Library post she began publishing her life story . . . how she was the progeny of the famous Wittgenstein family . . . what psychoanalysis had done to her . . . how she was virtually raped by her analyst. I drove over to her place in New Jersey and we stood on the front porch yelling at each other. When I got extremely angry she dared me to hit her, bouncing on the balls of her feet, fingers tensed and coiled like fighting shrimp. I restrained myself.

Sometime in the mid-seventies she began to practise herself and became a disciple of Melanie Klein. The rumours were that she had gone somewhere far away, probably India. They really needed analysts in India, I thought, what with all that Hinduism and Buddhism. Give them a dose of Western neurosis. Screw up the calm and equanimity. But it could have been anywhere. Liebmann said she might have gone to Australia. 'Somewhere outback anyway,' he said.

GMT—gross moral turpitude was not in the clauses of

tenure for Archival analysts. Many filmed themselves in the course of therapy. I made a couple of videos of Ludmilla and me, both looking virtuous in tennis whites, though not for therapeutic reasons. I expected terrible repercussions. I was known in analytic circles as a classic heterosexual, which was not the best credential. I was too hung up. I repressed things. I wrote a paper on the end of Freudian psychoanalysis at the hands of Feminism, but neglected to publish it.

So standing in that ancient Sorbonne toilet deafened by cataracts as terrifying as the Niagara, I duly gave out Liebmann's sheets and prepared to counter propositions from distinguished, uninhibited professors who were not averse to standing Freud on his head. It was not Freud they came to screw.

I found out later that the conference was concerned with one of his patients. A certain Sergei Wespe who was going to tell all. A wolf in the fold. A beast in the crease. A favourite son who was making for the margins.

Back in my hotel room I had a call from Liebmann. His voice was excited. He was ringing from a phone box in St Germaine.

'Artie,' he snuffled. He had a habit of clearing his nasal passages when he got excited, making little snorting sounds like a model steam engine. 'I've done a bit of checking. On you. Of course there's no question of incompetence . . . just integrity. I mean, at any institution you would immediately be given an honorary, believe me . . . after that book of yours . . .'

I didn't answer. He must have heard me breathing and assumed I was still on the line.

'*Fellow Traveller* put an end to several cynics. Not that Sigmund needed defending. But it was a nice gesture. A solid book. Indeed, more solid than the background of the writer . . .'

I knew what he was getting at. I expected the worst and made calculations. At least I still had the Mercedes. I could start again as a junior lecturer at a cow college, maybe in the Midwest. I was already working out the topic: the relation between grammar and schizophrenia. A GMT clause in my contract. But Liebmann was more excited than malicious.

'I've got a little proposition for you,' he snorted. I thought of the indifferent stares I received in the Sorbonne toilet. The proposition was finally being made.

Liebmann suggested we meet for lunch in a restaurant off the Place St André des Arts.

I arrived a little late, for a while unable to find the restaurant, wandering through back lanes and ending three times at exactly the same spot, in front of a bookshop which sold the translation of Liebmann's latest book in stacks on tables near the door. He had taken a chapter, almost word for word, from the manuscript of *Fellow Traveller*, which he had suggested I delete on account of certain American libel laws. 'You want to know your litigation when you publish in New York,' he said.

Liebmann was expansive in the little restaurant, which seemed to have been built for him. He was seated at the smallest table near the kitchen. The restaurant was full. I squeezed past several women in order to get to him. They put their hands on my backside as I went by. I felt to see if my wallet was still there.

'Artie!' Liebmann almost screamed. He stood up. The table tilted. When I sat down he pushed the table into my stomach. I had to break off the branch of a palm which stood behind my head.

Liebmann waved to the waiters. They ignored him. He looked like a baby, opening and closing his fingers against the light. After about two minutes he became frustrated and putting a fifty-franc note into the woman's lap, reached over and took her bottle of Côte du Rhone.

'It's not worth that much,' I said.

'It's a special occasion,' Liebmann snorted, and poured the wine. It was dark in the restaurant and he had to hold up the menu, fixing his half-moon glasses. There was a skylight above us and it let in a patch of smoky, brooding, Parisian winter sky. Pigeons made repeated sorties over it. At first it was charming, the shadow of wings, like having the Holy Ghost to lunch. But then I saw it was their crapping place, and they alighted there only to leave great globs of greenish slime right over our table.

Liebmann refused to talk until he had summoned a waiter. He ordered for us both. Wild boar, it was supposed to be, from Normandy. I poked at the fatty substance.

He began with a flourish of his fork. Gravy sprayed onto his waistcoat. Liebmann liked to dress, I could tell. Beneath the satin waistcoat he had on a claret coloured knitted tie and a cream shirt. His diamond cufflinks clicked at the edge of his plate and his gold watch slid halfway down his forearm when he waved at several women he knew. They flocked to him, especially French women, who bent to kiss his forehead and cheeks, negotiating the widow's peak and greying curls. He never smiled. Perhaps he reminded them of Napoleon. Historical memory was particularly strong in France. He was to charm the best of them: Cixous, Irigaray, Kristeva, Wittig. They would come to hate him as well. He had a kind of straight-faced humour, but there may have been other things. Maybe he was asexual or supercharged. His machismo was supposed to be legendary. Perhaps his height was no threat. But then others thought the same of Napoleon.

'There's a guy in Vienna called Wespe,' he whispered over his boar.

'Yes,' I said, 'Freud's most famous patient.'

'Yeah. Well, he's becoming kinda *assertive* . . .'

Liebmann shot up his bushy eyebrows at me. They moved independently, like performing rodents. Instantly recognisable, he once made a bit of a mark on a Parisian quiz show. That was the beginning of a glittering career.

'Like what I say, they're all the same. Reformed neurotics are the worst,' he said.

Liebmann looked around the restaurant. He was afraid of being overheard, but in this restaurant you had to shout to be heard at all. He leaned over to my ear.

'He's beginning to meddle with the Eternal.'

This he whispered in German.

'The eternal?'

'For God's sake, stop repeating that word,' Liebmann

153

scolded. His face was darkening into the colour of his tie. 'The man is biting the hand that feeds him.'

This was news to me. I knew one or two things. I knew that this Wespe was publishing periodic papers on his analysis. Bits and pieces of memoirs of Freud. But Liebmann wasn't going to tell me more. I waited until my boar was cold and watched him mop his plate savagely with bread. It was almost appetising to see the way he ate, like a dog, making the same sounds, except that his sweat was dropping into his gravy. He smirked with satisfaction after this brutal *fin de repas*. Wiped his mouth with the serviette. Glanced casually at the dessert menu. Waved away the by now over-attentive waiter . . . a miracle in Paris. We settled for coffee and cheese, with Liebmann misquoting Brillat-Savarin: 'A dinner without cheese is like a beautiful woman with glaucoma.' He squinted. 'You see a lot of that in India.'

What was he doing in India?

Ludmilla.

We picked over the cheese.

'The difference between active memory (*Gedächtnis*) and recollection,' Liebmann said with his mouth full, 'is emotion. The patient does the recollecting and the analyst is forever waving goodbye to this kind of memory. An analyst never mourns. He's always on a ship, going to Tahiti. The discourse of the analyst is pure art. But when the patient starts playing the analyst . . . the patient . . . ahem . . . is sullying the past, and he has to be . . . figuratively . . . I've been visiting him for some time now.'

'Who?'

'Wespe.'

Liebmann adjusted his tie and pulled a face. He began to make circling motions with his head. Suddenly his neck cracked. I thought something had broken.

'Let me offer you some clock tales.'

'Cocktails? It's kind of late, Ishmael.' That was the only time I had used his first name. If he needed a turbocharge at this stage, then he was getting serious.

'Call me Dr Liebmann,' he said, looking annoyed, and then softened. 'Just for in here, you understand.'

A pigeon waddled above us and pecked at some crap.

'This Wespe character is fuckin' around with Eternity. What I mean is, the guy's trying to re-write Freud. Making what he calls *exposés*. Now, that in itself is no big deal if he's incompetent. But he's got a nomenclature. It is thanks to Freud. It was Sigmund who gave the guy some backbone. *Wolf-Man* . . . can you imagine that? Conjures up snow, survival, wilderness . . . and later, Nazis. Sigmund was the great mastermind of this . . . tagging a simpering snotty-nosed aristo with a symbol of our great biological exigency . . . think of the 'old' brain, by God, that fossilised medulla still sending out signals of the hunt . . . Sigmund uniting Nordic myth with neurosis . . . what diabolicalness involved in this cure! What genius! Legacies! We're all connected to each other. And people, Catacomb, the *Menschen* out there, have had the temerity to label *me* a Zionist!'

Liebmann wiped his forehead, tapped the back of his neck, trying to pick up static from the past. He looked at the skylight and made a face.

'No, Wespe's one of the Elect, by God, and he's trying to destroy his father. And what's more he's claiming he was a *writer*. And as far as I'm concerned, only *one* writer has ever fucked around with Freud successfully. I'm talking about Borges, the Argentine writer. You know Borges?'

'Not personally.'

'I do. Or did. He didn't recognise me the second time . . . which is interesting, you know, because Jorge was violently anti-Freudian. You can guess where they all went after the war. Anyway, Borges has this story, essay, whatever you like to call it, entitled "A New Refutation Of Time". It's a little elaborate, like the ironlace in Buenos Aires. Anyway, in this piece Borges tells how one evening after dinner he was walking in a place where he's never been before. It's a place called Barracas, and he has this strange feeling that *he's been there before*, in his childhood, in the 1890s.'

Liebmann drew a deep breath through his nose, curled his lips and exposed long yellow canines.

'Borges says that he had "an indefinite fear imbued with science" at that very moment.'

155

Liebmann was in a trance.

'Borges was experiencing the Uncanny, but he was being over-philosophical.'

He grabbed my arm.

'Look at what Freud says in *The Uncanny*, standard edition, volume 17, page 245, to quote from memory:

> *It often happens that neurotic men declare that they feel there is something uncanny about the female genital organs. This* unheimlich *place, however, is the entrance to the former* Heim *[home] of all human beings, to the place where each one of us lived once upon a time and in the beginning. There is a joking saying that 'Love is home-sickness'; and whenever a man dreams of a place or a country and says to himself, while he is still dreaming: 'this place is familiar to me, I've been there before', we may interpret the place as being his mother's genitals or her body.*

'Borges,' Liebmann suddenly shouts, 'is coming up against his mother's genitals. Look, Borges also said: "I suspected that I was the possessor of a reticent or *absent* (Liebmann stressed this word) sense of the inconceivable word *eternity*." In other words . . . '

Liebmann is now standing up.

'ETERNITY IS A CUNT,' he roars.

People are staring. Liebmann sits down again. Scribbles something on his napkin.

'Destiny,' Liebmann sighs, 'is all we have, we think. But we've been there before, like Huckleberry Finn. We go there again and again. We can't let the irrational notion of some future time erode biological reason. Interpretation or sterility. That's the choice.'

He looked at me enigmatically.

'We've got to get this goat out of the clock, Arthur. Bring back the notion of the same. *Restore the status quo*. I mean, Freud is Freud . . . forever. He never abandoned interpretation, and his impact is eternal. Wespe's in the wrong time, the wrong tunnel, up himself, trying to make mileage out of the so-called "malaise" of Freud, my dear Catacomb, implying

156

that Sigmund went off into hocus-pocus, literary theory or some such thing because he thought he had been duped.'

'What do you want me to do?'

'Act as his double. Get all the copies and originals of his writing. Befriend him. Act as his ghost-writer. You know, the irrefutable psychological principle of the ego is that when self-love is overcome, the idea of the double becomes the signifier of death.'

'You want me to kill him?'

'Oy,' Liebmann said, shrugging, holding up his hands, smiling for the first time.

Vienna
1972

The thing that worries me more than anything else: Is my life a fact or a fiction?

Freud asked of me an impossible undertaking: both to narrate and to tell the truth about my childhood. In order to evade this impossibility, I needed someone else, other than myself or Freud, to whom I might refer . . . who would substitute for, and sustain my integrity. Someone, in other words, to vouch for me, without questioning me at every moment.

I found in Art Catacomb this particular witness.

I didn't want to be a fake, a counterfeiter, but everyone saw me as such. But if you breathe three times, deeply, Father, Son and Holy Ghost, you can disappear. If you breathe three times you can hide in a clock, in a vagina, in a closet. If caught in the open you can merge with the earth, and the body could be hidden in the earth and there will be no photos, no words, no tracks, and only the wind will be heard.

These girls Catacomb has around him are magnificent. They are sullen, but they are interested in me. They bring me dried flowers and read to me from books that I no longer care to read. They are thorough, beautiful in their seriousness. As an octogenarian one still has the desire to be caressed, to be loved, to fuck and to be fucked, but everything becomes a little desolate, a little slovenly and blurry, and one doesn't have such great ambitions for the real. The young, anyway, have their limits. They have not experienced the drift over the divide which opens another field of knowledge . . . fetishes, smells, excitement captured in the pot-pourri of an infinitely deferred love. Not many have experienced dispassionate skills, the arbitration of desires, the manual of sex from which no consequence flows. Like a massage, this doesn't involve frustration. But these girls make up for it with their seriousness. In my glass penthouse, all this is hidden from them, but they try so hard to understand.

I have an older girlfriend of course. She understands my desires but not my field. She tries to call herself a Communist to appear skilful in rhetoric, but she is a failure. Communists are not intellectuals anyway. They are ideologues. Look at the grey coat she wears. She comes here trying to steal my money. She wants to buy a new coat. Loulou has a plate screwed into her head. They had to take out a part of her skull after a car accident. She's a difficult woman. Whenever we go out together, shopping or whatever, she makes it a point to get lost in the crowd so that I will worry and start looking for her. She likes this, making me worry. This is her unconscious working at full steam. She wants to make me jealous, suspecting that she's gone off with another man, but she doesn't know that I never look for her, that I would welcome it if she went off. She thinks she's flirting, a coquette. But in reality she's a slut. I like this English word 'slut'. Artie taught it to me. It's a dirty word. You go slipping and sliding on it like on a wet road. I can handle sluts, not intellectuals. Artie's girls disturb me. They are intelligent and ruthless and I would like to be their slave without entering into their reality. But they don't know this, because something is always hidden and the right combination is never met. My sister Anna held the key to that. If she were here today she'd be twenty-one and driving a Porsche very fast on a wet road, her legs open for me, her mind testing all my limitations.

But Loulou is the opposite. Loulou wants to pretend to be lost, but all the time she's well within her limits, and her limits are narrow. I say to her: 'Loulou, next time you get lost, ring the police and tell them to bring a metal-detector. With that plate in your head they'll be sure to find you.'

She said I was angry because I was jealous.

We haven't been shopping for a while. Loulou used to come here practically every day to shoo Artie's girls away. But she's getting old and the stairs are too much for her, and she rings instead. I always get one of the girls to answer. The girls have nice names: Gudrun, Ursula, Ulrike, Grete. I don't fall in love that easily with names anymore.

The Catacomb Diaries II

Buying his confidence wasn't that easy. I mean, I literally had to refurbish the apartment he was renting on the Schüttelstrasse, turned that decaying hovel with its eighteenth-century walls into the aluminium and glass structure it is now. The Society met half the funds. I mean, it was now a livable space. Everything was in my name. The girls and I turned over some cash from Germany to make up the rest, and for a bonus we sold some old manuscripts we found in the roof to the National Museum ... turned out to be further works by 'Mozart', apocryphal, no doubt, since we now know Salieri wrote pretty good stuff himself. As I said to Wespe, I said: Sergy, this writing business isn't all it's cracked up to be. There is no origin and no real author half the time. Biography is being subverted. There are only ghost-writers and contracts. How about you let me take you in hand?

That was the wrong expression to use. He was old-fashioned. He thought I was going to steal his testimony. The whole truth or not, he said he was the only one who possessed it for all eternity. I said: Sergy, eternity is ... an absence. It's a paradox—both invasive and entered upon ...

He looked doubtful. I was surfing champion of Dee Why, 1955. One of the first goofy-footers on a six-foot plank with war shrapnel in his knee on the beach that summer. I rode on others' doubts. I said to Wespe, I said: Sergy, do you really want to bugger up the rest of your life by thinking about posterity?

I let him think about that for a few weeks and hopped across the border into Germany, to a bar in Charlottenburg called the *Wolf's Lair*. Some huge bastard with tattoos and a leather vest was my contact. He sold me some of that new stuff. A kilo of it would take out a whole building. When I returned, Gudrun was pregnant. It was *her* child, she said, and I had nothing to do with it. That was our contract, signed hastily on the lost steps of a basilica in Toulouse. She made it sound like a virgin birth. I was not to touch the child. Ever. For eternity. I would return, time and again, to eternity. I worried over it, not as an idea . . . the way it went backwards as well as forwards, sliding over inertia . . . but because it had no idea without movement. It ached in my chest. It pained, physically, don't ask me why. It united, created, remained incomplete and forever hidden, so resolved was I that I would carry this secret to my grave.

Odessa/Vienna

At the end of the war, in 1918, French and Polish troops occupied Odessa. Thérèse went back to Germany. Her daughter Else had died. I lost all my money. Everything. All my investments had turned to shit. Dr Drones had been fighting at the front because he said that a psychoanalyst must go through *absolutely everything*, and I wrote to him asking his advice. He replied in two words: 'Try baccarat'.

I lost several thousand of my remaining roubles.

I tried to make my way to Thérèse, and got stuck in the port of Constanta. I had to wait in Bucharest for two weeks before they would issue me with a visa. In Bucharest everyone was vomiting a sort of brown water, like gargoyles. The gutters were running over and there was a constant subterranean rumble, like an earthquake. I asked the officials what was wrong. Nobody told me. Some sort of plague. The fundamental equality of human bodies.

When I got to Vienna I immediately visited Freud. He gave me an autographed copy of *From the History of an Infantile Neurosis*. I sold it for several hundred crowns to a fellow who came to see me. His name was Jung and he said the inscription on the fly-leaf would be worth something in the future. After that Freud began lending me books with English pound notes in them. These bookmarks I kept. Freud said nothing. Every year, on the 16th of June precisely, I visited Freud and he gave me a book when I returned the old one. On one of the last occasions he could hardly speak, having just had an operation on his mouth. His face was distorted. He mumbled.

Everybody suffered.

When I saw Thérèse again, her hair had turned white.

Backsliding has been my destiny ever since. I'd never

worked before. To get a job now was the greatest agony for me, not because I was afraid of hard work, but because I had to become a fraud to find honest work. A cyst grew on my nose, doubtless on account of the stress and worry which dogged me from morning to night. When I woke in the mornings, *I didn't feel different*. Most people woke feeling slightly different. They were more optimistic, had new ideas, renewed energy. The worst thing in the world was waking to find that the world was the same. Always the same. As if something would change. Something besides words.

To lie here. Not think anymore. Not receive anything. To say nothing. Not to hope, which is not the same as hopelessness, because hopelessness is a change. For the worse. But indifference. Sweet indifference. Bitter-sweet indifference. A variety of indifferences. Indifference as the first effect of poverty. It paralyses. Makes you disdainful. Disdainful indifference. This is a new tack. Hating my illness. No. Be indifferent to it. How to be multifarious: be indifferent to everything.

I learned very quickly that I had to become someone else. I became obsessive about money. Mother gave me some jewellery she managed to salvage from Russia. I hoarded it. When I had to pawn it, the pawnbroker's disdain made me feel sick. I sat outside on the pavement. A sour bile rose. I was filled with such self-hatred, such frustration and anger that I took out my penknife and incised the cyst from my nose. When Freud heard about that he didn't want anything to do with me. I was a *fait accompli*, a cure, a success for him. He had written it. In fact, he wrote me a letter asking precisely about the wolf dream. *He wanted written proof!* Imagine that. Thou shalt not bear false witness against me. I wrote back. Made a statutory declaration. Testimony. Yes, Herr Professor, I was four years old at the time. Why doesn't anybody believe me? Why do they all think I made it up? You cannot make up dreams. (Otto Rank, particularly, was suspicious.) I think though, that I convinced Freud I was still of interest, still a force as the subject. (Under interrogation, you always have to give something, to volunteer the truth, but this is always at the expense of your own integrity. Lying is far more honest in controlling the external situation.) It was hard to rise above my indifference, to be someone else. Not to be honest, to be honest, it was all getting cloudy.

Freud sent me to Ruth Mack Brunswick. When I entered her consulting rooms she appeared in a page-boy outfit, in blue velvet breeches and stockings and ordered me to the couch.

'I'm a decent woman,' she said. 'I wonder if you can talk dirty to me.'

I was floored, couched, I mean. It was different with Freud. He always prepared the ground, jived around. 'Listen,' Freud would say, 'you're paying for this session, pal, so let's cut the crap. You ever heard of confession? Yeah, it's a Catholic thing. Makes damned good sense. Bless me father, for I have sinned. It's been three days since my last fuck . . . heh heh.'

Dr Mack was different.

'Why don't you free associate a little,' she asked, crossing her stockinged legs. I heard the susurration.

I wasn't attracted. I could never come at intelligent women.

'Is free association free?' I asked.

'Listen buster,' she said, 'I got overheads.'

So while I'm lying to Ruth Mack I freestyle a little, capture her from behind, take down her breeches. She catches me on the half-breath: 'I think you are going too far, Sergei.' She sways from side to side, a musk rising from her haunches. I find her passage, taste the bitterness of her ear, which I have in my mouth, (she sighs . . . beneath her breast, which I hold in my hand, beats the heart of a bird, tense, erect, promising), and together, in a state of tender piety, I offer to reveal to her my fetish. We part. I put her on my knee. She knows exactly what to do. She came from a nice family. 'Anna!', I say to her, 'maybe I will now tell you my story.'

1919–1938. Everyday life. *I couldn't stand it. The responsibility of it.* See this greatcoat? Vienna tailor, 1919. Restitched, turned inside out three times. Frugality. Didn't know the meaning of the word once. Thérèse and I sat out the winters of those days passing a kettle of warm water between us. Then I got a job in life insurance. I was there thirty years, learning to decode luxuries: if you say the words 'caviar', 'Mozart chocolates', 'herring rollmops', 'Goldwasser' many many times, like Buddhist incantations, you learn to do without reality. You can hide words by breathing them out of existence . . . as long as you have the *insurance* (life insurance is a foresight that never repays the past) that the situation itself—let's say the ultimate catastrophe—can be excreted from the word in a breath or fart, and though your breath may have once stunk like shit, the pure odour of nothingness can take the place of hunger, and ultimately, of desire altogether, and you learn to live by creating small excitements: little lives and deaths every day. Collections of trivial moments. Breathing. In and out. In and out. And out.

'What would you say if I ghost-write your memoirs?'

'I would say it was a therapeutic exercise.'

'Why?'

'To find some resolution in yourself.'

'Why do you think Thérèse committed suicide?'

'Why do *you* think she did that to me?'

'How come you have Nazi friends like Kurt, and Communist friends like Louise?'

'When you're as old as I am you have all kinds of acquaintances.'

'Kurt works in the National Archives. What as?'

'He's a sorter.'

'He's also the leading figure in the "Waldheim for President" campaign. You see his bald skull at demonstrations. He carries a weapon.'

'I have nothing to do with that.'

'Are you using him to search for your fragments?'

'Perhaps. Listen, you sound like a detective. Do you read Conan Doyle too?'

'No. Why?'

'Freud did. He used to get very excited about Sherlock Holmes. I saw copies of those books under his desk. When he went to England he bought a deer-stalker's cap.'

'No!'

'Yes. And a curly pipe. Though he wasn't allowed to smoke. His cancer, you know. And a heart condition as well. Yes, Freud thought he was Sherlock Holmes, and I was Watson. What I saw was elementary ... all was invention. I was a writer. What he saw was philosophy. He was tough as well. In 1923, after the death of his grandson, he became depressed for the first time. The postman only rings once. He didn't get depressed for nothing. It was abnormal without reason. He profited. He called it courage. What he saw, he saw. He was robust though he wasn't tall. Photographed with taller men like Jung, he stood on a box. Could handle himself in a street brawl, no worries. He was capable of pushing you over a cliff, said Ferenczi, who had an argument with him. Then Ernest Jones, Freud's biographer and faithful disciple, began a rumour that Ferenczi was homicidal. Freud had friends. He was tough. Like my sister Anna. He bought an Alsatian dog for his daughter, who was also called Anna. The dog he called "Wolf".'

'Wolf and Anna . . . '

'Common names.'

Crypt

What he sees he sees. Wespe's been writing a long time now, these secret notes to himself, chronicling this procession of so-called scholars and analysts and doctors who've come to knock at his door for a sniff of dust and time, peer at the cranking old machinery of a 1914 engine, still working magnificently, kept oiled and cleaned and hissing. Neurosis. Clouds of steam. They come, with names like Eissler and Abraham and Gardiner and Liebmann ... this last a four-foot-nine-inch wonder, a dwarf with a king-size ego, lugging it from room to room to watch over his unconscious. They're paying you, Catacomb, Liebmann says, puffing. Don't be ungrateful.

It's a year and nothing has been done about Wespe.

He's a survivor. They've besieged him for over fifty years. It all began with the few English pounds Freud left in his books. Small bribes can lead to immense corruption. Wespe's bought a plane ticket to London.

He sees what he sees. Artie Catacomb and a bunch of blonde girls giggling away as they filed out of the National Archives. Adjacent to the archives, the *Wolfsschanze* Club. First time he'd seen any of them smile. He steps back into the thick bushes. West Vienna. At the edge of the woods there are meadows. Long grass conceals mauve-coloured stones. You can walk on these stones across the damp meadows. Your shoes won't get dirty. Ghost-writer. Catacomb has the name for it. Together they've worked on these memoirs, brought them up to 1938. He can't stand Catacomb's style. It's distant, legal, antiseptic. He hates it in fact, but this is not therapy any longer. This is someone else writing, and if they criticise it, it will prove everything's in a name. Further ammunition for me

169

to destroy psychoanalysis. Your shoes won't be dirty. They'll shine them, in fact.

Wolf-Man by the Wolf-Man, Artie's going to call it. The name 'Catacomb' will not appear anywhere in it. No puzzle entombed in it. A secret celebration. This'll be a great joke. The literary hoax of the century. The psychoanalytic bungle of all time. A real time-bomb.

1938. There are Swastikas on the footpath. Thérèse is wasting away and he doesn't notice. Nobody gives a damn about Thérèse's mental and physical health. Freud gave her the once over in the Prater and his face took on a lewd expression. He'd like to see her with her clothes off. Marry her, he said to Wespe, I give you permission. Freud suspects she's insatiable. She's got the kind of voice you hear at the markets. Hoarse and low. Nobody cares about Thérèse. Artie Catacomb says it would be politic to keep her presence to a minimum. Let her speak just once. Maybe reproduce a little poem she wrote. Something about burying the heart deep.

February 12, 1938. Schuschnigg meets with Hitler. Thérèse stands in front of the mirror all day while Wespe's at work. She sees in the mirror all the things she's been . . . a divorcée, a gypsy, a nurse, a Spanish dancer, a caring mother, a loving wife, a battle-weary daughter-in-law, a fantasist. She didn't care about his money, but now, with the schilling devalued, frugality has become her pathology. She stares at the mirror. Outside, Jewish tailor shops explode like crystal goblets. Soprano screams. The newspapers say that the Jews are using a lot of gas. What seems like a soap-opera at first, has real consequences. Real blood. Real deaths. She stares in the mirror. She has become a Jew. She will be concerned. Take up the burden. We are all Jews. Do you know what we're going to do? What? We'll turn on the gas.

Outside the Swastika flag beats against its pole and slaps at the window. She leaves many notes, all poetic, under stones, all over the house. He prods the smooth riverstones by his feet outside the Archives, in a different time now, but the same attitudes.

They were both in possession of something, Thérèse and he, but not of each other.

170

Some men frequented bars. He frequented tailor shops. Spent most of their minute stipend and tiny salary on clothes. He thrilled to the tailor's tape, the measuring capacity, the way it imprisoned him as it encircled his waist, his thighs, his crotch. Thus measured, he became bold, impressive. Went next door to speak to the ladies. Procuresses, who came to order clothes for their charges. Placed his hands on the small and unclad buttocks of mannequins. They had reversed roles since their marriage. He dressed, she wrote, but in writing she revealed too readily her life beneath, while in dressing he wore the Emperor's New Clothes, and became the clothes, and there was nothing of him except the clothes . . . the formation of new inventions, new combinations. Beneath, there is precisely nothing except a set of desires, a fashion system, lines of escape. He spoke for Thérèse. She had become mute, or at least, monosyllabic. Astoundingly, she whispered. Once had a voice like a cheap megaphone. Silently, she began to beat him. Slaps first, then with a riding crop. As usual, he was his women. In love, they glimmered briefly as others. In lust, there was only himself. Procuresses in the Prater. Tall women in riding boots. She became invisible to him. There's Catacomb, in his Mercedes, heading downtown. The guy's dangerous, he tells himself. He has the crude passion of the materialist. A six-feet-four time-bomb with a short fuse. Catacomb is dressed like Father Christmas. Suddenly there is sound and noise, wind and rain and tailor shops have their vitrines shattered so that glass falls like crystal rain and the Archives erupt, the bowels of the building exploding, the ground shaking and the water mains spewing, debris floating on the rooftops in the overheated wind and the side of the building tilting and then recomposing itself and fires breaking out sporadically and then with a rush like jet engines, whining and thundering so ferociously the railings melt and wires topple and he can only stand there. He has to triangulate things. He needs to get the focus, the truth. Windows, staging, seeing. Slowly, he undoes his fly and urinates in the direction of the conflagration. He moves silently on. Why did you do this to me? Thérèse had left the gas on. When the ambulances arrive he sees a tattooed arm, quite pink, arteries splaying from the shoulder. They pick it up. It looks like an electronic prosthesis. Place it on the stretcher. Then the hindquarters of a man, pale and gleaming and pulsing, the femoral artery shooting like a hose somebody has left on the ground. Clouds of pink dust, the lawn strewn with offal. Walls crump over the firehoses. The sun is setting with difficulty in this red glow while the Allied bombers drone overhead. He catches something. Peels himself a mouse. Lives off fried banana peels and coffee rinds he boils over and over again. Burns the furniture in the stove. Kurt. The arm belonged to Kurt. The Death's Head tattoo of the Schutz-staffel. He walks home. People are rushing by. The bars are almost empty. Climbs the stairs. Finds his door open. Someone is there, sitting in his chair, rotund, draped in a red and white flag.

He's familiar.

'Artie?'

'Yeah.'

'Let me turn on some lights.'

And lights there are, spewing out of the walls, amber scallops washing into the miasma of tobacco smoke and a faint stench of vomit, air-conditioning still running at full blast to clear the foul breath, the cold like the emptiness of deserted movie houses, making him gasp that double intake he knew so well, pissing from the roof on snowy, sleepless nights.

When he looked up, dazzled by the lights, he was staring into the tube of a silencer, which was going up and down under his nose. The smell in the air had grown stronger. Artie's smoothly shaven skull loomed up like the moon, his smile crackling.

'Just a rehearsal,' Artie said, waving the pistol now from side to side. He clucked his tongue and squinted his eyes. He was shaking. He fired. It was louder than expected.

'We live in terrible times,' Artie said with pretended ease.

Sergei breathed out. Between the periodic eclipses of light, through the weaving and dancing rhythms of Catacomb's ner-vousness, he had seen the holes in the plaster and the flaws in the gun-hand. Artie had a weak wrist.

'Listen, Sergy, you were supposed to help me. I did everything I could to save you. All you had to do was to be there while I wrote your memoirs. That was the agreement. But you ran. Why, Sergy?'

Catacomb lit a cigar with one hand. There were burn-marks on his sleeve.

'The Association put such trust in you. Such faith. What about the subsidy every month . . . the star billing at the conferences, the articles you publish? Do you think every psycho who writes in gets selected? What about the spinoffs, the thrillers you write under your pseudonym? Who do you think paid the critics to slip in the words 'literary merit'? I know you don't need all that now. You make a tidy sum, nom de plume or not de plume. A feather in your cap to have known Freud. But if you want serious recognition you don't shit on his head now. No, not now.'

Catacomb shuffled and shifted smoke from one side of his cheek to the other.

Sergei looked at him with drooping eyelids.

'I'm an old man. It makes no sense to kill me. Freud would be protected anyway. All they have to do is to deny.'

'Would it make sense to cut my only contact? C'mon Sergy, I got two phials of explosive here. It's the latest stuff. Half a kilo can blow this building apart. You saw what happened to the Archives. You can have that or you can have the money. The money I'll get tomorrow afternoon. I don't carry any of that. What d'you say? Pulp your articles.'

Stick to pulp, Freud had said, unless you want to be a pauper.

'I don't know, Artie. What I said to Freud was the truth. I said I was a writer. If he wanted to make interpretations then that was his business. If I happen to be a bit of an entrepreneur, then that's what he owes me, man. Life's tough. Has been for half a century. Now put the gun down. I get nervous with firearms.'

Artie lowered the gun. He took two phials out of his breast pocket. He laid the automatic on the table.

'Our little rendyvous tonight was to erase some of that pornography you wrote when you were a sicko, comprendy?

173

Special investigators were snoopin' into them. That guy Kurt, the Nazi, he was leanin' on you, right?'

Sergei nodded. His head swayed. His eyes became a little weepy, as though from watching too many movies. Everybody leant on him these days. He was sick of being a victim. When he changed from Anna the Wolf to Wespe the Wimp he went from hunter to hunted. He lost command of words. The tough-guy detectives in his novels went to jelly.

'Kurt and I were also collaborating,' Sergei said. 'In his words: "To prove the Jew wrong".'

Artie took out a sheaf of yellowing paper from the inside pocket of his overcoat.

'This is hot stuff, Sergy.'

'Ungh ungh,' Sergei shook his head, grabbed at the paper.

'Not so fast.' Catacomb put them away and shrugged, walked to the door.

'What kind of perversities you doing here these days Sergy?' Catacomb was looking at a sketch on the wall. A contortionist performing something on herself.

The other man was sniffing at the glass phials. He snorted something up his sinuses and made a face.

'I paint.'

Goddamn, he seemed a prude when it came to some things, Catacomb was thinking. After years of being oversexed he began to hate the things he couldn't have. Arty-farty types always had so much energy, always onto something or someone else. He tried to imagine something. A model.

'She from the Ivory Coast?'

'Nah, man. She all ebony.' Sergei giggled, minced across the floor, amazingly agile for his age. Swivelled, seemed to be listening to something. Surprise. He spun around.

'This explosive does strange things to your head.'

'Shit!' Catacomb said. 'That's my coke. I've mixed up the tubes. The girls must be blowing themselves apart!'

Catacomb grabbed the phials and rushed to the stairwell. Firecrackers. Suddenly his coat was torn open. Two small black holes appeared. He turned, eyes dazed, struggled with the bannister. Cordite. The lights fell in. Two holes in his back. A red curtain. Contortions.

Convulsions. Dead already? The blood coming now, slowly, then all in a rush. Muscles twitching in his back.

A layer of gunsmoke washed beneath the light. Wespe prodded the body with a foot, taking care not to step in the pool of blood forming under Catacomb's armpit. He picked up the phials from the floor.

'Sorry, Artie,' he said, wheezing a little.

He carried the body downstairs, dumped it beside the trash cans. Another drunken Kriss Kringle. Then he puffed back upstairs. Cleaned the blood off with a sponge and soapy water.

He walked to the edge of the stage, sat down. God, what was the world coming to. There was something wrong when he had to remove scum like Catacomb before they did worse things to society. He cradled the warm pistol in his hands. Began to giggle. He saw little scuff marks on the parquet, five-cent size holes in the polished wood. Stiletto heels. He remembers now. The contortionist wore stiletto heels. He reached across to the lightswitch panel, dimmed the spots, began to contemplate his own excitement. Uncontrollable giggling.

Libidinal excitement. Yes, finally . . . this was his inheritance from his forebears. Strong instincts. Violent lives. Uninhibited sexuality. He suddenly felt free. He wanted to dance, up on his hind legs. Healthy instincts. Fuck society. Hoo! It's okay. He sees the other side. Hoo! The natural contrivance of desire. Free to roam. Hot dog. Released into contradiction, into wolfishness. Hoooo! The light reflects in his eyes.

It is his birthday tomorrow. The window creaks, then opens by itself. Outside there is a row of walnut trees. On one of them seven white wolves are sitting. They have huge bushy tails and their ears are pricked. They are staring at him. From a high and supple branch, looking like a wolf, his sister Anna is swinging. Behind them, the city is on fire.

'Course Wespe's got that artistic temperament. Makes it hard to take over from him. Imagines things all the time. Cock and bull stories. Mare's nests. Paranoid. Persecuted. He saw me as a threat to him. All I wanted to do was to interview him. What Liebmann really said to me was: *kill the rumour*. I mean, the rumour that Sergei Wespe was a writer before he went to Freud. Maybe he never met Freud at all. Maybe the whole thing's a fraud, cooked up by an old boy who needed cash. Look at some of the stuff he's publishing lately. Psychoanalytic thrillers, he calls them. Airport pulp. On the back cover of each there's a logo. A wolf's head. 'Paints in the harsh tones of reality—another Wolf-Man mindblower' it says beneath. But what if the Wolf-Man's little frauds were true? This kind of thing would have worried Freud. Not about the Wolf-Man, but about himself. All his life Wespe protected Freud, not the other way round. Protected Freud from himself. From losing his conviction. These are the Wolf-Man's mindblowers.

They could leave out the mind bit. (That reminds me, poor Ulrike disintegrated back in her apartment. I knew that explosive was unstable. It lets me off the hook. It's an open and shut case now.) Besides, the guy has had a proven record of lying. Well, maybe not lying outright, but of distorting the truth, of relaying it in a way that shifts the focus onto language. How do we *prove* anything? Freud made a heroic attempt. Only to be howled down by Jung and Rank and subsequently by my contemporaries. Wespe lives in a dream world with an escape-hatch. Take the famous Wolf Dream. Forget symbols, forget interpretation. Play him at his own game. Read the narrative:

Suddenly the window opened by itself, and I was terrified to see that some white wolves were sitting on the big walnut tree in front of the window.

In German, the words are balanced even more deliberately, woodenly, as though the curtain has just gone up. Jerkily at first, it uncovers a fear of movement. The sentence situates its fulcrum beneath a heavy inertia which distributes itself in an absurd balancing act. A part-act. The sentence is Freud's, not Wespe's. The latter could only draw it. Freud's rule: a dream transforms experiences into their opposite. The real thing was agitation and excitement. Freud's interpretation: it represented Wespe's parents fucking *more ferarum*. In the manner of wild beasts. But something is missing from this rather savage interpretation. An opaque window opens. (Double-glazed. *Glazá*, ('eyes'), Dimitri used to say, putting his hands in front of his eyes, when he told wolf stories.) The window is always there, guarding the sentence, *holding the reins of reality*. (When we take our hands from our eyes, we wake up.) Feel the cold. It is beginning to rain. Too warm yet to snow, though a few flakes drift by, are pasted on the glass. *A misty rain is falling*. It is the first line of one of Wespe's books.

The window may be the dream's way of saying that Wespe is waking up to watch this scene, but dreaming that he is waking up within his dream is really to die, to have no access to any other waking life. The window, therefore, is *a way back*. It is a rumination, not a dream. But in Freud, the window, the frame, the escape-hatch for writing, the process which rescues it from death, is always overlooked. The witness is overlooked in order to get at the evidence. Freud was aware of this. He wrote: 'I fear that this is where my reader's trust will abandon me.'

You cannot make a connection without a frame, a context. The dream and the reality both depend on the window. Picture the scene: Wespe is lying, very lightly, on the couch. Lying on a floral rug. Hanging on the wall, another rug. Lying on a clean pillow. He is thin. He hardly eats. Takes three or four enemas a day. Freud, with a grey beard, breathing heavily, is out of his line of sight, at the head of the couch. (Later, Wespe will change the white wolves to grey ones.) Wespe has to balance Freud. He stares at the window. He wants to die, to be embalmed in the scene. Death by defenestration. (Freud will later say to him: 'We had the wrong attitude to death'. Notice he doesn't say 'you' or 'I', but 'we'.) But the consulting rooms are on the ground floor, looking out on a courtyard which reminds him of a grey day in Berlin. No possibility of even hurting himself. For balance, Wespe says he is a writer. In the next room he hears the clicking nails of a large dog. There is a wind outside. The window creaks. Next to the window, on the wall, there are photographs of Freud's colleagues. They stare down at him with white beards. Wespe wants to die, to stop this process of constant becoming. Of going on in a line. Not to go on is his greatest desire. To simply *be*, which is the condition of being a wolf. He is not afraid of the wolves sitting on the walnut tree outside. He becomes them. They glimmer. But it is precisely that part that is missing, this *being*, which is oblique, unseen, whenever he writes. He shifts, from foreground to background and vice versa. From transparency to opacity. He glimmers. There is great pain in readjusting this blind spot, guarding it from merging with his intentions, which try to pull it from the luminosity of the present moment into the pale light of the crypt. He cannot delude himself for an extended time. If he is cured he will no longer be a writer in this sense. He will represent, become transparent, realistic. If he is not, he will forever be a patient, browsing on words, startled by their incrimination. Not to go on, but not to die. To be but not to mean. The only path left to him is that of recapitulation. Other people would say backsliding . . . that he lacks decorum, a sense of propriety, a trustworthiness in representing. But it is also the case that everything is happening at once. Somewhere else. A way back. Writing is always a return to somewhere else, the uncanny, never to be caught in a one-way street: a wolf is framed against the snow in a forest near Baden Baden. It glows and fades. He goes up to it. It has disappeared. There are no departing prints, no traces of what it was burying. There is no exact site, no movement, yet a wolf never loses his way.

Wespe stares at the window.

Behind him, silently doubling back on his own tracks, Freud

says: *We all desire inertia, but we are afraid to die. Fear is also a desire.*

Heroism. Action. Courage. The death-wish. Not to commit suicide is to desire fear for as long as possible.

In 1950, on the twelfth anniversary of Thérèse's suicide, Sergei Wespe wandered into the Russian zone in Vienna. He wanted to paint a bakery. He sat down on a crate, took out his box of paints, set up his easel. A party of Russian soldiers approached, detained him and interrogated him for two and a half days inside the disused bakery. He felt quite safe. The Russian officer who questioned him had the same kindly manner as Freud. But the language was warm. The language was Russian. The officer said to him:

'Psychoanalysis is a romantic view of life. A privileged view. To reject it is a social act. A profound gesture. All diseases are material, don't you see? It's all a matter of harnessing the conditions. Stimulus and response. Are we not all wolves, our savagery being also our solidarity?'

The officer was framed in the light of a large window. His cap had flaps stuck up on the sides like dog ears, and when he spoke, little sprays of saliva cascaded on sunrays.

After this lecture, Wespe was released. He made his way back to his zone, through streets still bearing the scars of the war.

What could be more abnormal than these shells of houses, these mausoleums which only a few years ago still stank with the decay of bodies buried in them? Yes, he said to himself, I will *regress* towards the social. I will die into the many.

During the interrogation the window had opened by itself. Only a few years ago he had seen dozens of wolves and wild dogs descend upon the city from the wooded slopes. They looked familiar enough, loping, thin, muzzles to the ground. They roamed in packs, they changed direction without warning, like schools of tuna in a grey sea. They nosed among the rubble for meat and dragged out shapeless bundles, the flesh trembling beneath their thrusts, the ruins echoing with their grunts. Then they, in turn, were hunted.

179

Mother

Mother lived with me after Thérèse's suicide. She took my mind off my tragedy. She pressed a seventeenth-century icon to my chest and told me never to be ambivalent. I didn't know what she meant. The beaten metal in the icon was like an X-ray plate, cold over my soul. I breathed in three times.

Now I know that she wanted me to reshape my life. There was only one path, she said. I needed strong instincts. Thérèse was a mistake. My whole life was a mistake.

My mother ate lettuce leaves. She was so economical we actually managed to save money. When I told her I was going to write a book she said:

'What for? So much effort and so little reward.'

One night she came up behind me in my room and spat on my page. She took to pinching me in the fleshy place under my arm.

'This is life,' she said.

Sometimes she waved a stinking fish under my nose as well. Life was stench and pain. I wanted to spin away from it, forever.

Nowadays we send out satellites which do their job and then, discarded, allow them to wing off into the infinite universe. But suppose that one day they returned, spinning slowly and bristling with antennae, to re-attach themselves to the earth. What would we do then? Revise our idea of limits, of eternity?

Mother lived to the age of eighty-nine. She had infinite resources. In that time she gave me, I calculated, close to thirty thousand schillings.

Everyday life

1926–1938: treatment with Dr Ruth Mack Brunswick
1950s: treatment with Dr Kurt Eissler
1955: three weeks in a neurological sanatorium
1956: treatment with Dr Wilhelm Solms
1960s: treatment with Dr Menninger and Dr Liebmann
1972–1973: treatment with Dr Arthur S. Catacomb

KATOOMBA

1978

The pure plateau air . . . Beckett. Excitement without climax. A madhouse sits atop here.

You are reminded of Wespe's many brushes with fortune. All his ups and downs. You, too, had known wealth and the wealthy.

For a while you were salvaged from the ash-heap by a woman, given a small reprieve on the harbour in Sydney, marvelling at fortune. You used to walk down Woolwich Point feeling the first breeze of autumn. Subtle. It came from the sea. The wish to fly came off that smell. An invitation to voyage. The need to go again, but not going. Contemplation. Reminded you of Beijing one high summer of dust storms when an intrepid bureaucrat collared you in a tea house and said: 'Any action, and money is action, is worth all the contemplation in the world. To contemplate is to be negative,' he shouted, smiling out of thick lenses, government-issue no doubt. Then he drove away in a luxury Toyota. You agreed at the time. They awarded you an honorary degree at the university. But ah! Woolwich Point. To enlist nature again. There, behind sandstone walls and stucco, Mediterranean terracotta and fountains, were exotic birds, groomed dogs, a stuffed wolf or two. The domestication of nature and a retiring disposition allowed privacy to fondle a lyric . . . 'I've got the world on a string . . .' Music as soft as the lawn. Whisky in the garden at dusk, a ceramic crocodile in a pond. All for contemplation. For it these things remained at their worth. But the woman who was lying on the deck chair, the woman waving at you with a finger from her glass . . . you've known her bed too, her worth. She was dying, like you.

Listen. Beneath frangipani and ferns a tennis court far

below, next to the glistening water. Listen. In short skirts the nation's débutantes strut their stuff and bend balls back across the net, a little stiff-armed, liberal-minded to an extent, understanding how to hard-nose their way in the world. That was their allure; their hardness. Curiosity about the rich. Allow a little self-righteousness. Between hedges retiring company directors sit becalmed, feeling their way along a new experience of senility. Schooners rock below the point, masts clanking, the voyages fewer even in memory. Think of all that aggression, brought to bear and then dissipated in the wind. You used to see them bending over ill wives. The moon must have played havoc among the arches when the blonde children unrolled their Porsches and spat gravel through the gate for the last time till the execution of the will. Bitterness. Limitations.

Somewhere in Strasbourg your blonde ten-year-old child may have been uncorking a bottle.

You had the strength once, to fly beyond, imagine things upon the field of art. You were closing in once. No longer.

So an interlude in the great divide.

You were through with therapy and it was through with you. When you returned to Australia the Vietnam war was over. You were conscripted to the outer suburbs of heat and terry-towelling, of Toranas and thongs. You knew that the West was tough. But mainly you found that it was sad. At the age of fifty-five, when others were thinking of retirement, you tried school teaching and encountered much blood. You rode a damaged Harley with bent forks. Wore a death jacket from St Vincent de Paul's. The victim had bled into the lining. Dead men's shoes. You don't get much as a school teacher. At the school they thought you strange and eccentric and then middle aged mothers started buying you clothes when they saw what you were wearing. It was out of lust. It was always like that. You were the incarnation of their imagined lovers. Clad like the walking wounded you haunted their dreams and revived their faded memories. If you had no potential, you had potency. Maybe the bike stirred them. Recycling. In their beds you heard them cry and moan for the dead. On long and lonely nights you listened for echoes from the other side. In the clapboard house you rented you stayed late on the patio waiting with a shotgun for the nighttime hordes circling in thunder to steal parts from your bike. Paranoia. On sports days there were cuts so deep you held pieces of flesh together with bulldog clips. Kids came to you with clubbed heads, bent noses, embedded beer bottles, dismembered scrota. Until one day. Yes, one day a fourteen-year-old nymphet sat on your knee and slipped you her smile and in return you gave . . . no mere return for courtesy. So the sack. Scandal. To tell the truth what passed between the two of you was epistolary intercourse. Yes, a letter was by far the greater evidence. It was the word made flesh; more solid than carnality. It was there in black and white. Literal lusts. Figurative fucks. She visited you later, a glowing sixteen, knocked up finally by someone else. Too old for any romance, you gave her a few hundred and moved house.

You check your diary for other times, other moves.

The Catacomb Diaries IV

I could have made you more than you were, Sergei; more famous than Freud. You tried to kill me off in your book, but I escaped the crypt. It's okay. You don't have to apologise. You thought you were Lermontov, protecting your sister's honour. A moment of delirium. Let's say the small calibre bullets missed any vital organs and leave it at that. No, I understand. I respect the paradox that is in you.

Freud didn't want to threaten society either. Oh no, he was a family man. But when you told me about your father I thought everything should have come out into the open. You would have exposed all fathers, all grandfathers, all patriarchs, all potentates . . . all psychoanalysts. You converted me to your cause, and then you withdrew from it. You sniffed, yes, morality, with the dedicated scorn of the true pornographer. But then you said *it was only writing*, leaving me with no choice but to say that Freud knew you lied in the beginning and that these fabrications were keys to your condition. I began to rewrite, and suddenly I saw . . . just a glimmer mind you . . . as I worked on your life . . . *The Wolf-Man by the Wolf-Man*, I would call it . . . I glimpsed that movement out of the corner of my eye . . . a wolf burying something in the forest . . . I perceived that *you and Freud were one and the same*. Birds of a feather. Prurient together. *Arcades ambo.* You lived by means of disdain. Ah, the pure plateau air. And when your fortune changed, he gave you money. It wasn't a bribe.

In a Berlin sanatorium in 1905, in a black courtyard soaked in drizzle, you had seen your father give Anna money in the same way, by handing over a book interleaved with banknotes.

I, too, took advantage. At eighty-five and fifty-five, we were both too old for sentimentality.

Spare a thought for me. You were Freud's most famous success, *and* a popular writer, for God's sake. I was there to correct you, erase the copula. Instill doubt. Promote myself.

When I finished your biography, which had nothing of the *auto* in it, coming to a standstill with its radiator boiling and the pistons seized up, Liebmann threw a fit. He read the draft in New York and rang me immediately.

'Catacomb, tell me this is a joke.'

'It's no joke, Ishmael.'

'Listen here, scumbag. This stuff is, well, it's kind of shit, Catatomb. There's no chronology to the Wolf-Man's life, no facts, no details of what the guy told Freud. For all we know this may have been written by Wespe himself. It makes Freud out to be, goddamit, *ignorant of truth*. I mean, there is reality out there, Catatomb, that's what we're in analysis for . . . to bring back the Reality Principle. Time *is* the Reality Principle, you get me Catatomb? A respect for history.'

'You mean time is money. Don't you mean that you're in analysis not to bring back the Reality Principle, but to bring back the bacon? The *Gefiltefisch*? Wespe's been used, taken, swindled all his life by analysts, social humbugs, families, associations, nations, and only now has the guy found his feet . . .'

'Victimology belongs in social work, Catatomb. You've fallen for the charm, the dog-like passivity. And I thought you were hard-boiled! Look, let's stop shouting. I can hear you clearly. It's two in the morning here and I'm tired. The manuscript doesn't redress the bad publicity. I'd like to suggest some changes, take out the chapter on primal scenes, add a whole lot more to 'Everyday Life', give the reading public something to hold onto . . . I want the public to see that this guy used to be a social misfit, Catatomb. I want them to see how Freud got him from being an ass-obsessed, degenerate wimp to a respectable family man who works in an insurance firm . . . a man beset by the tragedies of two world wars, the loss of a fortune, the death of a beloved wife, the remorse of an idle childhood . . . you know, that sort of thing . . . goddamit, Catacomb, I want a mini-series outta this.'

There was silence, then a sort of crackling. I thought Liebmann had hung up. Someone was gargling on the other end. I heard him spit.

'Look Art,' Liebmann's voice came back on the phone softer, almost purring, *'you're* the analyst and the writer. Wespe's only the subject. If you keep that in mind you won't go wrong.'

Subject and expression. Content and form. It wasn't like that at all. The Wolf-Man was the formal substance of bodily expression . . . lights blinking on and off . . . rhythms and intensities.

I suppose Liebmann gave me a chance to redeem myself. But when I told him he wanted soap instead of the truth he told me to go fuck myself and hung up.

It wasn't long before I received copies of letters from his lawyers. I had been fired from the Memorial Library, due to my *inability*, in part, *to fulfil the duties of curator*, since I spent too much time overseas. I realised now why Liebmann sent me to Paris. It was his escape clause. Apparently I ran up huge expense accounts. Sergy and I were supposed to have done a grand tour of the casinos of Europe. Baden Baden (too cold), the Riviera (too hot, too many old women with blue coloured hair and little dogs shitting on your shoes), Paris (the *nouveau riche* insufferably bourgeois).

Of course, this was what Liebmann wrote. Killing two birds with one stone. His articles came out weekly in *The New York Times*. There were bogus lawsuits and then real ones concerning my fake degrees. I countersued over Liebmann's scandalous report on Ludmilla Wittgenstein. ('A con-man insinuating himself into one of Austria's most famous families by exploiting its well-known strain of lunacy,' he wrote, though I knew nobody in Austria gave the steam off their piss for the Wittgensteins). Liebmann had had a bad run with Ludmilla.

All this cost me a lot. I kept the Mercedes, but lost everything else. In the end, I would lose that too, but wait. Don't be too greedy for tragedy. I did my bit in the meantime. Protected

Wespe from himself. Helped him excuse himself from human relationships. Take Louise. I mean, take her away.

Loulou comes up the stairs like Boris Karloff with a wooden leg. Dragging chains, that sort of thing. Only the sound the chains make is the sound of money. People who rattle loose change in their pockets or handbags have a deep problem. Louise is so mean she'd have the eye out of a needle. Anyway, Loulou comes up the stairs to Sergy's apartment in her inimitable way. In furs and bad teeth. She complains all the time, asking why he should rent an apartment up here instead of on the ground floor, why he wants to make her walk up four storeys. She has a scarf over her head, like the Polish refugee that she is. Her breath is terrible. When she coughs, there is a rumble of tanks in her chest. Warsaw Pact armies on the move. She fixes a bloodshot eye on me and spits: You! she shouts. How come you are always here? She has changed her tune since my demise. Since I have come down in the world. She used to sit on my knee, roll her stockings. No big thrill, I assure you. One thing she had was energy. She still possesses that, soured with contempt. I mean, it's really something when somebody as contemptible as she is looks down upon you. Beneath contempt. These days I drink bad coffee in Sergy's apartment and try to keep out of her way. But she rolls in like thunder: why don't you bring some food? Better still, a bottle of wine? I confess I have no money.

That's the crux of it. I hadn't known real deprivation for maybe forty years. Suddenly I was without a job, without prospects of a job, black-banned by the ASPS, *persona non grata* in Viennese society, outcast, derelict, spending my mornings sipping sullage from a coffee cup at the Bahnhof Café and my afternoons listening to Louise, whose real madness was becoming apparent. She said she was receiving signals from outer space, relayed through the plate in her head. Someone, perhaps God, was telling her that Sergei Wespe was hot property, that it was about time the Wolf-Man came out of hiding. She would reveal all, she said, about her life with him. All this retrospectivity was remarkable foresight. Wespe was pecking away in his room again. The noise came like birds in spring . . .

the sound of renewal, fertility and money as royalty cheques increased. Yes, the typewriter sounded like shit to my ears. She put a stop to his favourite pastimes: consulting psychoanalysts, going to tailors. She tried to prevent his paying them . . . tore up bills they sent. Out of all this industry, a tidy bank account was growing, for which she took credit. With this rampant affluence, failures could only stand in the way. Louise got nasty.

I couldn't match him. Not even with forty years of trying. I mean, he was a professional neurotic. I wasn't made that way. I took the robust view of life. You had your ups and downs and you had to know not to indulge the downers and quietly preserve the successes. I could have been a good family man. Writing Wespe's life, even under Liebmann's instructions, brought home to me one thing: that kind of sensibility evolved from money. Big money.

And Sergy was making it. From potboilers. Even to get close to the man, to understand what drives him, you have to know one thing: his tragic nature was coded in a game . . . he said Freud told him that once upon a time.

There was something cryptic in those sheafs, those fragments I found in his place, when I was fooling with that .22 automatic Gudrun lent me. By the way, Sergy didn't know it was loaded. Or did he? He thought he was pretending to fire at me, then he went into some kind of fit. I ended up in the emergency ward. I first met Louise there. She was Sergy's latest friend, she said. She hoped I wouldn't sue or claim damages. She wore a white hat and veil and touched me lightly on the shoulder when she spoke. My shoulder was burning. 'He gets a little worked up and becomes very dramatic,' she said by way of understatement. When she saw that I wasn't impressed, she asked if I were insured. She pulled out a cigar but neglected to light it. 'By the way, what did you find in his apartment that caused his paranoia?'

'Me?' I gasped. 'I was the cause of his murderous impulses?'

I wanted to put my hands around her scrawny neck, but I couldn't move my arms.

'Sure,' she said. 'He gets like that once in a while. Gets

189

violent with people who are trying to help him. I know. It could be his aristocratic nature. He doesn't suffer fools gladly.'

Louise had a way of insulting you when she came on side.

'He tried to kill his dermatologist once . . . back in '24 or '25. Something about his nose. Yeah, I remember him telling me. It was Dr Wolf he tried to kill.'

Those bits of paper I found, prints in his wastebasket, were the beginnings of a real autobiography. Suppressed material. Rejects. Raw stuff from the unconscious. Now Louise has been gathering all that. I've seen her rummaging through his garbage. Stuffing torn bits of paper stained with coffee and orange juice into her concave bosom. She pretended she was cleaning up. Maybe she was, because the apartment became sparser, cleaner, airier, lighter. The rest of the rooms now looked like the spotless bathroom. In the toilet wall, Sergy had inserted a painting in place of the slot for his typewriter. Loulou took me from room to room, exhibiting his landscapes. He had a habit of displaying these to his women after intercourse. 'These are all over five thousand apiece,' she blurted. Renaissance Man. Wespe would invent helicopters next. Discover that the earth was round. The trans-historical nature of artistic endeavour. Louise bought him an Italian leather lounge. (Where did she find the money?)

Of course, I had moved three times. I rented a room in the low-budget quarter. Rising damp formed wrinkles on the Johann Strauss wallpaper. A root from a tree had forced its way through the wall and into my room. I kept hacking it back with a bread knife, but it kept shooting tendrils towards my bed during the night. I spent more and more days at Wespe's (really mine) neat and now quite ornate apartment overlooking the Prater. Louise had stopped acknowledging my presence. She still lives apart from him, but makes the trip puffing and cursing every morning. When she looks through me I can see that her face is really dead. It is decaying. She looks like Sarah Bernhardt in her coffin. I mean her final coffin. Except smoke is coming from her nostrils. Those cheap cigars. Cigarillos these days. She thinks she has a chest condition. Hey, Loulou, I say, your thermometer's on fire. I think Loulou is trying to poison me. The coffee always tastes foul. I am quite dismayed that Sergy has kept her on. He complains about her all the time, but he won't do anything about it. This is his trademark. This is why he went to Freud in the first place. He cannot make a move himself. Was he simply surviving or was he gathering experience for this secret book of his which Louise thinks will explode forever the myths of the Wolf-Man? The collected fragments of his literary endeavours. It would destroy me completely by revealing me . . . making me obsolete in absentia. Not even the acknowledgment of a footnote. Back where I began . . . that's what comes of trying to keep up with the Joneses. Okay. Enough of these weighty matters. Louise really does look ill. I said to her: 'That'll be the day,' when she said she might have been ill. I don't know why I say these things. I cheer myself up despite her. I can't help being jovial.

After a while, a very simple truth revealed itself to me: Louise had become his latest analyst. She was getting the words out of him. She was playing his game, becoming his nurse, his Freud, his sister, his muse. I knew she had total control of his manuscript. As for me, it was time to leave.

Come to think of it, it was the best thing I ever did . . . pass Sergei onto someone else.

So, after years of ghost-writing, I'm abandoning the ghost. Holy or otherwise. The inspirator. Reaching for the last breath. Exhausted. It was too much for me to keep maintaining this double-game. I'm going to go it alone now, reaching back through the ganglia of determinism. Cutting loose. Severing the umbilical. Reaching for reality. The bottle. The gun. Whatever comes to hand.

No, not that so much these days. Beaten down by fear. By events . . . those last hold-ups the girls and I did in Germany, simply walking out of the bank and taking the *train*, by God. Just walked into the S-Bahn smoking cigarettes. You see stranger things underground. Women who burst out crying. The despair on the busker's face while he's trying to smile as he sings 'Pennies From Heaven'. The fat man in the sharkskin suit, the fare-avoider who's trying to kiss the feet of the woman ticket-inspector, lurching forward on his knees, his fingers as delicate as a concert pianist's, not quite touching. No, the terror in the banks was quotidian. Down there among the people, in the thick fog of cigarette smoke with the spittle slippery underfoot, it was comic despair, like the Third World discovering Modernism.

Whenever I confided these capers to Wespe, he began giggling for some unknown reason. I saw it as a game too, but I didn't think it was funny. When they got Ursula in a garage after they'd lobbed tear gas canisters through the window, Ursula with nothing on except her panties, when they dragged her out by the hair, her familiar breasts shuddering for the cameras as they handcuffed her, I decided to give it up.

It was no longer fashionable for academics to espouse an ideology that had no ideas. When I told Wespe this, he panicked. He even tried to get rid of Louise, in case she was *morally* preventing me from anything. It was the one thing Louise didn't have . . . morality.

So, after all these years, Sergy, of counselling you, of lending you money, my experience, my car (yes, you drove it without a licence all the way to Baden Baden and back without getting out of second gear—it was a miracle—I sent it to Frankfurt where they made an ad with it: 'a thousand kilometres without changing gear—at Mercedes Benz foolproof means foolproof'), of calming you in a crisis, counselling you, sending you cases of Château Lafitte, of doing odd jobs, of inviting you to the best parties, the best brothels, of getting you to come out, convincing you that your condition was *normal*, a universal predilection for *dirty sex* . . . after all these years of waiting outside tailor shops while you made long-winded overtures to slutty seamstresses as though you were Swann in Proust's nineteenth-century marathon-of-a-novel, I'm finally giving up. You will have to declare yourself. I can't be responsible. Go and confide in your Loulou.

I didn't expect him to take me literally. Louise sent the manuscript of his collected fragments to a Russian friend, S.C. 'Döppelganger' Pankeiev, who called himself a literary agent, with rooms on the Schüttelstrasse. He never returned it. One thing Pankeiev did do was to give him good advice against marrying Louise. 'If you marry that woman,' he wrote to Wespe, 'you'll turn on the gas tomorrow.'

It was Christmas when I finally readied to leave. I sold Sergei's apartment sight-unseen to an American couple for use as a holiday house. They rented it out immediately for two grand a month, advertising it in the *New York Review* as 'a three-room apartment within walking distance of Sig's (sic) house'. They hoped to begin charter tours, build a waxworks museum, conduct fake psychoanalysis sessions whence the client would graduate with a certificate of competence, to set up practice, no doubt, as soon as he or she arrived home. They were a nice, hometown couple in their fifties, and I recognised them as fakes as soon as I met them in Frankfurt. They both had wonderful smiles. They wore Alpine hats with feathers in them. I thought, though, that the waxworks was a little kitsch and told them so, but kitsch is a little hard to explain. They asked about the Wolf-Man. I said I didn't know any Wolf-Man. Now, there was the Wolf-Boy of Aveyron . . . but though he could have growed up, I said, cruising onto the dialect, I guess nobody's heard since. I'll let you know, I twanged, if I hear. You take care now. Something atavistic must have drifted over my unconscious. I was touched.

Christmas. The snow formed a dirty slush outside the big department stores. I bought a bottle of cognac and called on Wespe for the last time. In the crowded street a dirty child sang 'Stille Nacht' very badly over and over again while its mother, one eye closed over, smiled at drunks who wanted to take her (the child at lower price) to a nice warm place. Vienna was a tough town, forget the postcards.

In the pockets of my greatcoat I had a stun grenade and two pistols, both lightweight Steyrs, one with a hair trigger.

I climbed the four storeys to Sergy's door and listened, waiting for my heart to stop thumping. Good. Louise wasn't there. I didn't hear any barking. I knocked. There was no answer. I went to the landing and looked up towards his bathroom. The glass was fogged up. Good. I went back to the door. 'Sergy, it's me, Art,' I yelled. 'I know you're in there. I've come to say goodbye.'

I could hear him shuffling to the door. He unlatched. He was in a profound depression, I could see. The signs? The old faded overcoat that doubled as a dressing gown. He looked like one of his photos, striding . . . yes, striding out as though he had no time then hovering near Berggasse 19, watching as the Freuds departed for England. The furniture. The couch. The Gestapo ringing the building. Here he was in the same mood.

'So. You are leaving,' he said.

'I've failed, Sergy. Failed to live up to your expectations.'

'I do not expect.'

I didn't expect him to finish. When he was in deep depression that was always how it was. Half sentences. Cryptic phrases. Probably the product of some sort of amnesia as well. An old man's voice with no point of address . . . but to keep going it needs points of contact . . . assents, grunts, nods.

'Come and.'

I entered. Closed the door. He went behind me to latch it. I sniffed. No *odor di femmina*. Cigar smoke, that is. I sat down on the couch.

'I'm not feeling too.'

'It's okay, Sergy. No good getting sentimental.'

He'd been drinking foul coffee. He went off to get changed. This was his way. A gentleman to the last. I studied the wall of books. Insurance manuals. He returned in a pin-striped suit. He had a brush in each hand and was carding back his hair. He hunched down on the sofa. Fiddled with his spectacles.

'I didn't know you wore spectacles.'

I waited for a dumb joke to come to mind. Something about reading with two hands to prevent blindness. But he looked too depressed.

Here was Wespe, this grand neurotic, the king of dreams and prince of pulp sitting in what could only be described as squalor. Erotic magazines spewed out of the cushions. Cigar stubs flowered, mashed into the carpets. Empty wine flagons nurtured a slow growth of green mould. He's really messed his

194

nest. Must have had a fight with Louise. I can't quite bring myself to say it. That I'd sold the apartment. In spite of everything he was on the rise. Yes, that was the paradox. Maybe that's why I made a supreme effort and reassured him.

'Sergy, you don't have to worry about a thing. This place is yours. *Mi casa su casa.*

'What?' he asked.

Loulou would cheat him too. For a writer he had too many visitors. Too many people from Porlock, ghosts at the gate. Don't blame me. I tried to do my best.

'You know,' he suddenly said, 'literature killed me.'

Who did he think he was, Tolstoy? Tolstoy went and bought a peasant smock and thought he was getting down to the grassroots of life. He died in a railway station. The waiting-room. He loved his country, but he always had intentions of going somewhere else.

'Come on, Sergy, you're not ready for the Bahnhof yet, are you?'

'Steinhof.'

'What?'

'My Elba. Perhaps one day they'll call me the Napoleon of crime.'

'Yes, on second thoughts I'd love one.'

He went off to get two glasses. He opened my cognac. He looked like death. I knew the feeling. He was in the middle of a book. I was sensitive to the artist's suffering. Professional delay. It was rough squeezing the muse. Some days it's all cold comfort. Refrigerators. None of that for me. I wrote facts. Real life. Fuck inspiration. Stories. Hot air. Cheers.

'I'm so sad you're leaving, Artie.'

At first I thought he said 'glad'. He's warmed up at last. A roseate glow in his cheeks. Sign of a heart condition.

I smiled. 'What you writing, Sergy?'

He smiled. 'Have you been doing things lately?'

'What things?' What things did he mean? Dirty things? He made his fingers into a gun. Oh. Extracurricular stuff.

'You know me, Sergy, I'm finished with all that,' I said.

That's why I'm going back to Australia, where the air is

fresh and the beaches beckon and the women stare at you straight in the eye and call you 'mate'. Linearity. A paradise for the masculine. I hadn't been back for twenty years. I needed some *identity*. Yes, I needed to go where all the cows, kangaroos and rabbits were looking jittery . . . the land of meat and the *hunt*, by God . . . there's some fanaticism and evangelism there that calls me to it.

Twenty years in the cut and thrust of psychoanalysis, making it to the top of the tree. Then there was nothing to do anymore. I saw the same thing happening to Sergy. When the analysts finished with him they dumped him. I saw him giggle and take huge delight in my antics across the border. Every time I came back with the girls he asked for news, smacking his lips. I embellished things at first. But when I saw how happy he was, rubbing his stomach with that happiness that you got from Alka-seltzer, the relief of pain, as Freud said, which was happiness, I fed him the truth now and again. One reward you get as a therapist . . . you see the pure joy you can give to someone . . . and the good part is that you know it won't last and that you'll always get paid for it.

'There's something I would like to give.'

'Me?'

I didn't expect that. I was going to say no, but he had already stood up and was making for his study. I didn't follow. A man's study is his castle. I went to the bathroom.

There were curtains on the windows. I pulled them aside. Outside, Vienna smoked in mid-winter comfort. Giant Christmas trees blinked from the park. The roads were furrowed black and white. A horse-drawn carriage full of shouting people trundled up the Ausstellungs Strasse. There was a hole in the wall. No more typewriter. No painting. I went out after shooting at a bobbing cigar stub with piss.

'Say, Sergy, where's the IBM?'

'Oh,' he said, rummaging around still, 'I use pencil and paper now.'

Easier to keep it to yourself. Indecipherable. To scratch and to hide therein.

'I write more slowly.'

He did everything more slowly. He ambled back with some sort of ceramic dildo which he promptly broke in half on the side of the table. He handed me the top bit.

'What's this? A vulcanised penis from Pompei? A fossilised phallus?'

I was half-joking. He was serious.

'Freud gave that to me. The ancient Greeks called it a *Symbolon*. Whenever visitors left, the hosts broke something like this in half and gave the other bit to them. It ensured their return . . . or the return of the pieces.'

Fragments always turned up in strange places.

'Freud gave you this?' I was overawed. It was a good likeness . . . to a penis, I mean. The circumsised helmet looked like a Conquistador's. A few drops of powder fell out onto the carpet like pepper. 'How old is this thing?'

'Ancient Greece,' Sergy said. 'As old as Plato.'

I didn't dispute that. I put the piece in my pocket, carefully keeping it separate from the stun grenade. All this hardware made my coat droop. I looked baggy. I noticed Sergy wore a stained cravat. We sat down again. He put a finger to his nose, brushed his white moustache backwards and forwards. I knew this habit of his. It was confession time.

'Now that you're going I suppose I can tell you something I've told no one else,' he said, almost in a whisper. He seemed to be listening. 'Loulou will be back soon,' he flicked a finger at the door. 'She's voracious for gossip like this, you know.'

I knew. If she knew this was happening, the Steyr pistols might just be what I would need.

'Years ago, ' he said, 'I had a problem with ( ).'

He inscribed brackets with his fingers. What was the significance of this? Nothing? The world? Buttocks? Dramatic irony?

'With masturbation,' he explained. 'Whenever I did that ( ), something bad always happened afterwards. I can tell you the number of times that's occurred, the ( ) and the ill luck, the misfortunes, the curses.'

'But surely,' I said, busily making mental notes, I should have had a tape machine in my pocket instead, 'this was only superstition.'

'No,' he exclaimed, almost shouting. 'It was straight cause and effect. A little ( ) and the world went bad. Onanism was a kind of omission, you see. It left out the world, its content, swerved into the backside of the universe, and when the world caught up with me it let me have it with catastrophe.'

Deviating from home, a way back through a back way is also punishable, for ( ) is not fear of emptiness, but inspiration against the law.

'That's just a fanciful theory,' I said. I'd learned at graduate school not to pamper the patient. Bullying was better. If you bullied you got results.

'No, no,' he cried. He made some sort of Russian gesture with his hands. 'No,' he said, 'it's no theory. Maybe unconsciously I knew something bad was coming, so I indulged myself.'

That made sense.

'I did it before Father's death. I did it the day before both wars were declared. The day before Thérèse's suicide, on the morning before Freud's death. These are just the significant dates. Everyday life was filled with millions of minor hazards. I was insatiable for their history. ( )ing was not only preserving and controlling them, but setting off the world, the train of events.'

I laughed. Laughing in the face of adversity sometimes helped.

'You don't mean to tell me you indulged in this kind of obsessive and superstitious pessimism?'

'That's what it means to be a neurotic.'

Oh, my. Poor old Sergy. I felt a vast amount of sympathy for him. This was professional suffering of the worst kind. He looked at me.

'That's what I *did*. That was the cause of everything . . . that loss of secrecy. The world joined me . . . it *responded* . . . with a kind of malevolent delight. The first time must have been at the age of six. Can you believe that? Six years before normal puberty. Six years in advance of those muscle bound boys boasting of expositions . . . the first time was a great celebration of precocity. I was going to be the genius of ( ), the Mozart

198

of masturbation. But as luck would have it, Nanya told me it was dirty. 'You dirty little boy,' she screamed. Then she gave me a sly look. That was the look of the world. Suspicion. From that time onwards, everybody doubted me . . . everyone except Anna. That was because she knew it was triumphant foresight for someone as retrospective as myself. I knew disaster was coming. One of my best dates was October 24th, old calendar, 1917. I must have been in Odessa. At a concert, in my private box with Thérèse. They were performing the 1812 Overture. "Isn't it wonderful?" Thérèse screamed. It was the first time I'd seen her excited. "Terrible," I shouted. I knew disaster was coming. And of course the next day . . .'

'Ten days that shook the world.'

He shrugged. 'You pay for ecstasy. It got so bad I couldn't even go to the mailbox . . . in case there was bad news.'

He needed disaster. What's more, he had come out of his depression. Everyone knows when you're depressed you can't do it. Loneliness. This is what killed people. Writers. Holed up in their rooms half listening to the world outside and half despising it. He needed people, talk, a bevy of women analysts. He positively lit up when I used to bring around the girls.

The girls. Most of them are in German and Italian prisons, looking beautiful and suicidal. One has bought a Harley. She doesn't know when she'll get to ride it. Maybe in twenty years. The authorities were on my trail too. I knew that and spread some rust over my roots. I was only a bit player, and for a time they were confused about my status. If ideas killed they would have got me a long time ago. But now . . . now. I had to clean up after my friends. Dispose of things. Learn to forget.

'But what happens now, as an octogenarian? Things slow down. No more predictions, no more wanking-spanking. But you know what?' he asked, his eyes twinkling, 'The bills keep coming in.'

I asked what he meant.

'It's the way I act,' Sergei said. 'I can't help it. People think I'm terribly wealthy. It's part of my attraction, no?'

He took out a cigarette from a crushed packet and lit it. He sneezed. Let out a howl after the sneeze. Now and again he became a backwoods millionaire, like his Grandad. I've seen Louise and him slap each other around like a couple of raw-boned peasants. Freud called it phylogenesis. I stood up. Drained my glass. I adhered to the age-old interruption of the session, only this time I wasn't coming back. It was a good time to leave anyway, while he was exultant.

'Yes,' I said. 'One day your identity will fit your circumstances.'

We embraced. He wasn't really thinking of me.

'Ha! 1917. Life was simpler then. Everybody was dizzy with events. Nobody analysed, you know. Neurosis disappeared . . . .'

I left him standing on the landing waving me off with a handkerchief. He mumbled something about action and inaction.

'My greatest failure,' he said, 'was everyday life.'

I noticed through the railings as I descended that his shoes were scuffed. He made arabesques of smoke with his hand.

'I tried to break away, but I kept coming back out of habit. Routine is a great killer.'

Already a shadow, the world closing in. He left out any mention of his sister's suicide. He, of course, had become her, hiding her, encrypting her name, fearful of betraying poetic intuition.

'Goodbye,' I kept saying, until there was only my own voice. His mailbox was overflowing. The bills kept coming in. That was his hold on reality. As long as he was keeping the wolf from the door. Good for him, I thought.

Outside it was still snowing. I made my way back to my hotel. In front of the department stores the child and its mother were still singing. One of the stores was still open, doing a brisk trade. Last-minute shoppers who were ready to buy anything. I cruised the floors and found myself in the children's section. Huge stuffed bears gaped from the shelves. Clockwork tanks lined up. Replica machine guns were the most popular items. They filled bins and were topped with signs that had the previous prices Xed out. It mimicked the arms race: lower prices for better guns. This business of death moved me. There was a sort of generosity in society when it came to defense. It reminded me of the way some countries doled out rifles to every household.

I was like a doting father. I had misty memories of Gudrun's face when she told me she was pregnant and was returning to her parents' place in Strasbourg. She relented at the last moment and half invited me to go with her. I decided against it. I spoke the language crudely and she was by far too strong for me. I could see myself stranded with a kid giving English lessons in a tenement and listening for the cathedral bells to break the monotony.

Eager fathers become boys. Some of them were trying out the hardware. I walked between the tables and the bins and put the Steyrs among the replica pistols and the stun grenade beside the replica grenades. You couldn't tell the difference. Some kid would shoot his father for Christmas. No, there were no bullets and the grenade was disarmed. I'm through with taking chances. I wasn't going to walk around Vienna with all that in my coat pockets in terror of having my balls blown off.

The next morning I caught my Qantas flight for Sydney. It was strange hearing the accent again. The wine tasted of the sun. I vowed once that I would never return. As an orphan who never adopted anybody or anything, I felt slightly prodigal, winging to Mama when things got tough. But then I was mistaken. Things were going to get tougher.

The Catacomb Diaries V

Shreee. The wind. From about three-thirty in the afternoon these places become tombs. Something about the imminence of snow. A solitary child, singing and skipping, marks time. A deserted railway station. It is the hour of the telephone, its ring cleaving the world in two, brooding, black. Afternoons and evenings of another place. A dog barks.

The telephone was ringing in my boarding house in Katoomba. Nobody ever answered it. I listened to it ringing off and then heard it ring again. It was a morbid sound. When I worked as a gravedigger down the mountain a bit, I often had to dig up old graves. Sometimes folks used to ask me to pound down the bones a little, put the dust in a tin for them. Most times nobody claimed the sites and the Department of Health issued orders for body removals. I put 'BR' on a stake and drove it into the ground. Make room for others. I exhumed what was left of the coffins and put the bones, if any, in a chamber in a wall. It was one wall of what we called head-quarters, for obvious reasons. Sometimes I found things buried with the body. Once I found an old phone, Bell vintage with a crank handle, in a first-class coffin. I polished it up. Sold it for a good price.

Now it sounds like it's ringing. For me.

I doze a little. Think of the past. I've come a long way down. One thing about lying low . . . nobody bothers you. I can't stand it. I get up and pick up the receiver.

'Hello?' It's a woman's voice. Deep. Lived-in.

'Yes?'

'I would like to make a reservation for this weekend.'

The accent was high-ball. Tinge of foreign.

'Uh-huh.'

202

I played along a bit. Always try and see how far things go.
'Just for Friday and Saturday nights.'
When she said 'Saturday' I knew she was a Yank.
'What sort of hotel is it? I mean, are there views?'
'Family,' I said. 'And all the views you want . . . Three Sisters, Echo Point, Jamison Valley . . . all the breathtaking anxieties you need for doing it, you know.'
I could tell she was a DW. Dirty Weekender. You always get the women ringing for reservations, asking for family hotels. Most DW's make like they wouldn't stay even if it was the Hilton. Then they succumb, as if doing you a favour. That's what my landlady, old Mrs Harris says, anyway.
'Excuse me? Have I got the right number?'
'Sure. I mean doing the sights . . . taking in the air. It's the best time of the year.'
'Are you Leura or Katoomba?'
'Both. Bed and breakfast and meals too.'
'I don't know.'
'Like to make a booking? What's your name?'
'Are you five star? The Alpine Lodge?'
'No lady. We're half a star at most. But that don't mean we're not in the universe. In fact, we're an imploded star, a black hole. We suck them right in. I mean, we're cheap, but we got the best views for free if you walk a couple of miles. Okay. This is the Alpine, but it's not the Lodge. It's the Alpine-Aeneas B & B with outside toilets and bargain basement rooms, no windows, dodgy plumbing, bedpans and bugs . . . oh, and there's a surcharge on Sundays . . . and no blood on the sheets.'
She hung up.
Bad jokes. The peace and quiet forces you into it. Never mind. Her voice intrigued me. She'll no doubt ring the Lodge and complain. Nobody gives a damn. I'll get Mrs Harris a bottle of Hospital brandy and we'll have a good laugh about it.

Come Friday and I was thinking I'd mosey on over . . . take a peek at the Lodge, see if a Yank turns up. Nothing to do anyway. Sometimes . . . depends if Madame Fleury is watching the kitchen like a brooding hen or not, I saunter up the back and share a few aubergines or left-over *coqs au vin*, or *carreaux d'agneau* with Jacky Callucio, who's supposed to be a French chef, tossing things up in the air with half a cigarette in his mouth and dirty fingernails, but who's really an Italian railway cook who got lucky with Madame Fleury once on a long haul from Adelaide. Old Calluch tolerates me. Now and again I fence a few things for him . . . silverware, old lace, a couple of cases of Veuve Clicquot. I take them over to other hotels, work the bosses around, give Calluch seventy-five per cent. It's a good partnership. With fifty-fifty you got no pressure, no leverage, on either side. I liked the crowds, the conventions, the meetings. I couldn't do without this social agenda.

But now and again, not too often, after many glasses of cognac in the dawn's early light, Calluch and I ventured onto great themes in the kitchen of the Alpine Lodge. Calluch had the kind of capacity for living and dying you saw in Italian operas. Everything could either be farce or tragedy. I thought I could see a book in Calluch, perhaps a ghost of a chance. Then the idea faded with the mornings. But under the cloudless skies of the *petite champagne*, he became lyrical. 'At our age,' he said, waving his arms about, dressed in a dirty singlet (this was his attire for cooking. Only later in the night would he don his spotless white jacket and toque and mingle with the clientele), 'at our age women are like cheese. We develop a taste for the soft and the fat. The closer we get to death the closer we get to Mamma.'

Calluch had no illusions. If everybody were as open, psychiatrists would be queuing for soup. Verdi knew his minestrone. That's why he dispensed with psychological depth early. No lyrics to be found in the unconscious. Audiences didn't want it. But what am I saying? I once had that game mastered. *Nostalgie de la boue*. Calluch mixes with the rich and famous during liqueur-and-coffee time. He stands at their tables wearing his white jacket which covers an impressive belly. Sometimes he leaves the bottom button undone, revealing a hairy navel, which he has decorated with a diamond. When he pushes Madame Fleury's best cognac on the crowds, he is exhorting them from the very basement of culture. Reality is crudity. Like Brecht, he appealed a great deal to some women. The Alpine Lodge began to have a reputation. It serviced the rich, the famous and the infamous ... DW's all. Politicians dined there. The Yank, Calluch had discovered, was the widow of a former Minister. She was going to check in tonight.

So I hid in the shrubbery about eight with a bottle and it started getting cold when I'd finished it. I watched for Calluch, who would come out to empty stuff in the garbage. He would know, he said, when she arrived, because Fleury would be in a fluster. I didn't even see the car. It was a black Porsche, chauffeur-driven. (Was he the lover, sitting so intimately with her in the cockpit?) Calluch was banging on the garbage tins. 'That's she,' he shouted, *'La Signora della notte.'* He pumped his fist. I crept round to the front. She must have just stepped out of the car, bringing with her a fragrance of perfume upon fur, which is a very different smell from perfume upon skin. Peered in. Saw her back. She was tall, straight, her dark hair pinned up. She wore a black dress that made the most of her shapeliness. But then she sort of duck-walked over to the newspaper rack and stood athletically on her toes, up and down, up and down, like a ballerina. I didn't need to look at her face to know who she was.

'Ludmilla,' I whispered from the door, croaking like a frog from the night air and burning whisky. It was a sound only she could have heard.

'Doctor Ludmilla Wittgenstein,' she said without turning. 'What do you want?'

KATOOMBA

1978

And now it is snowing heavily. Although it is late afternoon it is almost pitch black. The main street of Katoomba powders its brick-faced severity and sports a truly alpine look in the street lighting. You turn right at the bottom of the street, creep along the hedges and fences muffled and slow and white and wait for a couple of Range Rovers to pass. Lost, they look for richer places to graze, arcing their high-beams through the snow. You stare at the occupants. Their smiles are ringed with wine and satiety. They will go back to their hotels to spend the evening fucking, swimming in the heated pools, testing each other's tensions. Friends. You've forgotten what they meant. How they felt. What solidity they had. You stand on street corners. You do not hear the moans and the grunts and the words which used to give you erections. You hear instead the rumbles in your stomach. These are more important.

It was like that the night you saw Ludmilla again. The snow caking your shoulders and hat, the rumble of your stomach. The ache of love, which was like a hand tightening around your testicles. It's difficult to say how it felt, to see someone with whom you were intimate so many years ago, to be prepared to be shocked at the ravages to her face, to be embarrassed at the old love you shared, to feel a tremor in the stomach at the sight of a smile you'd forgotten and to remember the idiosyncracies of her coming, the soft oh! and the oh, oh! and the yes! please, again please, she would whisper and the severity of the *coup de grâce* . . . lay me, oh, lay me, it began like a roundel . . . you fuckinsonofabitch!

She hadn't changed at all. She looked beautiful. Perhaps thinner, darker, more Indian. She looked short-sighted. She

206

had a few grey hairs. Everything else was in place.
'Who are you?' she asked, in the foyer of the Alpine Lodge.

The Catacomb Diaries VI

Artie, I said. Artie Catacomb.

I could see her mind flick through her Roladex. Where in the fuck had I met this tramp? She thought long and hard and then made her face smile. Hello? she asked, as if entering a strange and empty house. Then it clicked. I was thinking the same thing and held up my middle finger. Some sort of phylogenetic memory must have creased her unconscious then, some masterful finger of fate teasing and caressing her primal sexuality and she must have jumped, felt the icy imprint of a fossil.

Artie! she said, and approached and I thought of her tennis dress and the little pom poms on her socks and the frilly underpants, as she bounced across to me. Kissed me on the corner of the mouth. Still played a nice game. Madame Fleury cleared her throat. We went over. Shook hands with the vamp umpire. Ludmilla asked me to dinner.

What happened next I'm embarrassed to report. Suffice to say that Ludmilla held up a mirror to me and in the course of that evening and others, I sifted through shame, pride, humility and despair. Mostly despair. I had not realised how far down the chasm I had slipped. I stank, both physically and mentally, though the mental stink somewhat became me. I saw integrity there still. But this was vastly mistaken. Nothing was rounded and whole. Not even testicles, as Ludmilla said. We made up these things to feel good about ourselves. To shape identity. Yes, Ludmilla dragged me into the pits of myself, scoured the foetid tanks of my soul and for two or three days we dined and drank and talked all in the most civilized manner. We cared for each other without stepping over boundaries. I say this without irony, or even parody. In my state these were as salt and pepper and when your meal was dry bread you depended on them. But Ludmilla fed me emotion and substance. I dispensed with the grain of salt. I began to desire.

After hating myself a good deal and then smelling ambition which was like fresh air instead of the sewer, Ludmilla spoke about her life. I did not pry. She said very little. She came up to Katoomba to sleep. Not around, just to sleep. She had no lover, she revealed charmingly, rolling her eyes at the ceiling. She knew the place had a reputation. She suffered from a sleeping sickness. Something she must have picked up in India. That's why she had a chauffeur. Her face had hardly changed since the time I knew her as a young lecturer. It must have been all that beauty sleep. Ludmilla recounted parts of her life and fell asleep at the table. Callucio the chef was insulted. He brought out cognac while Ludmilla snored.

'She's quite a broad,' Calluch said.

'Sssh. Calluch, do you mind? She's an old friend, a dear friend.'

'Look at her sleep. Not many have witnessed this sight.'

'Calluch, if you go on like this I'll have to ask you to leave.'

'Do you think she'll wake if I touch her?'

'Don't touch.'

Callucio looked at me unsteadily. 'You'd better get her to bed,' he said, stroking the back of Ludmilla's hand. She woke, withdrew her hand.

'Let's go to bed,' she said, giving both of us the most disarming smile. The invitation was not ambiguous. We took her up to her room, Calluch on one side, his hand gallantly or lasciviously, it was of no matter, on her elbow. At her door she kissed both of us gently, and without a word, closed the door very slowly. Calluch tried to jam his foot in at the last moment. I pulled him back. I was in love with Ludmilla. There was no question about it. After all these years I suddenly fell irretrievably in love. It was not a pleasant sensation. I had to hold my chest to control the beating of my heart. I wanted to die. I wanted to write. Tears gathered in my eyes, refused to fall in that immense sadness. Through a kind of magnification

I saw Calluch adjusting the front of his trousers. He must have noticed my confusion. 'One man's meat . . . ' he said groaning slightly. I reached for what I thought was a small log near the fireplace out in the foyer. Love was the enemy of lust. I swung it at the back of his head. It was a sodden, rolled up newspaper. Outside, under the streetlamp, I tried to master my breathing. I thought of sending Ludmilla flowers in the morning. I had no money. It was winter. I unrolled the heavy paper. On the front page was a photo of Ludmilla. *Renowned psychoanalyst Dr Ludmilla Wittgenstein, once confidante to famous Freudian patients (among whom was the famous Wolf-Man), is to head a conference in the Blue Mountains*, the caption read. I knew of course that Ludmilla was too young to have worked with such patients. She had certainly never met the Wolf-Man. I read on. She had come to Sydney in the seventies, the report said. Married a Minister in the State government. He was killed in a car crash when Ludmilla fell asleep at the wheel. She occupies a chair at a university now.

She was a blatant liar and an immodest self-promoter. I was in love with her, probably on account of this imperfection.

But let's leave it at that. It's curious what attracts at my age. Perhaps vanity. Yet after that weekend I ploughed on alone, traced the furrows of the past five or so years with a stone in my heart, an irritation, this thing that might be love. I restrained myself from putting pen to paper. Maybe I should have. It would have sent me back a sharp message of bile and balefulness . . . or florid inanities. Three or four weeks passed. I was almost cured. The telephone rang for me again. It was an expression of loyalty, of faith to a chemical principle: requited phone calls. Her voice filtered down the line in accented English, deep, rich, with a singsong suggestiveness. A night out at the opera. I couldn't abide the opera. What you saw at the opera was death and farce. The farce was on the stage. When I used to go to the opera in Vienna I used to return home feeling as if I'd gone to a funeral. Grave-digging cured me of funerals for a while. But Ludmilla and the opera was a strange combination.

It's difficult now to recount in detail all those evenings spent with her. She bought me a new set of clothes, polished me up, filled me in on intellectual matters, theories, events since the time I left Europe. Nothing much had changed. There was of course a new terminology for old ideas. At first I commuted on the Harley-Davidson from the Mountains, but it wasn't before long that I was cohabiting with Ludmilla at Woolwich Point as her live-in lover, or, in the new langauge, as her partner.

She changed.

Of course I'd expected something like that. To be fair, I must have done so myself. My fastidiousness, my jaundiced view of the world returned. She became extremely untidy after a couple of days. Left her underwear in the kitchen sink, her tampons in the wastebasket. And if it wasn't for the maid . . . the less said the better. For a few weeks I was able to do something I was unable to do for a long time. Ludmilla had the most beautiful and complete library. It was wall-to-wall books in the front room right up to the French windows which opened out onto the lawn and the rose bushes and then the cypress hedge which guarded the place from the road. The salt wind pushed right up into the pages of my book. The Sydney winter had turned golden and crisp and time served contemplation and there was a sort of bliss which cruised along a foolish route in search of age-old ambitions. Ludmilla accommodated me. She was wonderfully calm in her untidy world. She slipped in and out of rooms, in and out of the house in the silence of silk and scent. We filled Byzantine afternoons gliding and skating on velvet recollections, wine and tender love-making. She was athletic but gentle. She grew old. She slept in my moments of transformation, between the folds of reverie and intention.

When I grew tired of reading and writing I began to walk. This was always fatal. Walking crystallised things. I saw that Ludmilla's smile was crooked. That her face was only fully symmetrical when she was frowning. I was shocked to recollect that she frowned almost all the time. I thought it was this love that made her sad, the guilt of the memory of her dead husband. She only lectured once a week. That was the privilege of occupying a chair. She really didn't have to teach at all. She attended meetings, did research, was writing three books. I thought all this must have pressed upon her. Sobriety taken

to extremes. It was like a bad memory. I was surprised I had
come this far. At the point of the peninsula a rounded cul-de-
sac of white houses and terracotta roofs made me unwelcome.
No access to the water. I retreated, sat awhile on a stone
stanchion near a park and watched the barges make their way
up the river. Over at the Cockatoo Island dockyard I heard the
steady pounding of steam hammers and the attrition of steel
and despite marking down the present moment, lost myself in
bending words. *Mon semblable, mon frère*, I said, seeing a small
boy read the ripples as he skimmed rocks over the water. I
turned and something caught my eye. Behind the privet a
movement. An old woman, almost doubling over, pushed a
manual mower over a green felt lawn and shooed away the
birds. She concentrated fiercely on the slanting rows of rolled
grass. She walked and pushed with such small movements it
was as though she were in Victorian garb and the mower was
a pram and she was in Hyde Park. I wondered at such propriety and care and obsession. Then she seemed to fix me with
a beady eye, and though I suspected she couldn't see me
because of the angle of the hedge, she spat directly at me.

I thought of my mother. She was like that. I interrupted her
routine, her life. I remembered that she always used to buy me
a shawl for Hanukkah, present it to me with the same propriety and ceremony and then as she put it around my shoulders she would grab my arm and pinch me hard on the inside
of my biceps, where it hurt most. 'Promise me', she would say,
'that you will never become *ambivalent* about your faith and
your people.' I promised. I didn't know what ambivalent
meant, and when I bound my arm with the phylactery and
only used my right hand for writing I thought I was following
her commandment.

Then one day I left forever, joined the Communist Party, and
began my life of fakery. I wasn't always called Catacomb.
When I went underground I changed my name.

I walked back to Ludmilla's place and savoured the thought
of an afternoon of books, Baroque music, a glass or two of
wine, and most of all, splendid isolation. No such luck.
Ludmilla was there, lounging on the settee wearing a pair of
very large spectacles. I suddenly felt alien, dispossessed. Rau-

cous birds, mynahs, were fighting on the lawn. Behind Ludmilla, on a small table, was a vase of Deadly Nightshade.

I lose faith sometimes, when faced with the almost instinctive dissembling of human nature. I gave up the Sergei Wespe Project because of a kind of transference which precluded objectivity. I gave up other solutions because of his charm, his passivity, the doleful simpering dog-like face. I thought the keepers of the flame of Freud had nothing to fear. How wrong I was! Wespe was a dissembler, so was Ludmilla, and, for that matter, so was I. Ludmilla looked at me with owl-eyes. She sprang lightly off the settee and made me a drink, a cocktail with an olive, if I remember correctly. At that moment I had a strange wish to kill her, even before she spoke. I had a premonition of what she was about to say, and knew suddenly in this plush living-room, in this high-class suburb where I was sure I didn't belong, in this love which wasn't love (indeed, was I capable, was I *honest* enough to find love, that *permanent* thing that people talk so much about? Wasn't love a momentary obsession which ebbed and flowed like the tide, amorphous, ill-defined and a function of error and loyalty to error?), in this relation which was nothing but a trade-off, in this exchange, I knew that she had ladled favours on me to lure back a spirit from the past.

'I'd like you to use your influence,' she said matter-of-factly, 'to see if you could invite Wespe to Sydney for my international conference.'

She jiggled her drink and tucked her feet under her like a duck.

I was adamant that I would take no part in this project.

'The trip would kill him,' I said. 'He's an old and frail man. He's not been out of Vienna for almost thirty years. And Sydney,' I sighed, 'what would he make of Sydney?'

'What do you care about that?' Tossing her head, she got up, padded to the French windows, stretched a leg out backwards, extended her arms back and forth, pirouetted, took the bouquet of Deadly Nightshade and made a mock proposal of them.

There it was, this seed of excitement wrought out of disillusionment with Ludmilla, the thought appearing immediately that she was using me as bait, that I was some cog in a long-term plan to set the engines of her career rolling again. More importantly, I was already manufacturing the visitation of inspiration: The Wolf-Man would visit Australia and the trip would be the final crowning glory of analytical success, and I would make my mark upon history in this celebration of Antipodean analysis by writing *my* memoirs, of a famous patient of *mine*. Yes, *The Wolf-Man in Katoomba* would be the first of many titles. One could imagine the rest. Without the balance of this condition, of this restoration of a missing narrative, there could only be catastrophe. Everyday life.

Thus, Ludmilla was offering, if not an Arabian night, then at least an arabesque. Her suggestion was keeping Wespe alive . . . keeping us all alive by repeating the past without returning to it.

Sergei would have appeared pale, loitering by the luggage carousel, a shadow of himself.

Ludmilla and I take him to the waiting car and she talks while he listens, deathly, the way a ghost listens, troubled by old age, forgetful, cantankerous. He puts on a pair of sunglasses and hardly takes them off again during the three days of his stay. He asks me several times what my name is, and takes Ludmilla's hand and presses it to his chest. She is delighted, in her new tight skirt and weightier hips . . . she has eaten for this. We take him to the harbour, to the beaches, and though everything sparkles and though we want to celebrate, Wespe looks dark. He is about to collapse at any moment. He says he has been thrust into the present too brutally. He did not like aeroplanes. He said he slept twice during the long trip and twice he woke within a dream and could not truly waken. All this had exhausted him.

At the Sydney conference a thousand people turn up, but he barely speaks. He mumbles about being disoriented, he repeats himself. Ludmilla is embarrassed and furious, and doesn't know which feeling is stronger. Up in Katoomba he is restored to some semblance of health. He is less absorbed. Up in Katoomba the élite of the élite of the world of psychoanalysis gather for this one and only occasion, to listen to

Sergei Wespe give his last speech on the subject of his analysis with Freud.

And so . . . in the Everglades Motel there is a large conference room. This afternoon there is standing room only. Outside, the leaves have turned golden and red and across the valley small groups of golfers pull their buggies towards escarpments, stand on the edge of sheer cliffs to contemplate their putts. Their smugness is alien, but the air is crisp with anxiety. Winter in these parts lights up the spirit. The sky is metallic with cold, blue that is deep, the blue of outer space, afternoons like this I may have nodded at my desk or listened for the distant freedom of a churchbell, or fought back from contemplation floating in solitude in the ambergris of lives fragrant with other people's happiness, which for me were morbid secretions, things they had discarded without digesting, the shape of time, love, abandonment, the imponderable sadness within beauty.

On a distant hill out along the Narrow Neck Peninsula, Ludmilla, Wespe and I had spent the morning, picnicking among the low heather tuned brittle and brown with cold. We sat, the three of us, in some sort of golden frieze, with the sun at our backs, and formed a triangle of worship, our bodies fusing and reforming under the changing light, a sort of Vincian metamorphosis which must have inspired the Wolf-Man, because then he rose and smiled and said that 'the scene we made was what Freud would have painted with his intellect', and that he 'felt that a wolf had been let loose in these hills' for that purpose.

At that point I had this terrible urge to push him over the edge. I wanted just a sign of his ingenuousness, a breeze on the surface of water, something never to be forgotten. But what I saw was a leaf being sucked down forever.

At the conference his speech was truly memorable, though few could repeat it:

'Between you and me,' The Wolf-Man said in part to his audience, 'between this time and that time, there is only you and me, interwoven; the orchid opening and closing its petals,

215

the wasp folding and unfolding its wings; the wasp becoming orchid. What is the point of such mimicry? Not life, surely, nor death, but a movement between, like two points of light flicking on and off alternately. The appearance of a path. Blinding speed. Dizzying, painful, never at rest, merging into each other.'

These were the templets of his character. Back and forth. The body's orientation. Parodies and paradigms.

The Wolf-Man went on. He spoke about Anna and their childhood games.

'We were framed,' he said, 'by the notion of performance, both our's and Freud's. And we destroyed ourselves with the notion of perfection.'

I understood what he meant that morning. Picture frames, stage borders, movie screens, window frames, primal scenes, margins.

Afterwards, at dinner in the Paragon restaurant, Wespe indulged in a little more of his performative. Sitting in the back dining-room decorated with bizarre badges and banners of past Rotary Conventions, we listened dolefully to a recording of Jacqueline du Pré playing 'The Dying Swan'.

'Jacqueline du Pré,' Wespe said. 'She died of a crippling disease.'

'MS,' Ludmilla said, wiping her mouth with a napkin and ordering more wine at the same time.

'My initials inverted,' Sergei Wespe said.

'Which is what swans do when they die,' Ludmilla said, cleaning her teeth with her tongue and pulling a compact out of a large bag, 'invert, that is.'

'At least the first part of the word, the S and the W,' Wespe said.

'The head and the neck,' Ludmilla observed.

It was the first time since he arrived that you saw a spark of life in him. Ludmilla's doe eyes were on fire. Atavism. Lost displays. Most of us had been blind to this fold.

'You know, you remind me so much of my sister Anna. You are a mirror-image.'

'And what about the tail-end of the word, the A, N and S?' Ludmilla asked, fawning, diabolical.

216

Wespe smiled. I had never seen him smile so much. This is a coup for Ludmilla. I saw my memoirs sliding into the chute of her bottomless handbag.

'Only U are missing,' Wespe guffawed.

KATOOMBA

1978

Of course none of this had really occurred yet. They were parts . . . synecdoches to be fitted together, tiles of recognition the ancient Greeks broke off for their guests.

When Ludmilla suggested a huge fee for Wespe's appearance in Australia, you lost your temper. Such pragmatics destroyed the idyll of transcendence.

'He's not a pauper,' you shouted.

'But *you* are,' she responded, cooly, truly.

You didn't really have an argument. Ludmilla fell asleep quite suddenly and that made you think things over in a more rational way. Which is the more vindictive way, something to which you never subscribed. So you shouted 'whore!' and spat at her sleeping form and left. Of course her life with you was over, whether you went ahead with her plan or not. You rode the Harley back to Katoomba, exceeding the speed limit by a uniform twenty kilometres per hour. Mrs Harris, the landlady, was delighted to see you. 'I knew it wouldn't last,' she said. 'You're one of us.'

Backsliding is a bulwark against loneliness.

He ( )s his eyes. The window opens by itself. There is nothing there.
No one. Nothing but a white expanse. Nothing.

KATOOMBA

1978

So now it is almost dark and the snow has eased to occasional tiny flakes and your poncho is soaked and your greatcoat is damp but you don't feel cold for you have walked quite a long way from the bookshop and the centre of town. You veer from your usual furrow, which is down to Echo Point, up Cliff Drive and off to Megalong Road, past the Ritz Nursing Home, back to Katoomba with a drink or two at the Metropole Hotel, another one or two at the Carrington, on the verandah, then along the main street peering into howling alleys which lovers favour, the girl's back against the slimy wall, legs around his buttocks, she groans, sees you, smiles, and silently you shuffle on thinking age is not despair but a basic drive to discover the centre of yourself, which, when it arrives, is a deserted aerodrome with grass sprouting out of cracks in the tarmac, empty, flightless, always with an impending drama which unfurls out of the past . . . a girl's shriek at the moment of climax . . . that is when something dies, she shrieks for you and not for you . . . and then back to the Aeneas guesthouse. This is life as an almost-tramp. In New Zealand, you understand, they advertise tramping as a tourist activity. But this evening you find yourself heading for Narrow Neck instead. Narrow Neck: the name strikes fear in the hearts of walkers who have braved it in winter . . . a sliver of a track running between sheer cliffs, rock walls slimy with icy water and moss, crumbling trails dropping off into the valley below in boulder-size subsidence, the weather beating from both sides, snow clouds, sleet covering the track and you have to inch along wary of wrong footing, switching back now, darkening now, foreboding, the escarpment rises above and shaves off below, the short scrub whitening and in the weird light some blossom

220

glowing yellow and blue and shivering in the night wind which whistles and squeals from the cornices of rubble spewing spindrift, the clouds sculling over to take you from the centre of your being and shaking, you ask what fool edges along this boldface razorback in such weathers? Come rest in foam, dive, sleep in my folds! Dark. But it promises to be fine in the morning, sun slicing out of a blue of *lapis lazuli*, bushes glistening with crystal, drooping with the shaving-cream of old snow, black cockatoos gliding and nagging, an owl hooting regular as a factory signal in the amphoric air and far up the mountain a lone eagle swoops on bush rats brushing out sleep and leaves, a scree of brief lives gathered against shadows . . . your bones on the leeward shelf of a still black cave.

You came up here to be honest.

But you think of tomorrow. The future.

To be done with all the writing. Of course you've been writing letters since you left Ludmilla, much to your shame, great long letters filled with rhetoric and persuasion, letters in which you pointed out to Wespe his predilection for giving all his money to women who betrayed him. Ludmilla, you said, was different. She was intellectual, sexual and rich, you wrote. You begged him to take the trip. You didn't mention that if he came it would restore everyone's fortunes. Restore the whole analysis industry. Europe was out, they were saying. Europe creaked with age, haemorrhaged from bad plumbing. Without Europe there was only Asia, ancient neglect, which sat uneasily in Western stomachs, of which there was scant evidence save for the one or two Chinese restaurants languishing ignominiously in a sea of dullness.

You wrote separately to Louise, who was still the Wolf-Man's companion. You promised her thirty thousand schillings if she could persuade Sergei to come. This was your worst mistake, writing to Loulou. She was part of your group once, always on the fringes because she felt she was ugly. It wasn't the fact that she was ugly, but her isolation was the result of her trying to outdo everyone. She was competitive. You wrote to a competitor. Louise knew there was a good chance she would get nothing. You spent weeks between your two rooms, walking back and forth between kitchen and bedroom, writing and washing and writing and cooking and writing again, and not once in those weeks did you touch a drop of liquor. You wrote to Liebmann in New York. You told him what you intended to do. You would take Sergei bushwalking, to Perry's Lookdown, and gripping him by the arm, force him to look down and recant, or look down no more. You were ashamed of writing this to Liebmann, but rationalised it as bending under the pressures of a mechanistic society. Orality. Presence. The bugle of belonging.

A week later, you received a cheque from Liebmann. There was no covering letter.

You wrote and walked up the street to post more letters, licking stamps with a parched tongue and you had no money left after about a week, which was just as well and then luck blew a little your way and you spent a couple of days with a labour gang up at Blackheath corduroying a swamp filled with icy shards and freshwater eels and they paid you well for stitching the right-sized timber back and forth between the rails leaving a soft matting of bark and leaves above the water-line, and you, happily, finding these skills again, in harmony with your body. At nightfall, while the whisky burned mellow and blue on the crumbling terrace of a nearby hotel you counted shooting stars in the metallic sky, these great symphonies of silence already placing you within Wespe's avenging emptiness and then you caught the train back to Katoomba and in the train a woman began to cry out of the blue, tears like falling stars, sobs shaking her whole body, and at Katoomba station an old woman sat on the concrete platform whimpering, beating her palms on the wet ground . . . everywhere people bursting out into tears, you see this more and more often. You walked across the level crossing, and, suddenly, paralysed again by the sight of a crying woman who has preceded you to change platforms . . . *going back*, you wanted to say something, but what? You walked across the street and stuck a couple of dollars into the palm of Willy the Wheel who was just a shadow rounding the James Building Circa 1925 . . . Willy's been there about as long, deformed in his rolling chair, his sofa on castors which he pushes with

chimpanzee arms and salivates at passers-by, a clattering
ghost in the night, but Willy knows you and you put the
money into his hand for luck and he passes a bottle of metho
but you decline knowing your luck would depend on a clear
head and knowledge of detail as you pick your way past
broken bottles and turds lining the back way to the Aeneas.

A month goes by and there are no letters. Two months. Your
letters to Wespe return unopened. In desperation you write to
Liebmann, and you learn from him that the Wolf-Man is ill,
lying almost comatose at the Steinhof. He had collapsed when
Louise ran off with ten thousand schillings. That really
knocked away the last portals of symmetry. Art no longer
sustained him. He was a cripple and she was a hag. No longer
Freud's famous patient, an old man preoccupied with trivia,
urine, blood clots, pain. You re-read the rough drafts of your
letters. In one you wrote: 'Your tragedy, Sergy, is that you have
already lived, without knowing it.'

The day after, you go to that antique store on the corner of
Katoomba Street and you sell the terracotta penis Sergei had
given you. Eighth Century B.C., you tell the woman. A
symbolon. A fragment of possibility. A *tessera*, a tile of recognition. Yeah, it's pretty impressive but we don't do dildos, she
says. But she has it examined anyway and when you return
two days later, she gives you twenty dollars. Your last twenty
dollars. You buy a bottle of whisky.

It is very dark now, on the firetrail out to Narrow Neck. The
snow covers your tracks. Dark. Your thin shoes leak and your
toes are numb and the sound they make is annoying, regular
and irritating. Dark. You stop and take a leak. Dark, your
urine. No, it's blood. You can tell by the viscosity. The snow
breaks open to receive it, throws up a black script as promised,
such cruel generosity, this final offering, these lost furrows of
memory. There's a lesson here about the romance of degeneration. About the romance of anything. You do it yourself.
Shake out the last drops of life for your own evaluation . . .
against yourself. You make your way up the side of the escarpment. Dark, but someone has left a large upholstered bench
here. You take a rest, brushing away the snow. You are soaked
now. Your eyebrows crackle, your nostrils are blocked with ice

and your beard grates. At the top of the hill you tear through the scrub in a direction only you know. Your poncho is torn. Your greatcoat is bayoneted by branches. Dark. You reach a small outcrop of rock which you skirt with the agility of a wallaby which you had seen bounding off black and urinous through the snow. You find the cave, sweep out some droppings. Animals know things that humans do not: like the fact that defecation is also warmth. They know it instinctively. Like the timing of their death. We can only guess, make assumptions. If you lie down you will sleep. It is harder than you think, sleep, that is. The ground and the night revolve with magnetic forces which tear into and wrench your sinews. It is impossible to be in control of your death. Master endurance and still your bones shiver involuntarily. It is the body which says: *absorb and rebel*. A mass of tendrils. Dry. Disconnected. There are some desiccated branches left here by other animals, some gnawed, some blackened from summer fires. You rub a twig along the centre of a grooved piece of bark which fits neatly in the cup of your palm and together the wood and your body fall into a rhythm that seeks out cadences long forgotten, the pleasures of rubbing, the erasures of the primitive returned to you like a palimpsest, and you rub, fascinated, you indulge patiently the urgings of your genitals, follow the long slow smoke of curiosity. No doubling back. Driving out from within. About to discover the momentous object, you found yourself. You gurgle with pleasure. Moisture forms on the rocks. It finds many directions. In your pocket you have *The Wolf-Man by the Wolf-Man*. The pages are thin with reading and human oils. You tear off a page, lay it over the wood as the night outside entombs this summation of the present . . . until finally . . . a spark . . . hot dog . . . a parody . . . the hand, the voice, a spark: only on plateaux did these evolve, out of the darkness of the forest . . . it crackles . . . it breathes . . . an origin . . . no longer these burning desires for shadows . . . and if this is anxiety then a greater event will surely follow . . . I . . . inseparable . . . many . . . a beginning . . . rubbing . . . and soon . . . fire . . . and music . . . et cetera.)

Postscript

The Wolf-Man died on 7 May 1979 at the Steinhof in Vienna, aged 92. A manuscript containing his literary fragments remains undiscovered.

Bibliography

Abraham, Pierre, and Torok, Maria *The Wolf-Man's Magic Word* trans. Nicholas Rand. Minneapolis: University of Minnesota Press, 1986

Catacomb, Arthur S. *Fellow-Traveller: In Praise of Freud* New York: International Universities Press, 1970

Gardiner, Muriel (ed.) *The Wolf-Man by the Wolf-Man* New York: Basic Books, 1971

Liebmann, Ishmael *Is There a Wolf in the Fold?* Harvard University Press, 1975

Lukacher, Ned *Primal Scenes: Literature, Philosophy, Psychoanalysis* Ithaca, New York, 1986

Obholzer, Karin *The Wolf-Man: Conversations with Freud's Patient Sixty Years Later*, trans. Michael Shaw. New York: Continuum, 1982

Strachey, James (ed.) *The Standard Edition of the Complete Psychological Works of Sigmund Freud* London: Hogarth Press, vols. 13, 14, 17, 21, 22, 23

Wittgenstein, Ludmilla (ed.) *The Catacomb Diaries* Minneapolis: University of Minnesota Press, revised edition, 1978.

WOMEN OF SAND AND MYRRH
Hanan al-Shaykh

Introducing a leading Arab writer

Hanan al-Shaykh is a mesmerising writer, born in
Lebanon and currently living in London. Her
latest novel, *Women of Sand and Myrrh*, lays bare
the lives of four contemporary women caught in an
unnamed Middle East country.

'In this intense narrative of passion, boredom, and
the cruelty of God as expressed in a patriarchal
society, she has accomplished her second major
literary triumph, put into English with consummate
skill by Catherine Cobham.'
International Herald Tribune

First Australian and New Zealand publication

OCEANA FINE
Tom Flood

*The Australian/Vogel winner in 1988; winner of
the Miles Franklin Award and the Victorian
Premier's Literary Award in 1990.*

Marvel Loch, Western Australia. Beneath a vast
blue and gold landscape lie disused mine shafts.
Above the ground rise silos. This is a place of
mysteries and myths: the perfect setting for a bold
new novel which is part whodunit, part
psychological thriller, part magical fantasy,
charting the lives and decreasing fortunes of the
Cleaver family.

'From realism to surrealism, this is a novel always
original, exciting, different.'
Geoffrey Dutton

PAINTED WOMAN
Sue Woolfe

Now in paperback

'An exquisitely intense book...This is such
robust, unpitying and honest writing about women
that it becomes writing for everyone.'
Thomas Keneally

Sue Woolfe has, with *Painted Woman*, established
herself as a novelist of the first rank. Commentary
on a woman artist's life in the present explodes
with new meanings as her past is revealed.

'Extraordinary, beautiful writing, like a bright
light, glancing and flashing across a canvas.'
Kate Grenville

First paperback publication

JF WAS HERE
Nigel Krauth

A major new novel from a leading Australian writer

'Krauth...combines a delicate argument about ethics and goodness, both personal and political, with robust story-telling, and gritty realism.'
Robert Dessaix, Books and Writing

From the Hydro Majestic Hotel in the Blue Mountains, JF recalls not only his own adult life, lived largely in contemporary Papua New Guinea, but also the life of his grandmother, an eccentric golf champion who, like John, paid a considerable price for the right to be 'her own person'.

JF Was Here is a novel of maturity and depth from the prize-winning author of *Matilda, My Darling* and *The Bathing Machine Called the Twentieth Century*.